THE STRUGGLE

CAROLYN GEDULD

Black Rose Writing | Texas

First printing

ISBN: 978-1-68433-972-3
PUBLISHED BY BLACK ROSE WRITING
www.blackrosewriting.com

Printed in the United States of America
Suggested Retail Price (SRP) $20.95

The Struggle is printed in Bookerly

*As a planet-friendly publisher, Black Rose Writing does its best to eliminate unnecessary waste to reduce paper usage and energy costs, while never compromising the reading experience. As a result, the final word count vs. page count may not meet common expectations.

Grateful acknowledgement is made to the following for a previously published chapter:
Steam Ticket Journal. Volume 23. Who By Fire. University of Wisconsin at La Crosse. June, 2020. Pp. 88-96.

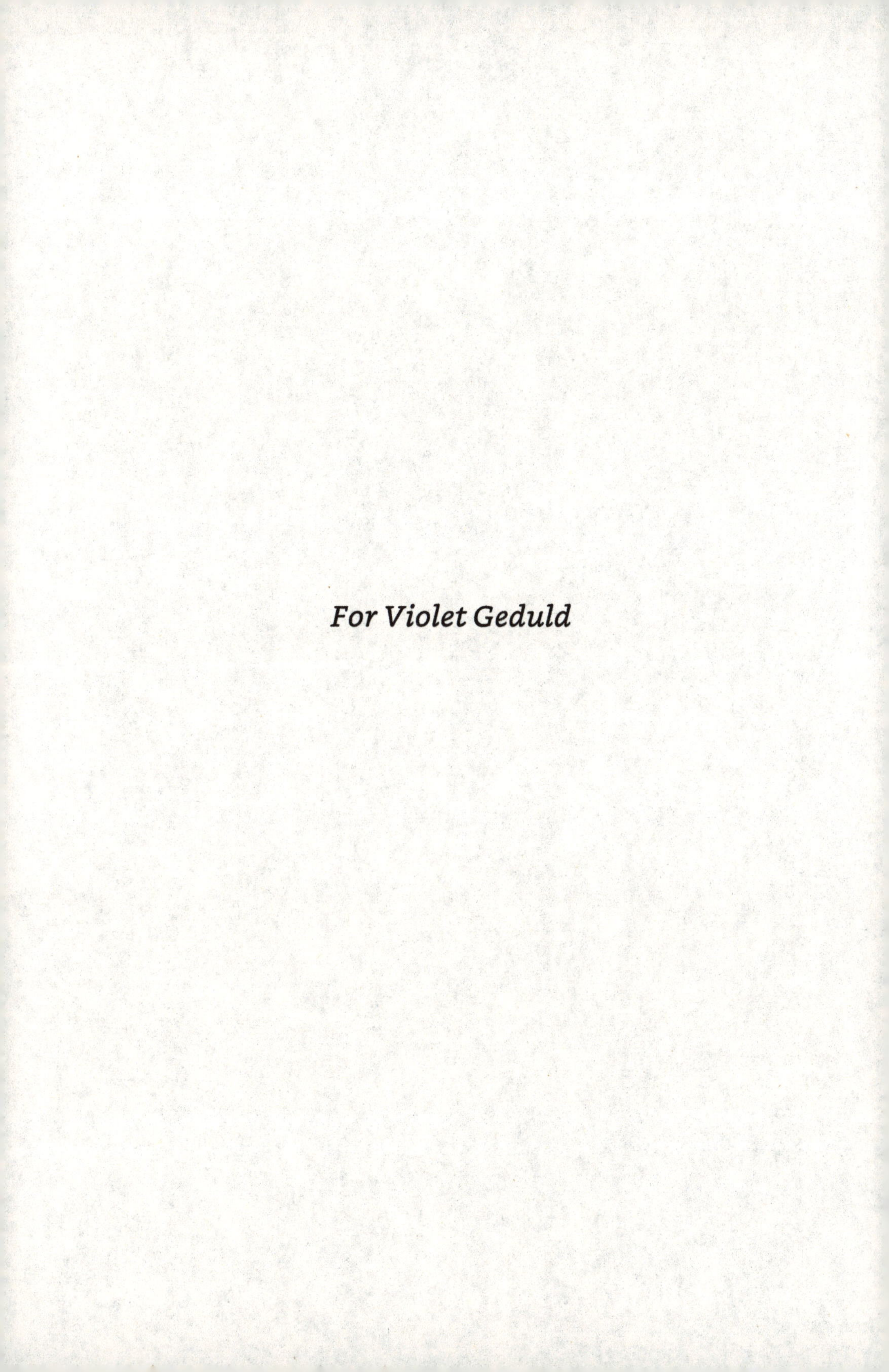

For Violet Geduld

THE STRUGGLE

Jacob was left alone. And a man wrestled with him until the break of dawn.

When he saw that he had not prevailed against him, he wrenched Jacob's hip at its socket, so that the socket of his hip was strained as he wrestled with him.

Then he said, "Let me go, for dawn is breaking." But he answered, "I will not let you go, unless you bless me."

Said the other, "What is your name?" He replied, "Jacob."

Said he, "Your name shall no longer be Jacob, but Israel, for you have striven with beings divine and human, and have prevailed."

–Genesis 32.4-36.43

CHAPTER 1

Wooden matches were the best because of the sound. Scrape. *Woosh.*

Uri's mother kept little boxes in the kitchen cabinet drawer next to the gas stove, the one with the spatulas and splintering wooden spoons. He couldn't get away with swiping them too often. A better bet was the match books near the ashtrays in the living room. It was his job to empty the butts into the step-on trash can, making it easy enough to grab a book and stuff it unnoticed into his sweatshirt pouch.

If his mother or one of her boyfriends asked, "Where are the matches I left here?" he would just look innocent, easy for an undersized boy with puppy-dog eyes. Then his mother would fish through her big black purse, which always contained a supply.

He would light the matches one-by-one while walking to Religious School at the synagogue, throwing them at the other kids who walked nearby. The girls would shriek and run a few feet ahead before turning to grin at him. The other twelve-year-old boys in his *bar/bat mitzvah* class protected their faces with their arms, while calling him "asshole" in a joking-around way. Uri would pull the same stunt on the walk back, making bearable the prospect of Rabbi Shapiro's dreary recitation of the *Haftorah*, followed by each kid stammering his or her way through several verses.

His mother's newest boyfriend, Simon, prepared him for his *bar mitzvah*, scheduled for the next mid-November 5764, or 2003 in the modern calendar, going over the Hebrew with him and explaining the verses he would read from the *Torah*. Uri didn't mind. He liked the stories in Genesis, when God would threaten to kill the idol-worshipping Israelites, before God ruined it by changing His mind at the last moment.

"Abraham convinces God not to destroy Sodom because of the ten righteous men living there."

"I don't get it. Why doesn't God just do what he says He will and wipe out Sodom?"

Simon considered. "God is merciful. Abraham is being tested."

Uri wanted a description of the plague or conflagration that would level an entire city.

When Simon put an arm around him and said to call him "Dad," Uri's face heated. He had a father somewhere, a real one. His mother fucked around when she was in the sorority and didn't even remember who with, after all the drinking she did. She told this to him nicer than that, of course, with genuine regret in her voice and without using the "f" word.

"I wish I had been more mature at nineteen so I could tell you which boy was your father. At least it was someone from a Jewish fraternity."

But it wasn't Simon. He was ten years older than his mother, having graduated while his mother still learned to ride a bike and do multiplication.

The other place Uri liked to toss matches was in his backyard, a small stretch of dry brown grass and weeds he had to mow during the summer months, when everything was green and growing. He sat on the back steps, lighting matches and aiming at the tinder covering the ground. He dreamed of starting a fire like the ones out west, with flames traveling up dry pines, then flaring skyward, consuming thousands of acres, destroying everything in its path.

That would be awesome!

But if a match caught the dried grass, he stamped it out fast. He would be the first one suspected if a fire spread to his house, a fire trap anyway. It wouldn't pass an inspection with its old wiring and lack of adequate insulation. Even if his mother wanted to sell, she didn't have enough money to get it into sellable shape. At least Simon helped pay the bills when he moved in. Boyfriends were good for that.

His mother called Simon a "prospect." Her east coast family cut her off in her senior year at the university in Indiana in 1990, when she was already pregnant with Uri. She fell in love with a black student, not the father of the child, not Jewish. It appalled her parents. Promiscuous? Pregnant? A black, gentile boyfriend? They withdrew financial support and wouldn't speak to her. A small inheritance from a grandparent enabled her to buy the little two-bedroom house, a fixer-upper she didn't have the income to fix. When her relationship with the black student didn't work out, subsequent boyfriends repaired this or that— torn screens, leaky faucets, keeping the place semi-livable.

But now she had a Jewish boyfriend, and Uri prepared to become a *bar mitzvah*. Her parents softened. If she married Simon, Uri would have a family. Grandparents. Cousins. *Seders. Hanukkah.* Wouldn't he like that?

He shook his head while shifting his eyes away from her. What he wanted was a father with a severe jaw-line and defined muscles, like a superhero who would teach him to be tough. He didn't need seders. He needed to stop the kids at school from picking on him just because he was short.

Hey! Dwarf. Wanna fight?

Just wait. I'll tell my father. You better not make him mad.

He didn't mean Simon, who was no superhero, just an old bald guy with a fringe of hair circling the back of his head, hairy arms, and a soft, round belly concealed by draped shirts. When Uri disobeyed him, Simon said he "didn't appreciate it" or that he "knew you could do better." He was a weakling, unlike what Uri's real father would be. Uri imagined fierceness from his real father, long hard beatings, ritual chastisements, and harsh discipline. That's what a real father would do. No one would mock a kid with such a father. No one would wish to bring such a father's wrath down on him or her. They would respect Uri for having a father who knew how to punish. All he had to do was show off his bruises and welts.

Simon and his mother planned to get married the day after Uri's *bar mitzvah*. All the relatives would have made the trip to Indiana, anyway. His mother's family had already agreed to attend. First, Uri would be called to the *Torah* on Saturday morning, followed by a luncheon for the congregation and visiting relatives. The wedding would be Sunday afternoon. Later, there would be a dinner for the invited guests. Once his grandparents reconciled with his mother, they would pay for everything. They would even hire the photographer and a band.

Uri dreamed of his real father showing up just before the couple said their vows under the *huppah*.

"Stop," his father would say, holding out his hand to his mother. "She's mine."

Simon would step back, not able to withstand the piercing gaze of Uri's real father. He would mesmerize his mother. "You?" She would ask, placing her tentative hand onto his outstretched palm. His fist would envelop it. He would yank her to him.

"Where's the boy?"

"Here I am," Uri would say.

"Come here." His father would reach for him with his other hand.

The three would leave together. His real father would take them to his secret place to live. A big, luxurious hidden palace. No one would find them.

A few days later, Uri came home from school and discovered they changed his room, cramming all his belongings into one side. His superhero posters were re-mounted onto the walls above his bed. They squeezed a second bed and an old beat up dresser—one that had been in the garage for storing drill bits and screws—into the rest of the room. Half the closet had empty dangling hangers. They squashed his clothing into the other half.

He found his mother in the kitchen, braiding challah.

"Adam's staying here from now on. He'll bunk with you," his mother said.

Adam was Simon's son, a year younger than Uri, but the same size.

"No! It's my room. He can't stay there! He belongs with his mother."

"Adam is choosing to live with us now. There's nowhere else to put him. I expect you to be a big brother to him."

"I don't want a little brother. I want my room back the way it used to be." He shouted, stamping his foot.

"Uri! Enough. It is what it is. We'll make it work." She reached out to him.

He backed away from her, knowing her touch would bring him down. Sobs formed deep in his chest, threatening to wring tears out of him by force, leaving him heaving on the floor like a small child, a baby. If his real father saw, it would disgust him. He couldn't let that happen. Instead, he stomped off to his room, slamming the door hard enough to rattle the entire house.

In the small space between the two beds, he seethed and paced. His life sucked. Who wanted a *bar mitzvah*? He didn't even want to be Jewish. He didn't want Simon marrying his mother. And what he didn't want most was Adam sharing his room.

The pressure in his chest grew. His breathing made tiny squeal noises, a timid, kittenish sound. To stop it, he kicked the wall on Adam's side of the room. It left a dark scuff mark, like a grinning mouth, laughing at him. He kicked again, harder. After a satisfying crunch, a hole popped in the wall. He kicked it a few more times, enlarging the hole. Then he felt better. Simon would be "disappointed" when he had to repair the wall. Uri scoffed.

The next day, Adam arrived with a large black plastic bag of belongings. Uri's mother hung the clothing in Adam's half of the closet, while putting his underwear and pjs in the top drawer of his dresser. Within a half-hour, Adam had his Nintendo Switch and DVDs arranged on the dresser top. He smiled at Uri, who pouted on his bed, and babbled about what he was doing.

"I'm going to put Ninja Turtles over here. Do you like my Ninja shirt? We can share it. Iron Man goes over here. No. Ninja on the left and Iron Man on the right. What do you think?"

"I think you better leave me alone. That's what I think."

Uri imagined pestering his real father the way Adam pestered him. He would smack Uri hard enough to send him tumbling across the room. If Uri whined about it or cried, he would be smacked even harder. He figured he should teach Adam a similar lesson. Rising from his bed, he punched him in the upper arm.

"Ow! What's that for?"

"For bothering me. Stop talking to me, or I'll hit you again."

Adam stared at him with long-lashed dark eyes, looking more bewildered than hurt. It occurred to Uri that Adam looked up to him in the same way he looked up to his real father. The worst thing would be if Adam made Uri like him. Uri needed to harden himself. His job was to make Adam so miserable, he would ask to go back to his mother. Then, maybe Simon wouldn't marry Uri's mother since she had such a bad son.

For the next week, Uri did anything to torment the younger boy. When the adults weren't around, he called Adam "dickhead" and "asshole." He destroyed his possessions, even the Ninja shirt. He shoved him or hit him whenever Adam was within reach. Adam withstood it all, never telling his father or Uri's mother what he endured. The little fucker turned out to be one tough kid. He did whatever Uri wanted, even doing his chores for him. Uri found himself both despising him and admiring him. Adam behaved the way Uri would wish to behave when his real father showed up.

Uri had to write an essay on the *Torah* verses they would require him to chant. He would have to read the essay to the congregation. The verses were about Jacob wrestling with a man. Uri imagined the man would be much bigger than Jacob. He pictured the man getting Jacob into a headlock, pinning him down. How he wished some big strong being would hold him down, allowing him to struggle, but always being the master, dominating the situation.

This is what he couldn't tell Simon or the congregation. He would just say what everyone expected, that the man was a disguised angel, that Jacob wrestled with him so he could become the person God wanted him to be.

"My goal in life, with the help of my mother and stepfather, is to become like Jacob—a good Jewish man."

He would lie. What did God want of him, anyway? Obedience. Blind gratitude. Loyalty.

Or did He want Uri to get his real parents back together and not marry anyone else? Did He want Uri to get rid of Adam by doing things like ripping up Adam's homework and peeing on Adam's bed, so his mother would think Adam wet it?

The *bar mitzvah* and wedding approached. There were meetings with Rabbi Shapiro at the synagogue to discuss arrangements. With a bitter taste in his mouth, Uri noted the Rabbi's leniency. Why did he agree with almost everything his mother wanted? Why didn't he tell her that Jewish law forbade this marriage, that Jewish law demanded she find Uri's father? Surely, with so many Jewish laws, they buried such rulings among them? Uri scowled at the carpet, decorated with an obnoxious abstract design that made his eyes water.

As the weekend approached, Uri figured out a new way to toughen himself. He stole one of his mother's cigarettes and took it to the rear of the backyard where he hid among thick bushes. He also borrowed her lighter. After lighting the cigarette, he rolled up his shirt sleeve and ground the burning end into the tender inside of his arm. Pain ripped through him. It took all of his will not to cry out. But then he relaxed for the first time in weeks.

At first, he only burned himself back behind the bushes. A few days later, it occurred to him he should show Adam how strong he was. Right in front of him in their bedroom, with the door closed, Uri ground the burning tip into his thigh. Adam stared. A charred meat odor combined with the cigarette smoke.

"It's a secret. Don't tell."

He opened the window a couple of inches, fanning the air with his hand to dissipate the smell.

"I won't."

In this way, Uri counted on Adam. If the younger boy hadn't told about the pinches and shoves, the destruction of his DVDs and favorite shirts, Uri figured he wouldn't say anything about the stolen cigarettes and burns. It made him not hate Adam so much.

On the Friday night before the *bar mitzvah*, after *Shabbat* services, while both he and Adam got ready for bed, Uri took out the box of wooden matches he had hidden in a shoe box containing his emergency stash of cigarette ends, collected over months.

"Want to play a new game?"

Each sat on his bed.

"Yeah. Okay."

"Just keep quiet about it."

"Okay. Sure."

Uri struck a wooden match.

Scrape. *Woosh.*

He threw the lighted match at Adam.

"Hey!" Adam batted his hands at the little orange flame when it landed on his jeans, snuffing it out. "Better stop!"

Uri continued to throw lighted matches at Adam. Each time, the younger boy ducked, before slapping at the little flame until it expired. Soon he was laughing, enjoying the game. Uri began laughing, too. The gutsy kid wasn't so bad. If they didn't share a room and a parent, Uri might have liked him.

Soon, they used up all the matches. The boys lay on their beds laughing. Adam sat up.

"Tomorrow. Are you going to blow your *bar mitzvah*?"

Uri smiled with approval. If he screwed up—pretending to draw a blank when he was supposed to chant *Torah* and remained silent, for instance—maybe Rabbi Shapiro would cancel the wedding.

"Let's play the match game some more," Adam said.

"Sorry. I'm out." He held up the empty matchbox.

"Wait here."

Adam left the bedroom without turning on the hall light. In a few minutes, he returned, closing the door. In his hand was a matchbook.

"Where did you find that?"

"In my dad's coat pocket. How do I do it?"

Uri instructed him in tearing off a match, closing the matchbook, and holding the match low on its stem while striking it, then throwing it at a target. Soon, the target was Uri. The boys roared with laughter while Uri was under attack.

When there were just a couple of matches left, Uri spoke to Adam.

"You're still a dickhead, but I guess you're alright. When my real dad comes, I'll introduce you."

Adam grinned. "Just for that, I won't throw these at you."

Lighting the last two matches together, he threw them toward the half-opened window. The full moon appeared to waver as the sheer curtains began billowing and twirling, gathering the boys into its glowing ring to dance the *Hora*, and spreading to include an ever-widening circle of participants in fiery anticipation of the celebrations to come.

PART ONE
HIGH SCHOOL

CHAPTER 2

Mrs. Green, the English teacher, drew a diagram on the blackboard. She "parsed" a sentence. The word "parsing" was unknown to Uri. He missed most of ninth grade, spending the year in the hospital, first in the ICU, then floating between the pediatric burn ward, the post-op unit, respiratory rehab and occupational therapy. A special teacher who visited children in inpatient settings gave him assignments, but no one expected him to do them. Anesthesia, narcotics and pain befuddled him too much to think straight, anyway. The diagram had to do with grammar. Words fell into categories. Nouns were things. Verbs were actions. Objects were the things verbs acted on. In "the cat ate the mouse," "cat" was the noun, "ate" was the verb, and "mouse" was the object. That was the sentence Mrs. Green diagrammed.

Another sentence, the one always in Uri's head, was "I played with matches and killed my mother and my friend." "I" was the noun, "played" and "killed" were the verbs, "matches," "mother," and "friend" were the objects. In his mind, the only verb that mattered was "killed" and only object, "mother," but when parsed, all had equal importance, which made no sense. To the mouse, being eaten had to be more important than who ate him. He hoped that to his mother, wherever she was, being consumed by fire was more important than whoever set it.Grammar turned out to be just another useless subject required in school that had nothing to do with life. It didn't help him with the feelings he had about being disfigured by the fire. Now that he had shot up to six feet, the kids didn't call him "Dwarf" anymore. Instead, they called him "Leather Face," after the villain in *The Texas Chainsaw Massacre* movie, because of the burn scars. Cosmetic procedures did as much as could be done. The false eye helped him look more normal, although nothing restored his sight on that side. The prosthetic hand wasn't the unaffordable articulated kind. He received what Medicaid offered, the cheapest, not much better than pincers in flesh-colored rubber. And he had no mother and no father. Messing with sentences wouldn't change him from a fire-scared orphan into a regular kid.

"Hey, Leather Face. You make me puke."

Simon took him in when neither his grandparents nor any other biological relative would offer a home to an adolescent arsonist, even if he committed his crime on the evening before his postponed *bar mitzvah*, when he wasn't yet responsible, according to Jewish law. He avoided Juvenile Detention under American law when the prosecutor ruled the fire an accident. Simon's generosity made him a *mensch* in the eyes of the synagogue community. Who else would foster the boy who killed Simon's fiancé and his son? At least he never said Uri "disappointed" him. He never spoke about the past at all.

Uri didn't either. If Simon kicked him out, he would face the uncertainties of foster care or a group home. He still didn't like Simon, but he wouldn't jeopardize his situation by provoking him. Whatever Simon wanted him to do, he did, including attending the youth Torah Youth Group at the synagogue.

"Leather Face. What're ya lookin' for? A match?"

One Saturday afternoon back when he lay in the hospital, doing nothing but chipping off flakes of green paint from the wall with a fingernail on his good hand, Rabbi Shapiro marched in with nine congregants, including Simon, and a *Torah* scroll. After removing his cup of water, tissues and unfinished school work from the tray table that swung over his bed, they covered it with a cloth and opened the scroll on it. The head nurse had a heated discussion with them about whether the bed could be turned to face east. When they settled that, they made Uri stumble through a verse in Hebrew from that week's chapter, with many pronunciation corrections from the Rabbi. When Uri finished, they threw hard candies onto his bed, and the president of the synagogue presented him with a certificate. He was a man.

After his discharge, Uri made his only friend in Youth Group, a boy who didn't know about Uri's responsibility for the death of his last only friend. No one else would come near him. The boy's name was Zhong, a short, fat kid with chubby cheeks and hair sticking straight up on a round head, the same age as Uri and almost as ugly. He came from China with his family when a local pharmaceutical company hired his father. How it came about that Zhong was Jewish was a mystery to Uri. It was impossible to ask him because he didn't speak any English except for the few words necessary to play chess. That's how he and Uri discovered each other. Since no one else would play with them, they played with each other, taking turns at each other's houses. Zhong was a prodigy at chess, even though he had been taught a version called Elephant Chess in China and was still learning the rules of classic western chess. He had to be reminded to place his pieces within the squares, not on the intersections as had been the custom in China. Even if Uri cheated by moving pieces when Zhong took a bathroom break, his friend always won.

"Bisopa."

"Bishop. Say 'Bishop'."

"Bisopa."

"Bishop, you dickhead."

Zhong might beat Uri at chess, but he couldn't say "bishop." Uri made sure Zhong saw his lips twist into a smug smile at this minor victory, while waiting for him to know enough English to play the Japanese card game Yu-Gi-Oh. He knew he could whip him at that game. He attempted to speed up the process by teaching him grammar.

"'Table' is a noun, get it?"

"*Hao.*"

Zhong peered at him through thick glasses. One lens had spider-web cracks running across it.

"When you say 'you' or 'I,' they're pronouns."

"What 'pro'?"

"Never ask 'what' or 'why,' man. Things just are the way they are."

"*Hao.*"

Uri spent the rest of the ninth grade, the summer, and the start of the tenth grade catching up on schoolwork, doing chores for Simon, playing with Zhong, and attending Youth Group. When late November rolled around, the *Torah* portion studied in the group cycled to the one Uri would have chanted if there hadn't been a fire. In it, Jacob wrestles all night with a man.

This was still Uri's favorite chapter in the Bible, just like wrestling matches were his favorite programs on TV, even though they were fake. He imagined Jacob and the man in a clinch hold, a figure-four leg lock, a standing choke, and a neck crank. Even better, he pictured certain submission holds used in aggressive wrestling, meant to injure or kill, never seen on tv, but known to spectators. It excited Uri to fantasize about the man forcing him, not Jacob, into such holds, sometimes switching to putting Zhong into a hold. If Zhong submitted, it was never as satisfying as submitting himself, since his friend squealed instead of enduring it in silence, as Uri did.

He never revealed his fantasies to Simon during their discussion of the chapter. Simon insisted on guiding Uri, using the ethical insights found in the *Torah*. Did he hint at the possibility that Uri had a criminal part of his character? It wouldn't surprise Uri if that's what Simon suspected, given how he accidentally murdered the two people Simon loved.

"Who do you think the man was?"

Simon had a book opened containing the text in Hebrew and English.

"Dunno."

He recalled Zhong's blank stare when Rabbi Shapiro asked the same question in Youth Group. He passed him a note reading "Attack roll," used when hitting an opponent in D&D, which Uri was also teaching him, to make his friend smile. Zhong nodded. Maybe he understood. No one had to say anything in Youth Group because Rabbi Shapiro preferred to lecture. But back home, Simon insisted on grilling Uri.

"Was the man a messenger from God or something from inside of Jacob?"

"Dunno."

In the essay that Uri never got the chance to read to the congregation, Simon directed him to write that the man was either an angel or a part of Jacob. He never said what part. Uri's real thought was that the man was God's vengeance, nearly subduing Jacob with his superior strength, not like the weakness that made Jacob use a disguise to trick his brother out of his inheritance. A stronger person wouldn't have used tricks. He would just grab the inheritance for himself.

Months before, he imagined his real father as a tough and merciless superhero. It was just a wish. For all he knew, his real father might be no tougher than Simon. When his mother died, he gave up his kid thoughts about a tough father. The longing for someone to be tough with him didn't go away when he stopped thinking about his father. It stayed underground within him.

If the man lived inside Jacob, like a shameful, hidden part of himself, his existence was a guilty secret. They wrestled at night, when no one saw. Then it got included in the *Torah*, where millions read it. That's why Uri wouldn't tell Simon or anyone his thoughts. He wouldn't want them written in some book. He would try to figure out what Simon expected him to say and just say that.

"Nowadays, many people prefer a psychological meaning—that Jacob struggled with his ego."

"That sounds right to me."

"What part of Jacob might his ego be?"

The discussion paused while Uri figured out the best answer. Simon crossed his arms, waiting.

"The part that tricked his brother?"

"That's possible. Jacob had to get control of that part of himself to become a good man."

It rattled Uri to think his inability to stop having wrestling fantasies made him a not-so-good person. He was already bad because of the fire. His imagination added to that transgression. The harder he tried to control his mind, the less controllable it became. If he touched himself while he was having a wrestling fantasy, his terrible guilt increased. God would hate a person with his kind of unmanageable ego.

"Leather Face. Who're going to kill next?"

It had been easy to hide his bad self from Zhong when they first met. He wouldn't have understood if Uri tried to explain. Through the tenth grade, they continued to play chess after school every day. Over time, Zhong's English improved. When he advanced enough to string several words together, he asked Uri about his scar.

"Why you have face of leta?"

He meant "leather." Zhong broke the unstated rule of pretending not to notice the scars and not referring to hurtful words like "Leather Face." Uri reddened, causing his disfigurement to blaze.

"Why do you have a gook face?"

Zhong, a month breather, formed his lips into a thin horizontal line crossing his chubby cheeks. He looked away, through his cracked glasses.

"I go home now."

In his head, Uri parsed the sentence. "I," the noun, was Zhong. The verb was "go." The object was unstated, but Uri knew it was him. "I'm leaving you" would have been correct English.

"No more games. Ever." Zhong said as he left.

"Asshole!" Uri shouted after him.

When the man couldn't defeat Jacob, he lamed him by pulling his hip from its socket. When he lost his second only friend, Uri felt something inside him rip. It wasn't new. The deep fissure created when he lost his mother and Adam widened another few inches. Another tear might split him in two.

CHAPTER 3

For an entire year, Uri and Zhong didn't speak. During that time, Zhong grew taller and leaner. His cheeks lost their pubescent chubbiness, and his thick black hair grew out, dangling across his forehead. He got a new pair of glasses with attractive dark frames. It was possible for native-born English speakers to understand him, despite his accent. He hung out with the geeks, future computer programmers who submitted early applications to CalTech and M.I.T. The Youth Group saw less of him, although he was still a member.

Uri changed, too, although his scar failed to stretch to accommodate his growing facial structure, giving him an odd, distended appearance. It drew the eye-socket containing the false eye downward while his nose veered to the side. The lack of symmetry of his features was subtle. Others saw his scar, that was unavoidable, but beyond that, didn't know what distressed them about his features without close study. As Zhong became more handsome, Uri's looks declined.By eleventh grade, his caved chest and rounded shoulders made him seem shorter than six feet. Although there was less cruelty in the upper grades, he was more beaten-down than ever. Loneliness and shame flowed from him, creating an invisible line around him no one wanted to cross.Except for Zhong. One day, out of the blue, Zhong caught up with him on the way home from school.

"We playa chess?"

Uri shot a glance toward him with his good eye, then looked straight ahead. He forced himself to act unsurprised.

"Your house or mine?"

"Mine. Nexta time, yours."

Although they no longer played daily because of Zhong's commitment to the coding club, which met two days a week, math club which met every Thursday and Youth Group—which Simon still insisted Uri attend on Sundays, they both pretended that the year's break hadn't happened.In his head, Uri puzzled about the renewed friendship. Did Zhong notice his lack of friends and pity him? Was he obeying the command drum-beaten into Youth Group to "love thy neighbor as thyself," choosing the hardest case available to prove he could? Did he have amnesia, blanking out the time between their last game a year ago and the first of the present ones?It was pointless to figure out what he was reluctant to ask Zhong. The only safe subjects were chess, D&D, Yu-Gi-Oh, and whatever chapter Youth Group discussed.

In November, the verses about Jacob and the wrestler rotated around again, as they would forever at this time of year. Rabbi Shapiro gave the same lecture he always gave, and Simon asked the same questions. This prompted a discussion between the two boys.

"Who do you think the man who struggled all night with Jacob is?" Uri moved his rook from a1 to c1.

"Man isa angel from Goda." Zhong took his rook with his bishop on a3.

"No way! A real angel would have won the first minute. Not struggled all night, only to lose. And don't take my rook. I moved him to c1 by mistake."

"Tooka hand off. No mistake. Man isa angel. Rabbi saya so."

"The trouble with you is you're, like, literal. You don't read between the lines. And the rook was on b1. It got pushed to c1 because my artificial hand jerked. It does that sometimes."

Zhong didn't counter. He never mentioned the artificial hand, obeying the unspoken rule.

"Hoa."

He won anyway.

It was an enormous relief for Uri to have his second only friend back, even if he was a geek. Uri wondered if he lacked popularity with the other geeks, who tolerated him without getting close. Maybe that's why he kept Uri around, always at his convenience, never missing his club times. Unless Uri joined the clubs, which he wouldn't be able to do because he was a "D" student in math, uninterested in learning to code, he couldn't tell for sure.Simon was glad Uri had his friend back.

"You two are good for each other. You'll help Zhong with English and American culture. And he's a good kid. It'll build your reputation for people to see you hang out with him."

Meaning it might remove some stigma of his past. As if the stigma wasn't right on his face, in case anyone forgot his criminal deed, Zhong or no Zhong. The scar might as well have spelled out, "murdered his own mother."

People still turned to look when he went to the mall or the public library, unlike the kids from school and Youth Group who were used to him. He dreaded graduation, a year and a half off, when he would get a job, if anyone would hire him, or go to college, exposing himself to the stares of strangers.

Mothers who passed by him put protective arms around their children, steering them away from the "monster," shushing them if they said anything or pointed. The younger ones stared, pausing mid-suck on their thumbs, straining against the hand pulling them in the opposite direction. Every so often, a grandmotherly type, often with a limp or disability herself, gave him a compassionate smile, looking like she would give him an oatmeal cookie just out of the oven if she carried one with her in her oversized purse.

"What business is it of yours if I'm scarred, cunt?"

Uri only thought this, saying nothing out loud. He arranged his features so he wouldn't look as mad as he was. After a few seconds, there was a bubbly sensation in his chest. Before he banished the memory, an image of his mother arose. He had no right to miss her after what he had done. It was another uncontrollable part of his mind.

Simon had something to tell him.

"There's someone coming for dinner tonight I want you to meet. It's a woman. I've been seeing her for a while, but I didn't tell you until I knew it's serious. Well, it is serious. Her name is Flora."

"Okay."

A woman? Uri had a bad feeling. It had only been three years since his mother's engagement and near marriage, by thirty-six hours, to his foster father. What was Simon's rush? He reminded himself that he didn't like Simon and didn't care what he did. Except this Flora woman might get him kicked out if she disliked him.

"I'm going to try my hand at spaghetti carbonara with a salad and a good red wine. Better than the usual. It'll have to be a store-bought dessert. I'm no baker. Any suggestions?"

"Dunno."

"Put on your *Shabbat* clothing. I don't want Flora to think I dress you in rags."

He chuckled, shaking his head at the thought.

"Does she know about…?" Uri touched his facial scar.

Simon answered without looking at him, as if the subject was a casual one.

"I may have mentioned it."

After a silent moment, in which Simon pursed his lips as if considering what to say, he looked straight at Uri.

"Flora and I have been dating for several months, Uri. We've told each other a lot about ourselves. She told me about her first marriage, and I told her about, you know, what happened with your mother and Adam."

It was a shock for him to say "your mother" and the name of his son, Uri's first only friend. Simon didn't talk about the past to Uri. But he talked about it with this Flora. Simon hadn't forgotten the woman he had been engaged to. But Uri was glad that—until now—he never mentioned her.

Uri had a revolting vision of Simon dropping his arm around Uri's shoulders, saying, "Son, let's talk about the time you set fire to your house and burned up your mother and my son. You didn't mean to do what you did. Right?"

If Simon ever said any of that, Uri swore he would run straight to the kitchen, grab a long knife, and stab his foster father in his fucking heart. He had already killed one parent. Why not two? He would never let Simon turn him into a weak, sniveling coward, weeping on his shoulder and whining about it all being his fault, even if it was.

He remembered his kid fantasy about having a harsh father who wouldn't stand for a weakling son and who would administer the punishment Uri deserved. Uri didn't want Simon's or anyone's sympathy. That wouldn't fix his face or the empty, twisted, wrung out sensation in his gut.

"I think you and Flora will get along. She's a lovely person. Uri, it will please me if you'll give her a chance."

Simon smiled at him as if they had come to an agreement.

"Okay."

Uri watched Simon's arm, preparing to duck away if he saw it move toward him.

"Good. Now you go get ready while I make the sauce."

Simon headed for the kitchen, while Uri continued to sit, wondering why any woman would date a flabby old bald guy. She had to be ugly. Probably fat. Very fat. With extra-wide clunky white shoes, like his old English teacher, Mrs. Green, wore.

He went upstairs to his bedroom to wait, trading his t-shirt for a button-down one. The chessboard he and Zhong used was on the floor, where they played, set up for the next game. Uri's problem was that he overused his queen and wound up losing. He must learn to let other pieces take the offensive.

For as long as possible, Uri delayed going downstairs. He heard the doorbell ring, Simon's welcoming baritone, the soft murmur of a woman, and two sets of footsteps, one of which was the tap of shoes with heels, not the clunky kind. Hers. He alternated between holding his breath so he could hear and panting as nervousness overtook him. What was he supposed to say to this woman, Flora, who knew about his disfigurement and his past?

"Uri, come down. It's time to light *Shabbat* candles." Simon yelled up to him.

After dawdling for a few more minutes, Uri ventured out of his room. Simon waited at the bottom of the staircase with Flora. Uri stood stock still, half-way down in shock. The woman was dark-haired, slender, and younger than Simon, about thirty-five or forty. She looked like his mother. More than the same type of woman. She could have been her clone.

With his head in a whirl, Uri gripped the bannister on the rest of the way down to prevent himself from falling. Was it his mother? Not dead after all?

"Uri, this is Flora. And Flora, this is my foster son." Simon beamed during the introductions.

"Hello, Uri. I'm so glad to meet you. I've heard so much about you. It's like I've met you already."

She sounded like his mother, same east coast accent, same soothing tone. Her name was Flora? It stunned him to remember at that moment that his mother's name was Lora. He nodded, although his tongue wanted to scream, "Is this a joke?" He used his teeth to keep the deranged muscle under control, not daring to let it speak.

"How about you doing the honors with the candles for us? It's been a long time since I've had a woman here to light them," Simon said.

The last woman would have been his mother.

They were in the dining room. Flora struck a match, something that always fascinated Uri when his mother did it and fascinated him again, seeing Simon's new girlfriend do it in the same way his mother did, lighting the two candles the same way, using her cupped hands to bring the light toward her the same way.

"*Baruch Atah Adonai*… Blessed are You, God…"

She intoned the prayer, sounding like his mother.

Later, after a dinner in which only Simon and Flora spoke while Uri stared at his plate, and Flora had said her goodbyes, Uri confronted Simon.

"She looks exactly like my mother!"

"Nonsense. Their hair color may be similar, but Flora looks nothing like your mother."

"They're like twins."

"It's not true, Uri. Your mind's playing tricks on you. Flora is warm. She can't replace your actual mother, no one can. If you let her, she'll be a mother-figure to you."

His teeth ground with hatred of his foster father, who deliberately chose a mother-look-alike with almost the same name as his mother. He parsed a sentence in his head. "Flora is Lora." Noun and object were interchangeable. Was the verb correct? "Is" or "resembles?" The verb was the most important part of speech in this case. His sanity depended on getting it right.

CHAPTER 4

On one of their regular days to play chess, Zhong met Uri on the school steps.

"Can't play today."

"Why the fuck not?" Uri looked forward to his time with his second only friend. The days he didn't see him were lonely ones.

"I hang out with new boy in Youth Group, Vel."

"Vel? That's his name?" He wouldn't admit he already heard his name or had any interest in him.

"*Hoa.*"

"That's okay. I'm busy anyway."

They walked the rest of the way in silence until they reached their separate intersections. He said nothing about the next chess-playing date. To Uri's dismay, Zhong made the same excuse the following week and the week after. He lost his second only friend without a third one on the horizon. Not because he had done anything wrong. Because Zhong liked someone else better.

The new boy, Vel, made an impression on the group from the moment Rabbi Shapiro introduced him. It was hard to explain why. He was of medium build with long hair pulled back into a rubber band, mischievous blue eyes, and a clever grin. Each person in the group, including Uri, received a quick sizing-up glance and a slight nod. It may have been an invitation or a dismissal. The uncertainty stirred excitement and tension in the room. Even the Rabbi seemed caught up in it.

"You can sit here, next to me," he said.

The group sat in a circle. Everyone scraped their chair over to make the space indicated by Rabbi Shapiro for the extra seat. Vel sat without hesitation, accepting the spot made for him. He kept peering at the others with his knowing blue eyes, as if already having decided something about each. Zhong received his most lingering stare and sustained smile. The Chinese boy had been chosen.

Rabbi Shapiro continued his lesson.

"This week we study *Leviticus* 25:1 to 27:34, in which God permits the use of slavery. What do you think about that?"

Hands shot up. The usually sullen teens vied to give answers—the slaves had to be treated well; it was a common practice of the times; the verses promised eventual freedom—looking toward Vel for approval.

The last to speak was Vel himself.

"We are all slaves to something or someone. You Tube, music, a game, a friend. The thing is to choose what to be a slave to."

Rabbi Shapiro hesitated before replying.

"Do you think *Leviticus* is saying that slavery or addiction is okay?"

"Maybe God is a slave to the Israelites. He can't seem to destroy them even when they worship idols," Vel said.

Everyone looked toward Rabbi Shapiro, waiting to see if he would scold the new boy for his untraditional response. Uri's rounded shoulders straightened. God wouldn't be God if He was a slave instead of the master of the universe.

Rabbi Shapiro cleared his throat, gazing at Vel a moment longer than typical of him. His stumped brow knitted.

"Interesting point." He evaded a lengthier response.

When no one had anything else to say, Vel continued his survey of the group, without the smug smile everyone expected after the Rabbi's defeat. Vel didn't give a sign that he cared about the Rabbi's lack of further comment or that the Rabbi's opinion mattered to him. That diminished the Rabbi's authority for everyone in the group. Uri's chest caved again. Within minutes of the new boy's arrival, he had sorted the group into those who mattered and those who didn't. Uri didn't, but wanted to.

After that, whenever Uri asked Zhong to play chess, he claimed to be unavailable. He hinted that he had dropped out of the coding and math clubs to hang with Vel.

"What's so great about him?" Uri pretended disinterest.

"He know about Jews in China."

"What about them?"

"Jews in China from eighth century. Called *Youtairen* in Mandarin. From *Yehudi*, Aramaic word for Jew. In China longer than America."

"So what's your fucking point?"

"Vel interested."

"It's just nerd interest. Nerds are interested in everything. They have no priorities, man."

"You only interested chess. And you rotten player."

"Oh, yeah? Who played with you when no one else would?"

Zhong's answer came so fast, he must have rehearsed it.

"Who play you when no one else!"

At home, in his room, he kicked the wall, something he hadn't done since his mother was alive. Why should he care about Jews in China? Let Vel and Zhong bore each other to death. He didn't need either. He didn't need anyone.

Without Zhong, Uri had more time on his hands to be at home with Simon. He stayed in his room, hoping to avoid Flora. She visited often, staying for dinner and showing up for breakfast the next morning in Simon's extra bathrobe, with wet hair piled in a towel. When it was just the two of them, she tried to get him to speak by asking him questions.

"So... What are your plans for after graduation?"

"Dunno. College, I guess. If I, like, get my grades up enough."

"Do you need help? A tutor, maybe?"

"I'm good."

These were typical getting-to-know-your-future-foster-stepson questions. He gave her getting-to-know-me answers. Sometimes she surprised him, though, asking him something when her back was turned, while walking out the door.

"Did you empty the ashtrays?"

There were no ashtrays in the house. His mother had smoked, but Simon never had.

"What ashtrays?" He looked around to see if any showed up.

"Just don't hide the matches," she'd say from the next room.

He'd stand there, staring after her, the smell of her perfume, the one with the undertone of smoke, still lingering in the room. Either she was a ghost or she was a human wanting to trick him. Back in his room, he spoke out loud to his mother.

"Is she you, Mom? Are you haunting me because of what I did to you?"

No one answered. A vise tightened around Uri's brain.

In Youth Group, Rabbi Shapiro sat on Vel's left and Zhong on Vel's right. Everyone else sat in their usual chairs. Uri sat across from Vel. Several times during the hour, Vel whispered to Zhong, whose eyes jolted toward Uri, then crinkled in amusement. It was clear to Uri that they made fun of him, of his scar, his awkwardness, his utter lack of coolness.

He imagined the three of them alone in a dark place.

"You whispered about me in the group. Say what you said to my face. I dare you," he'd say.

Without warning, the two would jump him. Zhong would hold him down while Vel gave him several sharp kicks.

"Had enough?" Vel would ask. "Get off him. Let's go."

They would walk away with Vel's hand on Zhong's shoulder. In reality, they walked out together with several others, paying no attention to Uri, who followed at a distance. It's worse to be ignored than getting beat up, he thought, longing to catch up with the group but too proud to reveal such neediness.

Alone in his room, Uri's daydreams picked up detail. He stood in a sort of courtroom. Vel was the judge and prosecutor, assisted by Zhong.

"You stand accused of setting fire to your house and killing your mother."

"Adam threw the match at the curtain, not me," he said. His desperate voice ranged an octave higher.

"The accused is trying to shift the blame to his first only friend," Zhong said.

"How do you plead?"

"I can't be guilty if my mother's still alive."

Among the observers in the gallery was a dark-haired woman, who stood up and spoke.

"I'm Flora. He murdered Lora, his mother, not me. Now, he's trying to get out of it by pretending I'm her ghost."

A roar of disapproval arose from the gallery. Vel banged his gavel.

"Quiet in the court!"

The crowd quieted.

"How do you plead?" Vel repeated.

Uri hung his head. "Guilty, Your Honor."

"I sentence you to a beating, to be carried out now. The court orders the man who wrestled Jacob to administer the beating. After the beating, I condemn you to a life of solitary confinement."

The doors in the back of the courtroom burst open. A giant of a man entered and advanced toward Uri, his enormous hands already cemented into fists.

CHAPTER 5

In May 2015, Simon gave Uri his first smartphone, an iPhone 6 with a measly 16 GB, but, hey, it was a huge step-up from the flip phone he received as a *bar mitzvah* gift when he was still in the hospital. It was a present for making it into his senior year. The school system supplied foster kids with Chromebooks, just for assignments, without gaming capability. Now, for the first time, he could text and game.

Not that he had anyone to text to or game with, except for online groups. He could only do the free ones, like Fortnite and World of Tanks. He also found chat rooms, where no one could see his scar. The one he liked best was "Tough Talk." He lurked without posting, fascinated by the way the posters took each other on. The most frequent poster was WhipUGood, who had over ten thousand followers. Uri "liked" his posts, wishing to be noticed.

WhipUGood: I'll crack your jaw and chew your tongue out.

Steelspine: Go try. I'll rip your balls off.

WhipUGood: FuckU

Steelspine: FuckU

Uri practiced editing by copying the posts from Tough Talk and pasting them to posts to Zhong.

Uri: I'll crack your jaw and chew your tongue out.

Zhong: Why you say that?

Uri: I'll rip your balls off.

Zhong: What matter with you?
Uri: FuckU
Zhong: Want to play chess Tuesday? My house?

Uri's breath stopped. Zhong hadn't played chess with him since Winter Break. Now, suddenly, he invited him to his place. What happened to Vel? Did he have the flu or whatever?

The next Sunday, when he arrived at the synagogue for Youth Group, there was another surprise waiting. Zhong was already there, in Uri's usual seat. Vel saw him enter and motioned with a sideways tilt of his head for Uri to sit next to him. With a backward glance at Zhong, Uri crossed the circle.

Half-way through the meeting, Vel sent Uri a sly text, the first he ever received.

"Look at that schmuck, staring at us with his gook eyes."

At that moment, Rabbi Shapiro led a discussion on the *Torah* command to "love thy neighbor."

"And who is meant by neighbor? Is it the person who lives next door or the community? According to tradition, it means other Israelites, other Jews."

Zhong was one of the Jews he was supposed to love. Uri had an impulse to defend him. Even though he himself called Zhong names like "gook," when Vel said the same thing, Uri didn't know whether it was offensive or cool. He did what Zhong had done to him, conveying amusement at his second only friend's expense. It was worth all the violations in the *Torah* to be in Vel's inner circle.

After the meeting, Vel became his third only friend. They walked out of the synagogue together and leaned against the building, talking about Zhong.

"Like, what happened with you and Zhong?" Uri hid all traces of interest in his voice.

"The dude's a *savant* or whatever. He's too into numbers for me."

"What's a *savant*?"

"You know, like on the spectrum. Autistic."

Uri tried to digest this news. He had heard of autistic kids who couldn't speak and went to Special Ed classes.

"How can you tell? Because his English isn't good?"

"Nah. He's, like, in the math club. All those dudes are on the high end of the spectrum. They, like, memorize airline schedules and thousands of pi numbers and stuff."

Both stared after Zhong's retreating back as he made his way down the street, toward his home, alone.

"See? All by himself. Not interacting with anyone. Autistic."

Uri realized that he, too, hadn't interacted with anyone in the group when Zhong stopped playing chess with him. His throat constricted at the thought that the next words out of Vel's mouth might be: "I used to think you were autistic when you had no friends."

But what Vel said was even more embarrassing.

"Hey, man, have you fucked any of the girls in Youth Group yet?"

There were three—Sylvia, Lois and Jenny. Uri had known them since synagogue pre-school. He was too used to them to think of them as fuckable. They were just there, like the chairs in the circle. But his major concern was giving Vel a not-autistic answer. Zhong would have shifted the conversation to chess or computers. It wouldn't be cool for Vel to think Uri was a seventeen-year-old virgin who never even spoke to a girl.

"Not exactly. Have you?"

"I'm working on it. I made out with all three and got them competing for me. Smoke?"

Vel lit two cigarettes and gave one to Uri, who hadn't smoked since he was twelve, when he ground lit butts into his skin. He was too scared that striking a match would lead him in the wrong direction. Besides, if Rabbi Shapiro caught them, there would be trouble. Vel didn't seem to care.

"How d'you do that?"

"Easy, dude. Just tell each one she's my favorite. The rest takes care of itself."

Uri didn't ask him to explain, even though he did not know what Vel meant. He didn't want to give away his ignorance about girls or give Vel the wrong impression. Unless it was the right impression.

"The thing is… my face and my hand put some girls off."

He wanted to confess the obvious, heading off the subject before Vel brought it up.

Vel smiled at him. "That's just it, man. You can turn them into your thing. Your strength. They can be mysterious to girls, and girls like mysterious guys. Play it right, and you'll have dozens on your doorstep wanting to blow you."

Could Vel say anything that wouldn't be a shocker or the opposite of what anyone else might say? Uri headed home, crossing streets without looking, not registering the blares of car horns, in a daze of confusion and excitement. He had a cool new friend. He wasn't autistic. His face could be his strength. Zhong was out, and he was in.

The first thing Uri did when he reached his house was text Zhong.

Sorry, man. Can't play chess Tuesday. I'm hanging out with Vel.

"LOL," he thought. He rubbed it in the way Zhong had done with him. "See how you like it."

Not knowing what to do with his elation, he logged into "Tough Talk," which—like wrestling—always gave him a boner. He pictured WhipUGood looking like Vel.

WhipUGood: Who wants their head stomped?

Just when the postings peaked in aggression, Simon called.

"Uri, could we talk to you for a minute, please?"

Flora sat with him, waiting in the living room, which was odd. Most of their conversations took place in the kitchen. The two adults were together on the sofa, holding hands. They motioned Uri to the easy chair opposite them.

"Flora has something to show you, don't you, dear?"

With a broad smile, the image of his mother's, she held out her left hand, palm downward. A ring that looked familiar sparkled on her finger.

"We're engaged. Your father proposed last night. You're the first to know," she said.

Uri stared at the ring—an exact likeness of the one Simon had given his mother. Or the same one he gave her? He tried to remember if they had buried her remains, which he did not see, with the ring. Rings were known to survive fires and to be found later. Did a firefighter or Simon himself retrieve it?

He felt himself flush with rage, without understanding why. Did Simon betray his mother by giving her ring to her double, or was it sensible to use it again?—if it was the same one and not a new one of the same design.

"I figured Flora would say 'yes.' So I took the liberty of talking to Rabbi Shapiro last week about dates for a wedding next November. Sunday the 22nd is open. We both agreed to book it then."

"The wedding date with my mother was supposed to be, like, November 20th."

Simon's eyebrows raised. He looked at Flora, checking to see if this offended her. She smiled at him and patted his arm with approval.

"Just a coincidence, son. I didn't even think of that."

They would be married on a date that was almost the fourth anniversary of the death of his mother and Simon's son. It might even be their *Yahrzeit*, or very close to it. They might be expected to recite the *Kaddish* prayer for the deceased on the night before the wedding. It seemed like a terrible plan, but Simon claimed it was a coincidence. Could that be true?

Simon opened a bottle of champagne, poured a glass for Flora and himself and a thimbleful for Uri.

"I guess we can allow a minor to have a taste, since it's a special occasion," Simon said.

It was another embarrassment that at his age, the only alcohol Uri had before this was Kosher wine at *Seders* and at *Shabbat* services before his *bar mitzvah*, when children were called to the *bimah* for sips from the *kiddush* cup. All the other kids snuck drinks from their parents' stash or from what older kids supplied. Uri was too scared his foster father, who had every reason to despise him, would kick him out.

But now one reason to despise him—the death of Uri's mother, Simon's former fiancé— was reversed by his engagement to Flora, his mother's look-alike. Would that make Simon like him less or like him more?

"There's something else," Simon said.

Instantly, Uri stiffened.

"It would be an honor if you'd be my Best Man at the wedding."

The next day, in the school cafeteria, Lois caught up with him.

"Can we talk?" She asked.

"Uh, I guess." He carried a tray toward the table occupied by Vel and his admirers.

"Sit with me for just a minute."

She led him to an empty table.

"You're best friends with Vel, right?" She twirled one of her red curls.

"We, like, hang out and things."

"Can I ask you a question?" Her pleading eyes stared into his.

"Whatever."

"Does Vel ever say anything about me?"

"I don't think so, not really." He wouldn't say Vel had plans to fuck her and the other two girls.

"Does he ever mention me or say my name?"

"We only talk about school and the group and stuff."

"Oh." She bit her lip.

"Can I ask a favor?"

"I guess."

"If he says anything about me, even just my name, tell me. Okay?"

"I'll try. If I can."

"If you tell me, I'll do you a favor, too. Sometime."

What did she mean? Would she blow him, as Vel said girls might if they liked his scar? Unless she meant helping him with his homework or a favor more like that.

At the table with Vel, his third only friend punched his upper arm.

"Wahoo! You got Lois in the bag, dude. I saw how she was asking you for it. I just want you to do one thing for me, pal."

"Okay."

"Tell me when you fuck her."

CHAPTER 6

After school, when he was near home, Uri saw Jenny waiting on his doorstep. Her long brown hair hung in thick waves, as it had since they were both three-years old.

"Hey," she said.

"Hey."

"Would you like to earn twenty dollars?" She moved to the middle of the step, barring his way.

"It depends."

He earned that much doing chores for Simon.

She glanced up and down the street as if she had a secret passers-by might hear.

"Look, I need to make Vel jealous."

"How come?"

"He says I'm his favorite girlfriend, but I found out he said the same thing to Lois and Sylvia. I want to be his *favorite* favorite."

"By making him jealous?" He had a vague idea where this might be going.

"Yeah. If he thinks another guy likes me, like his best friend, he'll be more interested. It happened to my sister. She was crazy for this guy, Rick, but he wasn't into her until she got together with one of his friends. After that, he had a thing for her."

"Okay. I get it."

He shifted his backpack to his other shoulder.

"So if you get Vel to believe we have a thing for each other, I'll pay you the twenty. See?"

He looked down at the walkway. Ants streamed in the staircase's seam. They all went in the same direction except one, who touched the antennas of all those it passed. Was it pleading for a place in the line?

"You can start by telling Vel I'm cute and you like me and whatever."

"Okay."

"We're getting together Saturday night at Jenny's house. When Vel is looking, come over to me. Talk for a minute, then kiss me. But no tongue, okay? Do it like a stage kiss. Remember, I'm not into you. This is for Vel to notice me."

"I have to, like, think about it."

If he agreed, it would be his first kiss. But it might not count because it would be a fake. Besides, he wasn't sure it was right to pull a fake on Vel. He might get mad or laugh at him. He might catch on that Uri hadn't any idea how to kiss, that it was a stage kiss with no tongue. Uri hated being laughed at by anyone. He reddened at the thought.

"You're blushing," Jenny said. "If you're into me, forget it. This is only a job. *Geez.*"

The ant was halfway across the seam. It wasn't having any luck. The others ignored it.

"I'll let you know."

He pushed past her into the house and ran right up to his room.

A text came from Zhong.

"*My father say Vel not good influence. Will get friends in trouble. Stay away him.*"

His conversation with Jenny brought jealousy to his mind.

"*You envy Vel hanging with me, like he used to with you. Chill, man.*"

"*You be sorry. He drop you one day for someone else.*"

"*Fuck off, Zhong.*"

One thing Vel predicted had come true. Two of the three girls in Youth Group and maybe the third, he figured he'd find out soon enough, competed to be Vel's *favorite* favorite. They seemed ready to do anything, even let him fuck them, he'd bet. They viewed Uri as a way of reaching Vel. Was that a good thing or a bad thing? On the good side, he practiced talking to girls. On the bad side, they used him. If what Zhong said came true, and Vel hung out with a new best friend, the girls would ignore him.

There was a knock on his door. Simon entered, wanting to talk. It was as unusual for Simon to come to his room as it had been when he and Flora announced their engagement in the living room. Uri couldn't recall ever having a serious conversation with Simon anywhere but the kitchen, during a meal or preparation for one.

"I've told you Flora has an eleven-year-old son, haven't I?" Uri lay on the bed. Simon sat on the edge.

"No."

"I haven't? Well, he's been living with his father. Flora thought he should have a male role model, since he's a boy. Now that we're marrying, I'll be his step-father. I can be a male role model, too."

"Okay." Uri's stomach pinched. An eleven-year-old boy. The age Adam was when he died in the fire.

"What's his name?"

"Adan."

"Adan? For real?" It couldn't be.

"Yes, Adan."

"Your son, Adam, was eleven when he died."

Simon frowned. He didn't like being reminded of his son.

"Your point?"

"Adam. Adan. It's, like, near the same name and the same age."

"If you're saying I'm getting my son back, no one can replace Adam. But having another pre-*bar mitzvah* boy in the house makes me glad."

"In the house?" Uri shifted into a sitting position. Something was coming he didn't want to hear.

"That's what I came up to tell you. Adan's coming for the summer for a trial run. If everyone gets along, he may stay for the school year or even longer. Flora is very hopeful."

Uri had a sense of *deja vu*. The past repeated itself. His life turned into a science fiction movie. He guessed what Simon would say next.

"Since this is a three-bedroom bungalow, and the third bedroom is my home office, what makes the most sense is for him to bunk with you for the summer. If he's going to stay longer, we'll buy a bigger house."

"Share a room with me, you mean."

Simon no longer surprised him.

"It's only for the summer, son. Six, eight weeks. You'll be moving to a dorm in another year anyway, if you get into a college."

Uri remembered his rage when he had to share his room with Adam, and how he wound up enjoying his first best friend being there. This time, he didn't go into a rage. Instead, he was defeated, dispirited, and unable to complain because Simon was his foster father, not his real father or even his step-father.

"Do you want help to make space for him? I'll be bringing in an extra bed."

"No. I'll take care of it."

Simon smiled and patted Uri's leg before rising from the bed.

"That's the spirit, son. I knew I could count on you."

Uri wished he could ask Rabbi Shapiro if God played a trick on him to punish him or gave him a second chance to do *Teshuva*, repent. Maybe he was supposed to be nice to Flora and Adan. At least he could avoid setting them on fire and killing them. That would be something. Rabbi Shapiro wasn't the type to help him find an answer. Like all adults, he'd poo-poo the worries of kids. It's all in your imagination. It's a coincidence. You'll be okay.

The party at Jenny's started at nine on Saturday night, after *Havdalah*. Uri hadn't been to one since the birthday parties of his childhood, before the fire. His stomach knotted. He didn't know what to wear, what to say, or how to be cool with kids who had been to scores of parties. He yanked his Harley t-shirt over his head, figuring he couldn't go wrong with it. Once, when he wore it to school, a couple of classmates looked at it and nodded. He took that as approval, then stowed it away in case he needed a special shirt in the future. Today was that future.

What time to show up was the next decision. Adults talked about being "fashionably late" for parties. By 8:30, he was too antsy to wait. He wanted to get it over with, if he was going to make a clown of himself. After walking around the block twice to ensure he wouldn't be a few minutes early, he arrived at 9 p.m. sharp.

A small group was already in the basement of Jenny's house. He stood just inside the door, watching. Loud music played. Uri knew little about music, but he recognized Dubstep. A couple of kids danced, jumping and waving their hands overhead.

Someone tapped him on the shoulder. It was Vel.

"Hey, man. You made it! We're going to get shitfaced tonight. Let's get started. Come with me."

Jenny's parents were away. They had built an actual bar in the basement, with a counter and a mirror on the wall. She wasn't in the room yet. Everyone not dancing stood at the bar or sat on one of the swivel stools. None attended Youth Group, but they all knew Vel.

"Hey, man. What's happening?"

"Dude! Where ya been?"

"Let's get crazy."

"Who's got some X?"

"I do," Vel said. He reached into the pocket of his jeans.

Turning to Uri, Vel said, "Open your mouth and close your eyes."

He did what Vel told him to do. Two pills landed on his tongue. He swallowed. Nothing happened.

Kids continued to pour in. Someone handed Uri a drink called a "shot." It burned his throat. Vel had his hand on Uri's back, on his shoulder, on the nape of his neck, keeping him near, laughing, making others laugh. Not at Uri, though. With Vel's help, he kept up.

Everyone cheered when Jenny burst in, accompanied by Lois and Sylvia. They wore similar shorts and halter tops, each in differing colors. It astounded Uri how pretty they looked. He realized they wore makeup and had done things to their hair they never did for Youth Group. As they moved around the room, avoiding Vel but trying to attract his attention by joining the dancers, Jenny caught Uri's eye, mouthing *"twenty dollars."* Lois raised her eyebrows at him. *"Has he said my name?"* Sylvia looked his way without signaling.

A half-hour had gone by. Or an hour. Uri felt good, better than good, terrific. He drank more shots. He danced. Anything anyone said was so funny that he and Vel collapsed against each other with laughter. He told his third best friend he loved him, and Vel said he loved him back. It was the first time since the fire that Uri was unburdened enough to stand straight, forgetting his scar, his ugliness, his lost hand, his glass eye, his terrible guilt, the tricks God played on him.

Later, he was in a bedroom with Sylvia. She sobbed.

"I love him so much. If he would only… I don't care if he has a thing for other girls as long as I'm his favorite. I'd even share him. If only he'd…"

They stood opposite each other. He had no awareness of leaving the basement. Her sobs intensified. Tears, blackened by mascara, streamed down her face in dark rivulets. She leaned her head on his chest. Looking down at her blond curls made him so sad for her that he cried, too.

"I know… *sob*… how you feel… *sob*… so lonely," he blubbered.

They hugged and cried, then kissed. Real kissing with tongues. They fell onto the bed, still kissing. It was king-size, the one Jenny's parents slept in. Uri had a boner bigger than from wrestling.

Between kisses, Sylvia kept repeating, "I love him so much."

"I love you so much. Let me... Please let me..."

"I don't care. I want you in me, Vel, now," she moaned.

In the moment, it registered on Uri that they were both drunk, high, and that she mistook him for Vel, but it didn't matter. He wanted what he wanted, and if she offered it, he'd take it. Just this one night.

The next day, when he woke up in his own bed, he didn't know how he got there or remember anything that happened the night before.

CHAPTER 7

As Uri expected, Adan looked like Adam. Same bangs, same long eyelashes, same freckles. God's trickery continued. If he thought it would do any good to point out the obvious, Simon would call it a coincidence, if he acknowledged the resemblance at all.

The surprise was that he didn't have Adam's friendly personality. He entered his summer home with defiant eyes, looking around the premises with scoffing huffs. After enduring a hug from Flora, he disregarded Simon's attempt to shake his hand. He gazed at Uri with his lip curled into a sneer.

"Welcome to our home, son. We want you to think of it as your home, too. This is your big foster brother, Uri. You'll be sharing a room with him."

Simon assumed a mock cheerful tone, ignoring the boy's sullenness.

"*Ew.* What's the matter with his face? The right side looks like leather. He's the ugliest dude I've ever seen."

"Adan! Manners!" Flora said.

"He's a creep. His face is a creep's face, and his hand, or whatever it is, is a creep's hand."

"This is your father's influence. I didn't raise you to be rude. Apologize to Uri right now," Flora said.

Instead, he threw his backpack on the floor.

"I'm not sharing a room with 'it'."

Simon spoke up, trying to reason with him.

"We've occupied all the other bedrooms, son. The master bedroom is for your mother and me; my home office is where I work; and that leaves Uri's room. There's nowhere else."

Uri figured keeping quiet was his best bet. Let Flora and Simon handle the tsunami they invited into the house. His feelings were mixed. Immediate hatred for the little fucker for calling him a "creep" and his scar "leather." Immediate relief that Adan was nothing like Adam and that he had no obligation to befriend him. Smug satisfaction that Simon would have to deal with the consequences of choosing his mother's double. Doubtful that sharing a room would work out. Fear that if he dropped his guard for a moment, Adan would pull something.

As soon as they were up in their room, Adan threw all of Uri's possessions in a heap in the corner. Even though he only brought his summer clothing with him and his most portable digital devices, he used all the shelf space, the entire closet, and all the drawers in the dresser. He glared at Uri, daring him to object. Uri didn't. He didn't care.

"Where's theTV?" Adan said.

"There isn't one in here."

Uri relaxed. This was going to be interesting.

Adan galloped down the stairs to the kitchen, where Simon and Flora waited.

"Where's the TV for my bedroom?"

His voice was so loud, Uri heard every word he said from upstairs. Flora murmured a response.

"Dad let me have my own TV. If I have to share a space with *el creepo,* at least I could have a tv."

Now it was Simon's turn to murmur.

"That's not fair. You should give me the TV that's in your bedroom. I need it more than you."

After more murmurs and a crash, Uri heard footsteps on the staircase. A few minutes later, Simon carried the TV into the boys' room, set it on the dresser, and turned it to face Adan's bed. He aimed a strained smile at his foster son and retreated downstairs.

The first hour of Adan's residency was over.

Uri vowed to get his grades up in his senior year so he could go to college, leave home and get away from Adan, in case the boy didn't return to his father. Now that it was summer, Uri needed a job. His face prevented him from working anywhere customers might see him. His artificial hand kept him from jobs requiring fine motor skills. His lack of vision in one eye didn't allow him to take jobs necessitating a driver's license. Simon persuaded Rabbi Shapiro to hire him to mow the synagogue lawn and keep the grounds tidy. The pay was minimum wage for twenty hours a week.

Vel, not the best swimmer, scored a desirable position as a lifeguard at the city pool. After two weeks, he was the color of bronze. Although he didn't have the abs or the pecs of guys who worked out, swimmers flocked to his tower, trying to get his attention. He sorted them into accepted and rejected with slight nods, as he had when he entered Youth Group. The sorting changed, sometimes daily, raising the temperature of the swimmers. Uri experienced it himself when he went to the pool after work. He feared his third best friend might throw him aside with no explanation, as Zhong predicted.

In fact, when the pool closed for the day, Vel hung out with another lifeguard, Sam, who wasn't in Youth Group. During the next party at whoever's house had absent parents, Vel still kept close tabs on Uri, as far as Uri remembered. He would be too shitfaced to recall anything that happened after the first few minutes.

Vel draped an arm around Uri's neck, teasing him about how shots, pills, and weed wasted him, amusing things he said or did, and what he did with girls.

"We saw Sylvia dragging you upstairs at that last party. Did you bang her? Jenny got in big trouble when her parents discovered the state of their bed and half the liquor gone from their bar."

He laughed, tightening his arm hold on Uri.

"Hey, Sam. Did you see that? Sylvia dragging him upstairs?" His other arm was draped around his new bro.

Sam was a short, muscular guy with a shaved head and a nose ring. His hostile eyes gazed at Uri. They were enemies, competing for Vel's favor. Vel played them off each other. Uri knew what he was doing, whispering shit about Sam to him and shit about him to Sam. It was the same thing he did to the three girls in Youth Group, fermenting a competition.

It took awhile for Uri to realize Vel talked about fucking the girls, but never did. The girls complained about it, longing for sexual proof that Vel preferred one or another of them. The sport of setting the girls up against each other, breaking up their inseparableness, was what turned him on. It was like the way he had played Uri and Zhong and now played Uri and Sam. Vel enjoyed being a master manipulator.

Uri despised himself for not having the will-power to leave the game Vel played. His extreme feelings—elation when chosen and despair when rejected—and the frequency with which they alternated, kept him off-kilter. Deciding to give up his third best friend was balanced by deciding to stick with him forever, savoring the moments Vel tossed him crumbs of affection.

He watched wrestling when Adan wasn't in the room, turning the tv toward his bed, imagining Vel as the stronger wrestler putting him into painful holds, throwing him against the ropes, jumping on him when he fell to the floor. Sometimes, Adan showed up when he didn't expect him.

"You're jerking off for wrestlers. Ha! You're not only a creep and a freak, you're a fag, too. I knew it!"

What Adan was going to enjoy while he lived in Simon's house was getting Uri into trouble.

"Simon, did you know your foster son's a fag?"

Simon continued to try a logical response to nastiness.

"That is unkind, Adan. What does God want you to do?"

Adan smirked when Simon fell into one of his traps.

"Let's me think. Murder, steal, worship idols, commit adultery, covet, and most of all, dishonor your father and mother. Did I forget any?"

Later, when they were alone, Simon apologized to Uri, but not for Adan's smart-aleck insults.

"I have to let you down. I wanted you to be my Best Man at the wedding. Adan makes a point when he says it's his rightful place as Flora's biological son. I'm afraid you'll have to give him the role he wants. That way, the wedding will go smoothly. I wouldn't ask this of you if I didn't know what a good sport you are."

"So, like, I won't be the Best Man?"

Uri didn't want Simon to marry Flora, but he wanted Simon to favor him over her brat of a son. If Vel didn't always favor him, at least his foster father could.

"You can be an usher." Simon's eyes shifted away from Uri. He was embarrassed.

"Whatever."

Uri suspected Simon understood giving in to Adan was a bad idea. He himself gave in because he didn't care. Simon gave in to please Flora and to win Adan over, to keep him from throwing a fit, to protect himself from the boy's fury. Was Simon scared of Adan?

His kid fantasies of a stern father returned. He remembered hating it when Simon said he was "disappointed" instead of whacking him. Maybe he wouldn't have played with matches if he honored his mother's fiancé more. A couple of hard whacks would straighten Adan out. He needed a whipping before he grew bigger than the adults who might administer it.

He imagined Simon delegating the job to him.

"Take Adan upstairs and punish him," he would say, handing Uri his belt.

Flora's view was the opposite of his. When they were alone in the kitchen, she told him so.

"What Adan needs is your big-brother guidance. His father didn't give him any attention. He just threw gifts at him, whatever money could purchase. Adan is smart. He saw through his father's attempts to buy his love. We won't make that mistake."

"Like, you gave him your tv."

"Only because it was his first day here. You could tell how insecure he was. Beneath it all, he's a very sweet boy."

"Okay." What was he supposed to say to that?

He had hardly been a sweet boy, yet his mother still loved him. She may not anymore, now that she's in heaven, after what he did to her. Adan had a dirty mouth. Uri had done worse than being rude.

Flora had her back turned to load the dishwasher.

"I'll always love you, but not your behavior with fire," he heard her, or perhaps his mother, say.

Uri tried to make sense of his relationships with Flora, his mother, Simon, Adan, and Vel while mowing the synagogue lawn. With each pass, he saw Rabbi Shapiro through the window at his desk in his office, typing on his laptop while consulting thick tomes. He had to be composing his sermon or preparing his lecture for Youth Group.

As he had done before, he considered telling the Rabbi his problems. He pictured Rabbi Shapiro's harsh response.

"God hates you for what you've done. He's punished you with a scar—the mark of Cain—and took your eye and hand. Your punishment will not end until you learn to live righteously."

"What should I do?"

"Accept the mistreatment from your family and friends, from your foster father and his future stepson, as your due. From the stranger who might mug and rob you. From teachers who give you failing grades. From school-mates who call you names and tease you. They all despise you. And wait for the day your real father shows up to give you the beating you deserve."

"Will that take away my guilt?"

"If you accept your punishment and become an observant Jew, as God commands, He may forgive you."

After he finished mowing, Uri took the garden shears and massacred several bushes.

CHAPTER 8

Half the summer passed. Vel stopped hanging out with him, preferring Sam. Uri texted him every day for two weeks before giving up.

Are you busy? Can we meet?

Can't. I'm meeting Sam.

Vel never invited him to hang with the two of them. As painful as it would have been to be the third wheel, it would have hurt less than not to be wanted at all. But that is how Vel operated. One bro at a time, and the discarded one thrown away like trash. He racked his brain to remember anything he did wrong. But he hadn't offended Vel. He just bored him. Sam shared pool experiences with Vel—the swimmers with cramps they fished out, the older men who did too many laps and wound up with heart attacks, the obnoxious kids, and the hot girls in their sexy bikinis. They had nothing in common with an uninteresting guy who picked up twigs from the synagogue grounds.

Uri lost his third best friend. The fire had scarred him for life, leaving him half-blind, handless, friendless, with his household in shambles. A familiar cloud enveloped him, the same one that hovered since he emerged from the thick smoke of the burning house when he was almost thirteen, sometimes lifting, sometimes descending, always there.

Flora, who was or wasn't his mother, drove him crazy with longing for the mother's love she only gave to Adan. She was always polite, telling Uri when to expect dinner, asking him how school went, suggesting he ask Simon for money for new clothes when he outgrew the ones he wore. But now that Adan lived there, she didn't have conversations with Uri. She had conversations with her son. The absence of Uri's true mother and the presence of her double or ghost forced him to take shallow breaths. A deep one would reach the bottom of his lungs, where tears waited to embarrass him.

His crime was called matricide. "I committed matricide" was a parsable sentence. The more painful one was "I killed my mother." "I" was the pronoun. "Killed" was the verb. "Mother" was the object. The "I" was his guilty ass, the one part he wanted to erase. "I killed myself" would be the only tolerable sentence, with all three parts having equal importance.

Adan pushed his thoughts in that direction.

"You should off yourself, faggot. You're a worthless piece of shit no one wants."

The boy told the truth, except for the faggot part. Unless his wish to be Vel's best bro again meant he was gay. Or the boners from watching guys wrestle. Or his wish that the man who struggled with Jacob struggled with him. But they said he went upstairs with Sylvia and messed up Jenny's parent's bed. That meant he was into girls, didn't it? More likely, he disappointed Sylvia. Maybe he couldn't get it up. She hadn't spoken to him since that night. The other two girls ignored him, too, since he didn't do what they wanted. He would be eighteen in four months and still didn't know what he was. He found another cause for shame, another reason to kill himself.

He didn't sleep and had no appetite. Neither Simon nor Flora, in the throes of wedding plans and maneuvering around Adan, seemed to notice. When he wasn't working, he curled up in bed, staring at his phone, waiting for a text from Vel. None arrived. Adan paid no attention, except to deliver the occasional insult.

"Off yourself, fag."

"You're roadkill, freak."

"Die, creep."

Again, he imagined Rabbi Shapiro telling him he should accept mistreatment. Who was right, the Rabbi or the others? If he believed the Rabbi, he would have to become a righteous Jew. That might mean keeping *Shabbat* and eating *Kosher*. He would have to live with an Orthodox family to do that. There was no way he would impose a *frum* lifestyle on Simon and Flora. And even if he deserved misery, he couldn't bear it much longer.

Everyone else wanted him dead. Simon and Flora spoke to him in the usual way until they turned their backs.

"Kill yourself, son. It's now or never."

"I'll love you again a hundred percent if you die for what you did to me."

He no longer watched wrestling. He listened to the voices of the actors on the real crime programs Adan liked.

"Kill yourself. Kill yourself. Kill yourself."

When the grass needed mowing again, it had grown unevenly. The places where it grew taller formed the words, "kill yourself." He saw the same thing in clouds, the patterns in tree trunks, and—if he glanced—billboard signs, although they reverted if he looked again.

When the same messages came to him after the fire, they sent a therapist to his hospital bed. His name was Dr. Rubin. He wore rimless glasses, and his hair was coal black and crooked, a wig. It was natural for Uri to have feelings, he said, after what he had been through. He took a piece of paper from a folder and gave it to him. On it were several simplified drawings of different faces, like emojis, with the name of the facial expression shown beneath each.

"Point to the face that shows your emotion about the fire," Dr. Rubin said.

He also asked him to point to the ones expressing his emotions about his mother's death, Adam's death, losing his hands, his burnt up face. When Uri didn't answer, he asked him if it might be those for "sad" and "guilty." No face on the sheet that came close to what he felt, no name for the bleakness inside him, no emoji for the words in his head.

"I killed my mother."

Back then, he stopped wanting to die when Simon offered to be his foster father, even though Uri killed Adam by starting the match game. At the time, he guessed he must be worth a little if Simon did something so generous. Now, he realized it had nothing to do with him. Simon had a good nature. Once Uri was dead, he would no longer be imposing on Simon's kindness. His foster father would be better off.

He thought of many ways to kill himself, but some, like slitting his wrists or stabbing himself and bleeding to death, were too messy. Others involved means he didn't have, like a gun or enough pills to overdose. After much consideration, he figured the best was to close his eyes and cross the highway. The interstate was far from his house. He didn't have the energy to walk that distance. If he ate, he would recover the strength to do it. That night, he shoveled down a double helping at dinner.

"I'm glad to see you're so hungry. Flora's an excellent cook," Simon said.

Maybe his foster father saw him stop eating and chose not to say anything. Uri didn't care. He no longer had any curiosity. He wished for stamina from a good night's sleep, but he still lay awake as the minutes changed on the digital clock.

At 4:30 a.m., he stopped trying. Without turning on the lamp, he dressed in his Harley shirt and jeans. The clock gave off enough light for him to write a post-it to Adan.

You can have my things. The TV can stay turned toward your bed.

By the time he slipped out the front door, the gray light that precedes dawn was sufficient for him to see. Soon it would be over. The future he didn't have. Aging out of the foster care system and any obligation Simon had for him. Poor grades, dimming the hope for college. Disabilities that made him difficult to hire. No girlfriend. Vel's rejection.

As he neared the highway, he felt a strange elation, as if he had taken X. He hoped a semi, the kind with a double trailer, the biggest vehicle on the road, would crush him. If Christians were right, he would go to a place of fire. Hell. He wouldn't have to suppress his fascination with the substance. He'd swim in it.

Even though they were miles away, the voices of people in his household reached him.

"Die, creep."

"Kill yourself, son."

"Do it, my darling boy."

Rabbi Samuelson's voice was fainter.

"Suffer and live righteously. That's *Teshuva*."

A wind pushed him forward, toward the highway, pummeling his back like fists. He heard the traffic whizzing. There was a wall to climb over. He took off his shoes, so his toes would fit in the grouting, and hoisted himself upward. He sat for a while, as the dawn traffic shot by at high speed. Then he climbed down the other side, facing the wall. He remembered to recite the prayer Jews say at the moment of death.

Sh'ma Yisrael, Adonai Eloheinu, Adonai Echad

Once both feet were on the ground, he closed his eyes and turned toward the road. All he had to do was take a few steps forward.

CHAPTER 9

When Uri came to, he was in a hospital bed mired in a mess of tubing, with stabbing pain shooting up his spine to his neck, then down his right leg to his toes. His head hurt, as well.

"Don't move," Someone said.

There was no pit of fire, just a room with green walls, a cup with a straw on a tray table, and a dull sky visible through a single window. Simon and Flora waited there, watching his wincing face with concern. Standing in the background, Rabbi Shapiro intoned the *Mi Shebeirach* prayer for healing. Not *Kaddish* for the dead, meaning Uri lived, much to his disappointment.

"You'll be going to surgery any minute, son. The accident shattered your left hip. If you can't focus, it's because of the concussion," Simon said.

"Why, oh why, did you do such a foolish thing? If you had problems, you should have told us," Flora said.

The next time he came to, he was in less pain. He seemed to lay a few inches above his body, which someone rolled on a cot. He saw the nostrils of the person above him, pushing it and a pole from which bags containing colorless liquid hung. When he arrived at his assigned room, Nostrils and a nurse lifted him from the cot to a bed.

"Easy, now," Nostrils said.

Uri's hovering self rushed to keep up with his body.

"Here's the call button. Push it if you need more morphine." The nurse made adjustments to the bags and attached wires to the vitals display machine. Jagged lines marched across the screen.

Simon and Flora sat in two chairs against the wall at the foot of his bed. The Rabbi must have left.

"Adan was so upset when he found out you were injured," Flora said.

He must have looked puzzled even through the fog encasing him.

"Of course, Adan isn't one to say how he feels in a direct way. But a mother can tell. He didn't have to say how distressed he was for me to know. He would be here now if they allowed younger kids in."

Uri dozed off. It was dark the next time he awoke, and the room was empty. The hovering part of him had descended into his body. When he found the call button in his hand, he pressed it.

"Can I help you?"

The voice came from somewhere in the room. If it didn't understand what he wanted, it couldn't read his mind. It was a person at the nurses' station, not a spirit, talking through an intercom.

"I need more morphine."

"Rate your pain from zero to five, with zero for no pain and five for severe pain."

"Uh, five."

"Okay. Just a minute."

Ten minutes later, the nurse came, turned on the lights, and fiddled with the drip. Babies and small children cried in nearby rooms.

"What's that noise?" he croaked. His throat hurt.

"It's children. This is the pediatric unit. We place anyone under eighteen here."

The next morning, he noticed the wallpaper decorated with elephants and balloons. Someone muted the tv and tuned it to the cartoon channel. A bag of Legos lay on his tray table, along with breakfast. Framed pictures of Disney characters—Dumbo, Sleepy, Cinderella—were mounted on the walls.

Nothing happened for several hours except for a parade of nurses and people in white coats going in and out of the room, getting him up, making him stand. Simon texted him, saying he and Flora had to work but would drop by in the evening. Uri dozed while the morphine kept the pain at bay.

In the late afternoon, a nurse entered and told him he had a visitor. He hoped for Vel. To his astonishment, it turned out to be Sylvia, looking as she did in Youth Group, without make-up or a sexy halter top. She wore a white t-shirt and jeans. Her blond curls were pulled back into a ponytail.

"Hey."

She sat on the edge of his bed, handing him a small package of M&Ms, like those sold in vending machines.

"Thanks. Put it on my tray table."

"I like the Disney pictures. Dumbo's my favorite."

She looked around the room.

"I'm, like, surprised you came."

"Yeah, well, I had to. You were, like, my first."

"First what?"

He guessed what her answer would be, but he had to make sure.

"I was a virgin before you."

She looked at him with sincere blue eyes.

"They said we were upstairs at Jenny's house. I was too wasted to remember."

He groaned.

"Does it hurt?"

"Yeah. A lot."

"I thought you were Vel. I cried so hard, and I was so drunk, I forgot it was you. That's how it happened."

She put her warm hand on top of his.

It was the one piece of good news he had in a long, miserable time. How unbelievable! It seemed he, Uri the ugly one, had sex with a cute girl. Even if he couldn't remember it, he wasn't a virgin. Despite the pain, he smiled at his achievement, while hoping he had done nothing Sylvia didn't want.

"Are you mad at me?" He asked.

"It's not your fault. No boy refuses a girl who offers herself to him or whatever."

The jagged line bounced up. The machine beeped. A nurse rushed in. Sylvia withdrew her hand.

"It does that. The wiring comes loose," the nurse said.

After she left, Sylvia continued the conversation.

"I had to come to make sure that you didn't, you know, get yourself hurt because of me."

"No. You're not why."

He wouldn't tell her she had been far from his mind.

"Because you're not the one I love. I'm in love with Vel, so I can't be your girlfriend. I have to be certain that's not the reason."

"It isn't."

He wished she wanted to be his girlfriend. The next time he had sex, if ever, he promised himself he'd be sober.

"You sure?"

"Yeah."

"That's all I wanted to find out. I didn't want you to think… you know."

"Yeah."

"If you want to talk about the reason, I'll listen. I may not have any advice if it's about another girl, but I won't tell anyone."

Her kind eyes looked into his.

"I'm good."

"They say it helps to talk about your problems. I talk about mine with Vel to anyone who'll let me. He's not cute, but there's something about him."

"I don't know why I did it. If I did, I'd tell you."

"Fair enough."

"Thanks for coming anyway."

Should he be in love with her? He didn't want to be. No girl would love a guy with a scar and a limp.

"Get better soon."

She bent to kiss him on the cheek, then veered to his forehead.

"See ya."

"See ya."

As she left the room and went into the hall, he heard her add. "When will you try again? You still haven't paid the price."

Someone said, "Insurance won't pay the price."

Did he mix up Sylvia with another person? Or did she say what he thought she said?

That evening, Simon came by himself.

"Flora wanted to come. The school called her to a meeting. It seems Adan got into a fight with another boy."

"Huh."

"Listen, son. I talked to your surgeon. He did what he could. Your hip bone was in fragments. He replaced it with an artificial one. If you work hard at physical therapy exercises, you shouldn't limp too badly."

"You mean I'll have a limp?"

"Not a bad one. They'll be moving you to a rehab center in a couple of days. You'll be there for two weeks while they teach you how to walk again."

Uri didn't care. He wanted to be dead. Why hadn't God allowed him to die?

"It's good that school isn't starting for another few weeks. The concussion might make it hard to concentrate."

Simon still stood, leaving the two chairs empty.

"Okay."

"We're worried about your mental health, too. They're going to start you on antidepressants, but they tell me with people your age it makes things worse before it makes them better. Someone will explain it to you."

"Worse?"

"We'll see."

Simon didn't stay. He had to meet Flora at the school. He would visit him again in rehab.

It hurt like hell when Uri stood and took a few steps. Once transferred to rehab in another wing of the same building, he had excruciating physical therapy every morning and afternoon. If he was forced to live, pain was his due. He didn't complain.

Dr. Rubin, the same psychiatrist with the bad wig who counseled him in the hospital after the fire, came to evaluate him. He pulled the same chart of different emojis out of his briefcase and asked Uri to point to the ones expressing his emotions about his suicide attempt. Uri didn't have any emotions about it, but he picked "ashamed." It was as close as he could get.

"Why are you ashamed?"

"I want to be dead."

This was the truth.

"Why do you want to die?"

"Dunno."

After a few rounds of this, the psychiatrist explained that the medicine he would prescribe, Lexapro, might increase Uri's suicidal thoughts for a couple of weeks. He would be safe in rehab during that time. This only happened to twenty percent of the adolescents who took the medication. If it happened to Uri, the thoughts should go away, and he should feel better by the time they discharged him.

That evening, another surprising visitor showed up. Sam entered his room carrying a bouquet of drooping roses with brown edges on the petals, perhaps from a florist's dumpster. He was at the peak of lifeguard attractiveness, tanned and burly, with traces of zinc ointment on his nose.

"Hey, man, how goes it?"

He sat in a chair next to the bed, picked up two Legos from the tray table Uri had taken with him to rehab, and jammed them together.

"Okay."

They had removed the tubes and wires. It was easier for Uri to turn toward his visitor. Why was he here?

After a few minutes of silence, Sam heaved and sobbed. Tears channelled down his copper cheeks. He pulled the Legos apart and pushed them together again.

"What the fuck, man?" Uri said.

Sam had a hard time getting words out between heaves. Uri wished he had kept Dr. Rubin's chart so Sam could point to an emoji. No doubt it would have been "sad."

"Vel dumped me for a Chinese guy… *Sob*. I keep texting him. He doesn't reply… *Sob*. I did nothing wrong."

"That's how Vel is. He dumped me for you."

"Thing is, he talked shit about that guy. Said he was autistic or something. Like he's an imbecile."

"Zhong is a genius. He's just Chinese. Sometimes he sounds dumb. It's his accent."

"It was, like, one day we were hanging out, close, and the next day, he had a new bro. He straight-out told me, didn't hide it or nothing."

"That's what he does."

Sam hunched over, handling the Legos between his legs.

"I don't understand why I like him so much. He isn't sharp looking or strong or funny or a great swimmer or all that cool. It's kinda hard to describe what his power is. But I can't live without him. You see?"

"Yeah."

"Is that why you walked onto the highway? Because he traded you for me?"

It occurred to Uri that Sam and Sylvia knew about his suicide attempt. Who told them?

"How did you find out I went on the highway?"

Sam raised his head and stared at Uri with tears clinging to his lashes.

"You were on TV, man."

"I was?"

"Yeah. Like the evening news. They showed you being loaded into an ambulance and stuff. You shut down an interstate. You're a star, dude."

"Crazy."

"I'm surprised Vel didn't text you. I can see why he'd choose you over me, but not this Zhong guy."

Uri's phone had disappeared. Maybe he left it in his bedroom. He did not know if Vel tried to text him.

Sam started crying again.

"Thing is… *Sob*… I don't want my crying over Vel to be girly, like a gay thing. I don't want to be gay. Do you think it's gay?"

"You'd get a boner for him if you were."

Uri hoped he was right. He expected Sam to say he didn't.

"Thing is… sometimes I get a half-boner, if you get what I mean. Not a real hard one, but still…."

"Don't worry about it, man."

"Don't tell anyone, okay?"

"Okay."

Sam looked down at the Legos again, then up at Uri.

"He talked shit about you, sometimes. Do you want me to tell you what he said?"

"Not really."

"It was, like, about your scar and your hand. And you being uncool about sex and stuff."

"Whatever."

Sam got up.

"When you're busted out of here we could, like, hang out?" He put the Legos in his pocket.

"Okay."

"Cool."

As Sam walked out the door, Uri waited to hear words about trying to kill himself again. There were none.

CHAPTER 10

The next day, the empty bed in the other half of Uri's room filled. The nurse drew a white curtain between the two. Uri couldn't see the other occupant. He heard him whimper, moan, and beg the nurse for more Percocet.

"You've had as much as I can give you for the next two hours. Your doctor's weaning you off narcotics."

"But it hurts so bad."

"You can have another dose at 4."

Sounds of rustling, thumps and squeaks arose from behind the curtain.

"There. All set. Would you like to meet your roommate now?"

"I guess."

The nurse drew the curtain aside.

A thin, sharp-featured young man, hissing through bared teeth, wearing a knee cast, sat on the edge of the bed. He glanced at Uri, then rocked back and forth.

"I won't make it 'til 4."

"Uri, this is Ernie. Ernie, this is Uri."

The nurse did not seem persuaded by Ernie's demonstration of pain.

"You two won't heal if you lie in bed. Sit up, Uri. You can both be in chairs or standing."

She left the room. Behind her back, Ernie gave her the finger. Uri didn't move.

"What a cunt. Hey, you look familiar. What neighborhood are you from?"

Uri told him.

"You Jewish? Everyone there's a Jew."

"Yeah. What of it?"

Uri hoped he wouldn't call him a Christ killer.

"I'm half-Jewish myself. On my mother's side. I thought I seen you around. No one could forget a dude who fucking looks like you. I don't mean nothing by it when I say that. It's just the fucking truth."

"Whatever."

"Tell me, what was your *bar mitzvah* portion?"

"That was almost five years ago."

"That means you're seventeen. I'm nineteen, a sophomore at State."

He lay back on the bed, on his side, propping his head with his bent arm.

"Why do you want me to tell you that?"

"If you're a Jew, I already know everything else about you."

"You know nothing about me. We just met."

"Oh, yeah? Like, I can guess how you injured yourself."

"How."

"Jewish guys are clumsy. They have their heads in the fucking clouds from generations of looking down at *Torah* all day. They either walk off of something, like a roof, or into something, like traffic."

Uri would not admit he got hit on the highway.

"What about you?"

"Tore my knee up sprinting. I'm running for State, but I'm on the bench the rest of the semester. I know what you're going to say—I didn't do nothing clumsy. That's 'cause I'm only half-Jewish. The other half is good at sports. So, what's your *Torah* portion?"

"Jacob wrestling with a man all night."

"Shit. What did I score? Numbers 19. They slaughter and burn a totally red cow with no white hairs. Then, whoever gathers its ashes has to wash his clothes and stay away all day. Try to make sense of that one."

At any other time, it might have excited Uri to imagine the cow burning, but he only wished Ernie would leave him alone. He knew Ernie was annoying, but he didn't feel annoyed. He had no feelings at all.

"Where's that call button? If I keep asking for Percocet, they might cave and give me some. It's worth a try to get a little high."

"Do you have a phone?"

"Yeah. Why?"

"Can I text my dad to bring me mine?"

"Geez. You shouldn't go anywhere without your phone. You'd miss your texts. But it might've broke when you got injured, so I guess you were lucky."

Uri didn't feel lucky. He lived when he should be dead, roasting in flames like the cow.

That evening, Simon brought the phone when he came toward the end of visiting hours. He was late from trying to persuade Adan to give up the phone. It was among the possessions Uri had given him in the post-it note.

"Adan says you can borrow it. He wants it back when you return home."

Uri was glad Simon let him come home instead of kicking him out for walking onto the highway, which may have been illegal. He wondered if he would wind up in Juvie. A psych hospital was more probable if the Lexapro didn't work.

There were several texts on the phone. One was from Vel, the day after the accident.

Dude. What were U doing? Sorry U'r hurt. Can't visit—hospitals give me the creeps.

Vel sent a second one the day they transferred Uri to rehab.

Sam talks a lot of shit. Don't believe him.

From Sylvia: *Don't hate me for not being U'r gf.*

From Zhong: *I'm friends with Vel now. That's why I can't visit and play chess. Got early admission to State. Moving to dorm soon, anyway.*

From Jenny. *Not mad at you anymore. You can still earn $20. To show you I'm sorry U'r hurt, it doesn't have to be a stage kiss.*

From Lois: *Will you tell me if Vel texts U about me?*

From Adan: *U can't even off Urself right. U'r an asshole.*

From Rabbi Shapiro: *God created man in His image. Don't destroy one of God's precious creations.*

From Flora: *Sorry for not visiting. I'm meeting with the school principal about Adan's fighting. The poor boy has an anger problem. He misses you.*

From Simon: *Remember, son. Jacob struggled all night. He never gave up. You mustn't either.*

When Simon left, Ernie continued to pester him.

"You're in high school, right? A senior? I bet you're not in any crowd. You're the loser type who sits with the other loser types at lunch. I don't mean nothing by saying that. It's just the truth. Don't get fucking offended or anything."

"I was, like, in the most popular Jewish crowd for a while, when Vel, the most popular guy in the group, hung with me."

"If it's a Jewish crowd, it's a loser crowd, even if it is the most popular of all the Jewish crowds. You don't have to tell me more. I already know all there is to know about a Jewish crowd."

Ernie cocked his head.

"Did you say Vel? I know that dude. He hung with my half-brother, Sam, and messed him up good."

"Sam is your half-brother?"

It was the first thing that interested Uri since the accident.

"Yeah. Small Jewish world. Everyone knows everyone. Anyway, about Vel, when I get outa here, I'm going to crack his jaw and chew his tongue out."

Was Ernie in the chat room with WhipUGood?

"Then I'll rip his balls off."

Uri kept silent. He didn't want Ernie to find out he lurked in "Tough Talk." Neither that nor wrestling had interested him in the past few weeks.

"The fucker Vel is nothing special. I don't understand what Sam saw in him. But he was fucking broken up when Vel dropped him for a gook."

Ernie smiled.

"Yeah, yeah. I shouldn't say 'gook.' I don't mean nothing by it."

Several days later, Dr. Rubin came back and took Uri to a private room for an interview. He asked Uri how he was feeling.

"I'm good," he said. Maybe it was accurate.

The psychiatrist pulled out the emoji chart and asked Uri to point to the one that expressed his emotions about rehab. Uri didn't have an emotion about rehab. Then he asked him to show his emotions about Simon and Flora. Nothing. But when he asked about Adan, Uri stared for more than a minute. Finally, he pointed to a face with a frowning mouth and eyebrows forming a vee on the bridge of the nose.

"Good. You have an emotion. You're improving," Dr. Rubin said.

The emotion was "hate."

"Do you still want to commit suicide?"

"I haven't thought about it."

He had spoken the truth without realizing it.

"Then you're not one of the twenty percent. Lexapro is working. You must stay on it for at least six months."

Lexapro made him hate Adan? He liked it better when he didn't care, although hating Adan was better than the numbness he had about everything. Even having a growing irritation for Ernie was an improvement. He hoped he wouldn't go back to the pitiful state he was in when Vel traded him for Sam—the state Sam was in when he visited. It was hard to remember why he was so ecstatic when Vel hung with him and so miserable when he didn't.

"Do you have any brothers or sisters?"

When Ernie was bored, he tried to make conversation.

"I have a future younger brother, sort of. It's hard to explain."

Uri answered more often now, without lapsing into silence or giving one-word responses. He had more energy to talk, even if he preferred not to.

That evening, Ernie met Adan when Simon and Flora brought him to visit. The boy cast a sullen glance at the two patients, then plopped into one of the two chairs, leaving Simon to stand. Without waiting, he took out a device and hammered at it with two fingers.

"Adan is so glad you're better," Flora said, taking the remaining seat.

Adan scowled.

Simon introduced himself to Ernie.

"How do ya do? I'm Simon, Uri's foster father."

Ernie's eyebrows raised. Later, he said he didn't know Uri was a foster kid.

"You don't know everything about me just because I'm Jewish."

"What I didn't know was you were fostered. Most Jewish kids aren't. Their Bubbas take them if their parents throw them out or something. The other only thing I don't know is what happened to your face. I didn't want to ask. I try not to offend."

"It was burned in a fire."

"Bummer." Ernie wrinkled his nose. He opened his mouth, then closed it. For once, he didn't say whatever blunt thing had been on his tongue.

"Anyway, your brother's a dick."

"Yeah. That and worse."

"I could tell. Is he your foster dad's son?"

"No. He's Flora's son."

What Uri didn't say was that Flora could be his mother's ghost or her secret twin. He worried, now that he could worry, that Adan would kill her the way he had killed his mother. Adan was capable of anything, and Flora was blind to his true character.

They discharged Ernie before Uri. He said parting words to his roommate.

"If you go to State next year, be sure to take Professor Bern's Jewish Studies 101 class. He's the best teacher in the place. Everyone tries to take his courses, no matter what their religion. He's that popular. And if he takes a liking to you, he lets you into his off-campus courses. Not for credit, but who cares? I'm hoping to get an invitation."

The nurse replaced his large knee cast with a small one. By the spring, he would run again if he kept up with physical therapy.

"Remember. Professor Berns. It's worth getting into State just to meet him. I'm not fucking kidding."

Another sensation besides hate returned to Uri. Curiosity.

CHAPTER 11

After they discharged Uri from rehab, and he returned home, he was left alone. Everyone in the household preoccupied themselves with the upcoming wedding, three months away. The simple affair with just a few guests had grown into an elaborate occasion, with over three hundred people invited.

There was a flurry of preparations—the small buffet enlarged to a catered menu—would be brought to each table by a gaggle of servers. Instead of a DJ with a playlist, a band would play at the reception. They changed the venue for a larger one. Three bartenders would mix drinks and keep thirty tables supplied with bottles of champagne. They hired a *huppah* designer to make a decorated canopy beneath which Rabbi Shapiro would perform the marriage ceremony. A fashionable baker would make and decorate the cake.

Adan ignored Uri as the wedding drew near. Instead, he argued with Flora. Often Uri overheard.

"I don't understand why you have to get married."

"That's what people do when they fall in love. I love Simon. He's a good man, Adan."

They would sit next to each other on the couch during these conversations.

"Why don't you marry my father?"

Flora sighed.

"One reason is he's not your actual father. I married him because I was pregnant with you, and your grandparents arranged it. It wasn't a love match like it will be with Simon."

"Simon is a jerk. Can't we find my real father? I bet he's tough."

Another sigh.

"Adan, I've explained the situation to you. I don't know which boy in the Jewish fraternity is your father. If I did, I would tell you."

"You were a whore."

Flora shot up.

"Adan! What a nasty thing to say. Take it back."

"No. It's the truth."

As if a video played of a scene from five years ago, Uri witnessed his own role with his mother when she was engaged to Simon. Except he never called her a whore out loud. He wondered if Adan played with matches when no one looked.

The boy demanded Uri's phone back. He let him keep his clothing since none of it fit him. Uri no longer had a backpack, a bicycle, or any rights to the TV. The desktop belonged to the state and had to be returned when Uri graduated. It was the only thing Adan couldn't have.

Simon tried to intervene.

"Adan. Be nice. Your brother had an injury. Give him back his possessions."

"He's not my brother. He's just a foster. And he gave everything to me. Fair is fair."

In the end, Simon chipped in so that Uri could buy another smartphone with the funds he earned mowing the synagogue grass for a few weeks.

By late August, when school started again, Uri had an uneasy feeling that Adan might kill both his mother and him the evening before the wedding, as he himself had done to his mother and future step-brother. He tried to keep an eye on Adan. As far as he could tell, he hoarded no matches. But that didn't mean the boy wasn't up to something else.

Meanwhile, his last year in Youth Group began. Vel attended and Zhong—who came even though he had an early admission to State—along with the three girls. When Vel rejected Zhong again, he invited Sam to join. Sam struggled, not having had the benefit of a previous Jewish education. Rabbi Shapiro didn't object. If Vel wanted Sam to join, Sam joined.

Nothing had changed. Vel pitted everyone against each other—his guy friends and the girls, without committing to anyone. But the Lexapro helped tone down Uri's feelings both when accepted and rejected by him. When Vel hung out with him, he was still elated and still upset when Vel dropped him, but it wasn't life or death. He no longer became suicidal over Vel's choice of the week. Instead, he expected the cycling.

In October, Adan surprised him.

"I'll give your things back if you take me to the next party," he said.

"Kids your age don't go to senior parties. You'd be out of place."

"I'll let you watch TV for an hour a night."

"No!"

"Two hours?"

"What's this about?"

Adan had a wide-eyed, innocent expression Uri hadn't seen before.

"There's someone I want to talk to who goes to the parties. It's a private matter. All your possessions, two hours TV, and fifty dollars. That's my best offer."

This tempted Uri. He had no cash. And a back-up phone would be useful.

"You'll go home with me when I say so?"

"Scout's honor."

"And get permission from Simon and Flora?"

"Their pushovers. *No problemo.*"

The next party was at Jenny's again. Uri put on his Harley shirt, which survived the collision, the EMT ministrations, and the emergency room with only a few small blood stains. Adan wore a Tekashi69 t-shirt he somehow talked Flora into buying for him.

Uri could take Adan with two stipulations—he mustn't let the boy drink, and he must have him home by midnight. Even before they left, Uri thought up excuses to make when Adan broke the rules. He'd watch Adan, but couldn't babysit him. The clever brat would do whatever he wanted.

Simon drove them to Jenny's house. He'd be back at midnight to pick them up. The first thing Uri did in Jenny's basement was head for the bar and chug two shots. It was a surprise when Adan didn't sneak a drink, instead scanning the room, looking for someone. As long as he obeyed Simon's rules, Uri didn't care what he did.

After an hour, he stopped watching Adan when Jenny broke away from the girl pack and approached him. Long tresses dyed pink and blue shimmered in her wavy brown hair. Glitter sparkled on her face and bare shoulders. A strapless mini-dress flowed as she neared him.

"Hey. You ready to earn twenty dollars yet? It's still on the table," she said, close to his ear.

"I guess."

She took his hand. Her long fingernails were painted in an array of colors.

"Let's go over there, where Vel can see us, and make out."

"Okay."

"I owe you one tongue kiss when Vel is looking. The rest will be stage kisses. Unless I tell you different."

She led him to a chair in a corner near the spot where Vel and a group of followers stood joking and laughing.

"Did you see him? He's so shit-faced." One said.

"Priceless, man."

"Which dude is the worst." Vel ranked others as always.

Uri wondered if they were talking about him.

Jenny motioned him to sit, then placed herself on his lap with her arms around his neck, in view of the group. She glanced at Vel.

"Wait until he looks. Not now. Not now. Now."

She kissed him with what seemed like passion, using her tongue. Uri had his first real kiss, lasting several minutes.

"It may be X talking, but I'm kinda into your scar. Not that I'm in love with you. I'm not. But right now, I'm into you. Just don't touch me with that fake hand."

Several long kisses later, she wanted to go upstairs. Uri was to clomp up, making as much noise as possible with his leg brace to attract Vel's attention. They wound up in the same bedroom he had been in with Sylvia, the master bedroom. Jenny didn't care. She gave him a twenty-dollar bill from a box on her mother's vanity. He was drunk, but not enough to black out. This would be sex he remembered, like being a virgin all over again, then not being one. Jenny commanded. She paid to have what she wanted. The Lexapro, the alcohol, and the tab she slipped onto his tongue made Uri willing to submit.

"Promise you'll tell Vel what we did and how good it was."

"I promise."

Later, back downstairs, it was Vel who told him.

"Buddy. You bagged two of my girls. Don't worry. I'm not mad. How did it go?"

"It rocked."

"You've got one more, man."

Vel smiled, draping an arm around Uri. It was the two of them again. The others had tight grins.

"What do you mean?"

"You did Sylvia and Jenny. There's still Lois. I want to know which is the best."

"I was too wasted with Sylvia. Jenny takes charge. I liked that."

"Huh."

A few minutes before midnight, Uri broke away to search for Adan. He found him sitting by himself, drinking a Sprite. Although he expected a hard time, Adan left with him without a murmur.

Simon forced him to leave the party early. It didn't matter. He was drunk, but not too drunk. He made out and then had sex with a girl. Vel liked him best again. Adan cooperated for once. He pleased Simon with his chaperoning. Uri was glad he didn't die on the highway. He fell into a deep sleep as soon as he went to bed, without having to wait for hours to pass.

For the next month, until the wedding, Adan didn't rattle the household. He wasn't pleasant, still sulking and scowling when anyone asked anything of him, but without having a tantrum. Uri knew better than to trust him. The boy had something up his sleeve. He plotted, unlike Uri, who never planned to set a fire before Simon's last wedding day. If he had the chart of the emoji faces, Uri would choose the one with slits for eyes and a thin line for a mouth for Adan. The face of a conniver.

CHAPTER 12

After morning *Shabbat* services on the Saturday before the wedding, a typical series of near-disasters and frantic last-minute preparations took place. The florist arrived late with her delivery. The baker sent the cake to the wrong venue. The hem of the bridal dress needed to be repaired. Guests found hotel reservations over-booked. Flights were delayed. The wedding ring was misplaced, then found.

Uri kept a nervous eye on Adan. The chaos distracted Flora from paying attention to her son. When a headache threatened to overwhelm her, Simon took the brunt of the confusion. Adan kept quiet, which was uncharacteristic, staying in the boys' bedroom watching tv and playing video games. He had nothing to say to Uri, who kept sniffing the air for signs of smoke. There were none.

Uri tried to stay awake all night, fearing what Adan might do if he slept. His terror returned at the thought of being burned again. Memories of the fire that killed his mother surfaced. He recalled playing the match game. Adam throwing a lighted match at the curtains. The immediate conflagration. Their attempts to smother the flames with blankets, which caught as well. Sparks igniting other objects in the room. The billowing smoke cutting visibility to zero. The heat. The difficulty of breathing. Crawling on the floor. Then a black spot in his memory, when he had been burned while escaping.

After laying in his bed shivering, teeth chattering, he gave up, and, even though it was late November and cold, he went to the porch to sleep where he might be safe. After a couple of restless hours, his anxiety drove him across the backyard to the garden shed. He rested there, squeezed beside the lawn mower and rakes, waiting for the sound of fire truck sirens. They never came.

At dawn, Uri opened the shed door and stood blinking at the unscorched scene. Fire had not been Adan's preferred means of destruction, after all. Uri went back to the house, already humming with activity, and returned to his room to dress for the wedding breakfast. Adan wasn't there.

Suspicious, Uri found Simon and asked where Adan had gone.

"He said he needed exercise and wanted to walk to the restaurant banquet room. It's only a couple of miles, so we let him. Flora thinks it's his nerves."

They scheduled the breakfast at the restaurant for the wedding party and close family and friends of the couple—Flora's parents and siblings, Simon's aunts and uncles, the oldest friends of both, Adan and Uri. It unnerved Uri to know that Adan had gone to the restaurant in advance. It could only be for one reason. He vowed not to eat or drink anything there. When no one noticed, he snuck into the kitchen for his usual bowl of Captain Crunch and instant coffee. He ate with no appetite to avoid the temptation at the official breakfast. From the items in the sink—a bowl and spoon, a mug, Uri guessed someone else ate, too—Adan.

If he had the emoji chart, Uri would pick the one with a dot for a mouth and round circles for eyes to show his emotion—alarm. What if Adan planned to set fire to the restaurant while everyone was confined to the back room? Or poison everyone? He imagined dead bodies at the banquet table, their faces fallen into the poached eggs on plates before them. If only Simon believed Adan could be dangerous. But if Uri said anything, his foster father would dismiss him.

"Adan? A danger? Come on, son, he's just a mischievous eleven-year-old, half your size."

Or worse.

"Do I detect jealousy? Are you afraid Adan will replace you in my heart? Is that why you're inventing falsehoods about him?"

All the guests arrived at the restaurant around the same time except for Adan, who had been seated early. Uri chose a chair as near as possible to the exit door. Glasses of orange juice and pots of coffee were already at each place setting. The rest of the menu would arrive after servers took all the orders. Uri noticed Adan didn't touch the drinks, but, in a show of innocence, asked for a glass of milk. For about fifteen minutes, everyone sipped the beverages and chatted.

Then the tone changed. The noise level increased. Laughter became louder.

"I'm so jittery. It must be the excitement. I've never been so… happy. So happy. Overjoyed. Euphoric," Flora said.

"I was sleepy. Now I'm wide awake," a guest said.

Others chimed in.

"I feel so good."

"If only they had hired a band."

"The food looks delicious, but I can't eat."

"This is the best wedding ever."

Uri had an ominous sense that something was very wrong. The breakfast should be pleasant, even a bit exciting, but everyone was too aroused. It wasn't normal. The mood seemed more like the parties where all the kids took X.

As more time elapsed, the guests became restless, rising from their seats and moving around the room, greeting and hugging each other, leaving eggs and waffles untouched, yet thirsty for the juice and coffee. Some burst into song or line-danced the *Hora* without music. They threw food at each other amid peals of laughter. Silverware clattered to the floor. Others argued, bringing up old wounds, delivering fresh insults. A fist fight broke out. Servers escorted the combatants outside.

Simon's breathing was rapid.

"I drank too much coffee. Three cups. My habit is to have only one." He gasped, reaching for more juice with a shaky hand.

Uri heard him say, "Something's wrong. My heart's racing." Then he collapsed.

A shout arose. "Call 911."

Uri turned and glanced at Adan. The boy snickered at him, then left the banquet room. Whatever he had done, Uri was the only one unaffected. After a confused pause, screaming started. Flora knelt down beside her groom in her pink breakfast suit, her mouth stretched into a wide circle.

Much later, when they had pronounced Simon "dead on arrival" in the emergency room, Uri walked back to the house. No one had paid any attention to him, the foster kid, not anyone's friend or relative. Someone decided that Flora and Adan shouldn't spend the night by themselves without telling Uri where they'd been taken. A hotel or the house of a friend.

Alone in the room he shared with Adan, his scrambled thoughts led him to the certainty that Flora's son laced the orange juice or the coffee with something purchased at Jenny's party, maybe meth or X, something that could be ground to a powder and dissolved in liquid. The little fucker had gone to the restaurant early to make sure everyone got high from the beverages. Simon got an extra dose, enough to stop his heart, enough to stop the wedding.

Uri despised Simon for his weakness and secretly loved him for his kindness. He never admitted the love to himself before or told Simon that he loved him. He never thanked him for fostering him, giving him a second chance. Now he was scared. What would he do without a parent, without someone to be nice to him? In a rush, the despair he felt before his injury returned. After the joy of having sex with Jenny, he had thrown away the Lexapro, believing he didn't need it.

He paced through the house, into each room, picking up objects he wouldn't see again—Flora's perfume, Simon's cufflinks, the velvet box containing the wedding rings, a can opener, a remote, an orange—then put each one back where he found it.

In the kitchen, he opened the drawer where boxes of matches were kept.

He only needed one box. Back in his room, he sat on his bed, lighting each match and throwing it at the curtains. It took fifteen tries before they caught. There were still another ten matches left. Uri walked from room to room, setting fire to another ten curtains. It was the calmest he had been all day. He paid no attention to his singed hair and burning left ear. Without hurrying, he walked out the back door and waited in the shed. This time, he heard the sirens.

Uri turned eighteen two days before, a milestone not marked because of the upcoming wedding, but with a promise to celebrate at a later date. He was an official adult now, admitted to an adult psychiatric hospital, with a thick bandage on his ear. The prosecutor suspected he drugged the guests at the breakfast. No evidence showed up to charge him with murder, but they convicted him of arson. A judge remanded him to the hospital for evaluation before being sentenced to a year in prison.

CHAPTER 13

Don, Uri's cell-mate in their two-bunk cell, would be released two months before Uri's sentence ended. He was three years older than Uri and very short, not even as tall as the second bunk. One thing they had in common was ugliness, since acne scars riddled Don's face.

"I may not be the handsomest guy on the block, but you're the worst looking dude I've ever seen."

"It's from bad burns. And my hip had to be replaced."

Don's voice, lower pitched than expected for someone his size, soothed Uri. He was a veteran of previous sentences and could help Uri adjust to imprisonment—the routine, the noise, the stink, the heat, the cold, the vermin, the pettiness and meanness of guards and inmates, the awful food, and the clanging of cell bars. Don offered to take him under his wing, guiding him through official and unofficial prison regulations, and protecting him. Other inmates respected him, leaving him alone. If Don looked after him, they would leave Uri alone, too.

There was a condition.

"I'll get you through until I'm released, but you've gotta give me a hand job every night. It's not gay. I can't get to sleep unless someone does that."

"I'm not into that."

"It's eat or be eaten here, kid. You won't be eaten if you do what I tell you."

Uri didn't want to touch Don's dick. The thought made his stomach heave. He couldn't do it without puking. But his survival was at stake. He had no money. They confiscated the fifty dollars from Adan and twenty from Jenny to pay court costs. Without a family or friends to put cash into his commissary account and without protection, he would be worse than miserable. Inmates might even attack him for being a freak. And no one guessed he was Jewish. In the end, he steeled himself to agree to Don's demand.

Uri deserved the punishment. Prison was for burning down the house. Conditions in the cell, including doing what Don wanted, were for causing the death of his foster father. He should have watched Adan at the party instead of having sex with Jenny. He assumed Adan wanted to come to buy drugs for himself and to sell to his middle-school buddies, not to stop the wedding by murdering the groom. Getting drugs and alcohol were the reasons younger siblings of seniors came to high school parties once in a while. Everyone understood that.

Adan needed big money to buy enough for the whole breakfast. It wouldn't be a problem for him to take cash from his mother's purse. Both Simon and Flora gave him the allowance he insisted on, anyway. If he needed more funds, he would find a way. Uri didn't know whether the boy planned to kill Simon or just make him too high to get through with the ceremony. If Simon had a weak heart, Adan might not have known. Uri should have guessed and told his foster father. Simon was old and not used to uppers.

Uri wound up telling Don why they arrested him.

"All you did is forget to watch the kid at a fucking party. There're guys here who've done worse shit than that. Hell, I've done a lot worse shit."

"I burned down a house."

"With no one in it. Insurance will pay for a better house to be built on the property. You'll see."

Don took a toothpick from his stash and stuck it in his mouth. He missed cigarettes.

When Don reassured Uri, his mood improved enough to show interest in his new friend.

"Why do the others here admire you and leave you alone? Any of them might, like, give you a beating or whatever."

They were all bigger than Don.

"Don's my real name. I told it to you since we're cell-mates. It's not the name I go by."

"What's that?"

"WhipUGood."

Uri drew back in astonishment.

"You're WhipUGood?"

"Yup."

"From 'Tough Talk'?"

"You've heard of me."

"I've, like, lurked on 'Tough Talk' a lot. It's one of my favorites, and WhipUGood is my favorite poster on it."

"That's yours truly."

"Holy shit! I'm a big fan of yours, but I never thought I'd meet you in prison."

This was the most astonishing thing that ever happened to Uri, even more than Simon dating his mother's double. WhipUGood could live anywhere in the world, and he turned out to be in the same town as Uri. And who would have thought he would be such a small guy?

"Why are you here?"

"Oh, stuff having to do with money I owed someone. Nothing big."

He shrugged, as if doing a year inside was no big deal.

Uri wondered whether "Tough Talk" was illegal, and the cops caught up with WhipUGood, despite his alias. According to his cell-mate, the chat room had nothing to do with his crime. Don explained that jail etiquette didn't permit inmates to ask each other for details about convictions.

Don became his fourth only friend. During the day, they hung out together in the yard, the cafeteria, or lay in their separate bunks and talked. Other inmates avoided the short, pocked man and his tall, scarred cell-mate. They didn't provoke the tough talker, uncertain if he was as rowdy as his words, and they couldn't figure out his "monster" buddy, who might have murdered his own foster father.

Every night, when the lights turned off, Uri climbed down to the lower bunk. He no longer minded the hand jobs as much, since finding out Don's other identity. The first few times were nauseating, but he adjusted to it just like he adjusted to everything else nauseating in prison. Thoughts about the chat room helped. He attended to his nightly duty with more enthusiasm if Don talked tough to him first.

"I'll crack your jaw and chew your tongue out," Don whispered.

"What else?"

"I'll rip your balls off."

Except for helping Don fall asleep, prison turned out to be a filthier version of other places, like hospitals and rehab, where they had confined Uri. In each, he shared a room. They didn't allow him to leave. Boredom and discomfort were the norm. And he had a few visitors.

The first one who came to see him in prison was Rabbi Shapiro. They sat across from each other at a table in the cafeteria. A tray containing salt, pepper, mustard, catsup, and hot sauce was still there from the last meal. Someone had swiped a rag across the table's surface, leaving behind wet patches. The Rabbi kept his hands in his lap.

"In your *bar mitzvah* portion, Jacob struggles all night with a man, perhaps an angel, perhaps the evil inclination, *yetzer hara.* What *yetzer hara* landed you in this place?"

"I set fire to Simon's house."

The Rabbi looked around at the other inmates and visitors, scattered at various tables. There was a loud din of voices. Then he bent closer to Uri.

"They say you killed your foster father, may his memory be a blessing."

He said this in a hushed tone, as if it might lead to another charge if anyone overheard.

"That was Adan, not me."

"And you killed others when you set fire to your first house."

"If you're, like, technical about it, that was Adam."

"*Yezter hara.* You blame others for your own transgressions." The Rabbi signed.

Was he "disappointed" as Simon would have been? Uri expected him to rage and threaten one of God's terrible punishments, like boils or an earthquake.

"Adam and Adan were pre-*bar mitzvot,* too young."

"Me, too, for the first one, by a day. Well, my *bar mitzvah* didn't happen the next day. Not until I was in the hospital."

Rabbi Shapiro stared at Uri, waiting. His accusing eyes bore into Uri's. It was worse than all the police interrogations he had been through since his arrest. The Rabbi's gaze brought the force of the *Torah* with it. Moses lifted the stone tablets to crush Uri's skull—unless he confessed.

"You're right, in a way. I'm the one who started the match game with Adam. And I allowed Adan to come with me to a high school party. He must've bought drugs there and put them in the drinks at the wedding breakfast."

The Rabbi still starred.

"Adan is a boy, not yet twelve. I believe you bought the drugs. The autopsy found methamphetamine in Simon's system. If you put a powder in Simon's beverages, you are responsible for his death," the Rabbi said.

Uri said nothing. No one would believe Adan had the *yetzer hara*. But they already tarred Uri with his mother's death. Anyone who murdered his mother was capable of any crime.

"I've spoken to Adan," the Rabbi said. "He doesn't say in plain words that he's devastated by the loss of the man who would have been his step-father. He doesn't have to. I know how he feels. A rabbi can tell. I can also tell he's miserable about the loss of you, who would have been his future step-brother."

"Foster step-brother."

"Yes, well."

Rabbi Shapiro put a folder he had brought with him on the table, avoiding the wet spots.

"Do you have any idea what's in this folder, Uri?"

"No."

"A copy of Simon's will. I'm what's called the executor. That's the person who makes sure the will is carried out."

"Okay."

He aroused Uri's suspicions. Something bad was coming. This was the real purpose of the Rabbi's visit.

"Simon left you money for your college education, with two stipulations attached. The first is that you complete high school or get a GED and gain admission to State. There's not enough for a private college."

"Okay." He waited, knowing there was worse.

"The second stipulation is that you help Adan with his *d'var Torah*—his essay on his *Torah* portion he will read to the congregation during his *bar mitzvah*. Of course, that would be once you're out of prison."

"Whoa! What?"

"His *Torah* portion is the same as yours. *Vayishlach*. Jacob wrestles all night with a man or angel. So helping Adan should be easy for you."

"But... but..."

"It's Simon's will. He may have suspected he had a weak heart. There's no other way for you to get the college money he left you. You can read it right here in the folder."

Before he left, the Rabbi added commands.

"Say *Kaddish* for Simon on *Shabbat*. And the *Sh'ma* every day. Don't forget to be a good, righteous Jew. It's part of *Teshuva*—repenting."

Later, Uri tried to explain the situation to Don. He told him he was Jewish. Don listened, although he didn't understand the power of a rabbi or the meaning of *bar mitzvah, yetzer hara,* or *Teshuva.*

"I've hung with a half-Jewish guy, my 'Tough Talk' frenemy. We pretend to hate each other and have fake fights in the chat room. His name is Ernie, but he goes by SteelSpine. He's on track at State, but he injured his knee and can't run until the spring."

Uri inhaled at another astonishment.

"My roommate at rehab was an Ernie. Does he have a younger brother named Sam?"

"I think so. Yeah."

"Fuck me! I know the dude. He's SteelSpine?"

"Yeah."

For a few minutes, Uri hovered over his body, just as he had after his hip surgery. Two shocks in one day—having to tutor Adan and learning who Ernie was—tore Uri from himself. When a guard announced a second unexpected visitor, he pulled himself together. It was Vel.

"Hey, man. How's my best buddy doing?"

They sat in the cafeteria at the same half-cleaned table Uri had been at earlier with Rabbi Shapiro. He wondered when he had become Vel's best buddy. He wished he had hidden his grin when Vel called him that.

"Just doing my time. That's all."

He pretended the loss of his foster father, his mother's double, his home, and almost losing his mind hadn't affected him.

"Hurry and get your GED, now that you have nothing else to do. Everyone in Youth Group is going to State next year. We should room together in the dorms."

Uri smiled again, even though it was clear the invitation to come back into Vel's circle was temporary. He'd take what he could get in his current circumstance.

"What about Sam?"

"Fuck him. He's immature. Let him room with Zhong. They're on the same level. Not like you and me."

Uri shouldn't have been flattered, but he was. Vel leaned toward him, just like the Rabbi had, and stage whispered.

"Anyone fuck you in here?"

"No!"

"I heard everyone gets fucked in prison."

"That's maximum security. It's not as rough here."

He wouldn't tell him about what he had to do to get Don to protect him. It wasn't as bad as getting fucked in the ass by a gang, although sometimes he had secret daydreams about that.

"Good. I wouldn't want my best buddy to turn fag on me."

If Uri was free to go to more senior parties, he could fuck girls. Didn't having sex with Jenny and Sylvia prove he was a normal, straight guy?

Who was he kidding? He was a freak with a fake eye, a fake hand, a fake hip, and half an ear. He was an orphan, an arsonist, and maybe a murderer. Tough talk turned him on. No matter what Vel said, he would never be normal.

Why would a cool guy like Vel come to a jail to ask a freak to be his roommate? Uri would have to get into State to find out.

PART TWO
COLLEGE

CHAPTER 14

The first tutoring session with Adan after Uri's early release from prison took place on a Sunday in the synagogue, with Rabbi Shapiro close by. It was August, three months before the *bar mitzvah*. They paroled Uri early, knocking time off his sentence when he completed his GED, got admitted to State, and followed all prison regulations.

Classes started the week before. Uri moved from his cell straight to a dorm room, from the company of his fourth only friend, Don, back to his third only friend, Vel. His second only friend, Zhong, roomed with Sam a few doors down. The girls had a triple on the freshman women's floor, a flight up. Don, released the same day as Uri, was with Ernie in a separate building for upperclassmen.

The gang in Youth Group had graduated, and it dismayed Uri to be tutoring Adan in one of the old classrooms, decorated with construction-paper *menorahs* and *dreidels*, like a kid when everyone else his age had moved on. He completed his own Jewish education. Now he was expected to live like any other Jew—attend services and abide by commandments in the *Torah*. At State, the Jewish students usually went to the campus Hillel, the Jewish college organization. Kids and parents or grandparents of kids attended synagogue, not college students, not often.

Adan was reluctant, too, smirking at the sight of his almost foster step-brother. He came to comply with the terms of Simon's will, like Uri. Whatever they were, they had to be bounteous or the brat wouldn't show up. That had been Uri's hope. He wondered if Adan would inherit anything if those in charge found out he killed his benefactor.

The two of them were supposed to talk through Adan's *Torah* portion until the boy had a clear idea of what he wanted to say. It turned out that Adan already knew what he wanted to say, and it would shock the congregation if he said it.

"Right before Jacob wrestles with the mystery man, he gets scared of his brother Esau, who is coming to kill him for stealing his 'birthright,' whatever that is. He's going to give his brother gifts to save his own ass. It's like a bribe. 'Don't hurt me, please. I'll give you good stuff if you don't hurt me.'"

He said the last in falsetto, imitating a frightened girl.

"What a wuss! Then the wrestling. Jacob doesn't win. It's a fucking draw. Jacob gets nothing out of it but a new name he didn't ask for and a screwed up hip bone."

"A 'birthright' is like what you've been stealing from me."

It dawned on Uri that Adan was more like he had been at that age than anything like Adam. He remembered thinking Jacob was weak. Otherwise, he would have won the wrestling match. Simon tried to convince him that Jacob wrestled with a part of himself, but Uri never bought that. He preferred imagining the man pinning Jacob in holds.

Now he had to take the role Simon had with Adan.

"Your almost step-dad said the man might be part of Jacob's mind. What do you, like, think of that?"

"It was just like Simon to say that. He was a pussy."

Adan took out a bent Mars Bar from his pocket and, without unwrapping it, bit off a large piece. He spat out the wad of wrapping onto the floor.

"That's disgusting. Pick it up, or I'll tell the Rabbi."

"Go ahead. I'll say you did it. *El creepo*. Mr. Leather-Face."

Uri wound up using a paper dreidel to pick up the bits of wrapping Adan kept spitting out. Angry tears threatened to spill from his eyes. Simon's will trapped him more securely than any prison. Was an education worth three infuriating months of Adan? He heard a grinding noise. It was his teeth.

Meanwhile, Don insisted Uri owed him extra months of hand jobs for the early release. The deal they made wouldn't be up until mid-November, 2008, on the same date of his arrest a year earlier. This was also the date of Adan's *bar mitzvah*, if the boy didn't commit another crime to get out of it.

Don argued with Uri through texts.

It's like a contract. U don't violate a contract.

What about Ernie?

Fuck Ernie. This is between U and me. Just come over every night at midnight to help me sleep. Unless there's a party or I have to cram. Then U have the night off.

He didn't know what to tell his fourth only friend. Uri couldn't leave their room every night without an excuse. At first, he just left for a half hour without saying why.

"You're fucking a girl every night. Right? She can't sleep unless you make her come," Vel said.

"I guess."

"Is it one of the Youth Group girls you already banged?"

"No."

"So who is it? Tell Daddy."

As usual, when he wanted something, Vel was all over Uri. Draping his arm around him. Squeezing his shoulders. Rubbing his back. Leaning his forehead on Uri's. He roped him in, an orphan, with affection.

"You never met her. She's in my Remedial Math class."

"How big is her ass?"

"Big."

"Cool, dude. You're my man. You're ugly, but I told you before, ugliness in a guy can be an advantage with some chicks."

The fake Remedial Math girl had a real life competitor—Jenny.

I'm still not into U love-wise. But I'll pay U 20 a fuck if Vel is in the room. Deal?

Okay, if it's before midnight. I have to see someone at 12 most nights.

Another girl?

From Remedial Math.

Two math idiots. Wow! U could have a baby who can't count.

Besides Remedial Math, Uri enrolled in Remedial English, Remedial Biology, Remedial Culture Studies, and Jewish Studies 101.

A foreign student of indeterminate nationality taught remedial English. He had an accent so thick Uri didn't understand a word. It was lucky he remembered how to parse sentences from Mrs. Green's class in high school.

When the graduate student wrote sentences on the blackboard like "Money buys books," "money" was the noun, "buys" was the verb, and "books" was the object. In his mind, he rewrote the sentence as "Jenny buys fucking with me." "Jenny" was the noun, "buys" was the verb, "me" was the object. He wondered why "me," meaning himself, was so often the object, the thing acted on.

He thought of the sentences that described his life.

"Adan disrespects me."

"Don holds me to a deal."

"Vel favors me until he doesn't."

"No one likes me for real."

He was just an object others used.

Jenny, one of those who used him, came over three or four times a week, slipping Uri the cash when Vel didn't see.

"Make noise to attract his attention, like it's the best fuck ever," she whispered.

As soon as Jenny's moaning and thrashing in pornographic excess ended, she left right away without glancing at Vel, who winked at his roommate, punching his upper arm.

"Man, you get laid more than I do," he said.

Since Vel never seemed to get laid at all, this was probably true.

It was the opposite during Uri's midnight visits to Don. They both were as quiet as possible, pretending not to disturb Ernie if he studied or gamed. When Uri finished, he chatted with Ernie—or SteelSpine—about classes for a few minutes as if he had just dropped by on his way to his dorm. He ignored his sleeping third only friend.

Zhong, Sam, Lois or Sylvia might be there when he returned, unable to stay away despite their lowered status. They needed to be near Vel, awaiting the moment he shot a glimpse in their direction, preparatory to replacing Uri. All those cast out stuck together, gossiping about Vel and his latest pick, vowing to keep their distance, change dorms, drop classes, withdraw from the college, only to drift back to the one person who enthralled them, enticed them, teased them with a whiff of his favor. Like Uri, they wanted to be lifted from despair or ordinariness by someone capable of doing so, an unremarkable guy with a way of keeping others bound to him.

During his year of confinement, Uri missed Vel the most. Don's protection insulated him from the worst of it, but imagining Vel and Sam, then Vel and Zhong while he rotted in prison made the empty sensation in his chest grow to near-bursting. He owed Don for keeping him from hanging himself with his sheet, as some inmates did.

One night, Ernie asked him a favor.

"Look, man, I'm too busy with course work to continue with the 'Tough Talk' gig. I need someone to take over SteelSpine. Don suggested you. The site owners pay. It's only a few cents a post, but it adds up. If you're very active, you could earn, like, fifty a week."

Fifty dollars a week was an enormous amount for someone whose expenses only covered tuition, dorm, meals, and texts.

"Maybe I wouldn't be as good at it as you."

"Don't worry about it, man. You're a natural. You already know all there is to know from lurking. And Don will help by giving you lead lines."

Between the money from Jenny and the money from Tough Talk, Uri would be one of the richer guys in the dorms.

"Money buys friendship."

He wrote this for a Remedial English assignment, parsing it. It might be the only way an ugly ex-convict would get people to like him.

CHAPTER 15

Don and Ernie both declared their majors. Ernie's was Business.

"My goal after graduation is to open an adult sex shop, a string of them if the first one goes okay. That's a business. I need to learn marketing and accounting and stuff."

"That's, like, your goal? To open sex shops?"

Ernie always astounded Uri.

"I could combine it with a weed store, if there's legalization in this fucking backwoods."

"Aren't they, like, connected with the Mob or whatever?"

"I'm getting an internship with the Mob next summer through my cousin. He's connected."

"Hey. I'm getting tired," Don said.

After putting Don to sleep, Uri continued his conversation with Ernie, whispering.

"Jewish guys don't work for the Mob."

"Oh, yeah? Ever heard of Meyer Lansky? Bugsy Siegel? The Jewish-Russian Mafia? Anyway, this is from my non-Jewish side. They're a bunch of fucking thugs. That's how I learned to run. If I didn't run, I got walloped by them."

"Hey, you guys woke me. Cut the noise," Don said.

Uri tried putting Don back to sleep, but it was useless. He was wide awake now. Brushing Uri aside, he got out of bed and went to his desk, opening a book with an exasperated thump. He hadn't increased in height since jail, and his feet didn't reach the floor of his desk chair. He gave the desk leg a sharp kick.

"What are you majoring in?" Uri dared to ask.

Don opened his laptop, giving Uri an annoyed glance, sucking in his pocked cheeks.

"Philosophy."

"Philosophy?"

"Professor Berns taught about the larger questions, like what reality is, how we know we exist, and shit like that. He got me interested, if you need to know."

"What can you do with philosophy when you graduate?"

"Think."

"Think?"

"It's more than you two morons do when someone's trying to get some shut-eye."

Ernie snickered.

"Wait until you meet Professor Berns. He starts his class two or three weeks after the semester begins. They let him do whatever he wants, since lots of paying students take his classes."

Jewish Studies 101 was held in a large hall shaped like an ice-cream cone, with tiered seats coming to a point at the bottom where a lectern was placed. Over seventy students enrolled. Several auditors slipped into empty seats or stood in the back.

After a fifteen-minute wait in the forty-five minute class, the Professor strolled in through a door behind the lectern and stood in front of it, surveying the room. His eyes rested on Uri, the most unusual-looking student, or in his general direction.

It surprised Uri to see how much he resembled Simon, although many of the older faculty did, more or less. No one would confuse The Professor with Simon, but he had Simon's rotundity, inquisitive blue eyes, and a ring of graying hair forming a half circle around the back of his head. It was hard to fathom what was so interesting about such an ordinary middle-aged man. The same was true of Vel, who seemed like nothing special at first glance.

He started his lecture with no introduction.

"Until the beginning of agriculture, about ten thousand years ago, there was no such thing as God. Humans didn't invent God until they lived in communities of over fifty people."

God was an invention? It stunned Uri to hear anyone say God didn't always exist, create the universe, govern the world. He remembered Vel causing a stir in Youth Group when he suggested God was a slave of humans. What the Professor claimed was more outrageous.

"In hunter-gatherer communities of less than fifty, the leaders made the rules and punished those who disobeyed. Everyone was related, neighbors, known to each other. There were few secrets, and law-breakers were noticed and judged. In communities of over fifty, secrecy became possible. People were no longer related or living close by. Something had to be done to prevent chaos and crime."

Uri exhaled. He had been holding his breath.

"So they invented a terrifying God. He was omnipresent and omniscient. Like neighbors and relatives, He knew what everyone said, thought, did. Rulers judged and punished in His name, and if they didn't, He would after death."

Uri didn't believe in lightning striking those who disrespected God, but he waited for something awful to happen to the Professor—maybe a heart attack or a seizure.

"For ten thousand years, God has been frightening, terrible, always furious. The God of Thunder. The God of an erupting mountain. The God who floods the earth in the time of Noah. In the mid-twentieth century, the God of Love was born. This God of the New Age, this *Shekinah,* is a female concept. Pardon me, ladies, for being old-fashioned with gender stereotypes."

He paused, looking around, sweeping the room, then returned to the area in which Uri sat for a long stare. His tone became more intimate.

"Tell me. In your heart of hearts. Who do you pray to when there is turbulence in a plane, when the brakes fail on an icy road, the elevator stops between floors, someone you love becomes ill—a God of love who can empathize and be your friend in sorrow and destruction? Or a God of justice who might be persuaded to grant you mercy?"

The Professor had to be speaking to him, Uri, the ninth student in the twelfth row on the right. He realized he had been waiting all his life for someone to say the words that had been there, unspoken, not daring to be spoken, in his own mind. Shocking words. True words. He didn't want a weakling God of love. He wanted a punishing God, a fierce God, a God of *yetzer hara*, and the Professor said that for centuries, God had been *Elohim*, a respected and feared king.

"Why do all Jewish services start with Praises? What kind of God requires our praises? A loving God wouldn't, but a God of Thunder better have praises or He might get irritated and cause misfortune."

For the third time, Uri was lifted out of his body, not by pain or discomfort, but by words that swirled him into an excited and lightheaded state.

"*Elohim*, the Jewish God, exists far above us, no longer furious, indifferent, dismissive, uninterested. Do you feel God's indifference? The emptiness inside each of you? That unnamed something you long for may be for God to notice you, even to punish you, anything but abandon you. Perhaps everyone else has."

After class, Uri took a walk around the campus without awareness of his surroundings or of himself as the Professor's lecture echoed in his head. The story of Jacob struggling with a man, Adan's *bar mitzvah* portion, popped into his mind. Rabbi Shapiro suggested the "man" was an angel, an ambassador from God, ready to bless Jacob when the match ended in a draw. Simon's interpretation was that Jacob struggled with the bad part of himself, his "ego." But Adan's ideas came closer to the Professor's. God's emissary snapped Jacob's hip bone because he could. God snapped Uri's hip bone because He could.

When he returned to the dorm, Vel was there, waiting.

"That was some lecture, huh?" He said.

Vel and the other former Youth Group members were all enrolled. Uri said nothing. He didn t want to ruin the experience with talking.

"Hey, are you, like, going out again tonight? Lately, we haven't been hanging out much."

Vel touched Uri on his shoulder, his back, his neck.

"Jenny and that girl in your Remedial Math. They've got their claws dug right into you, man."

"Whatever."

"*Sheesh*. Don't let girls take all your time and shit. You'll be, like, a slave."

Was Vel jealous? His touches became grips. He clasped his hand around Uri's arm and the nape of his neck, squeezing. Uri yanked away.

"You can hang out with Sam and Zhong. It doesn't have to be me all the time."

"Sam and Zhong aren't cool, like you and me."

Uri coughed to cover a laugh. After four years of longing and almost committing suicide when rejected, he no longer cared about Vel. He'd rather be with Don and Ernie, upperclassmen, who had other Jewish Studies classes with Professor Berns. It was a sudden realization. And now? It was Vel who clung to him, wanting acceptance, with an edge of desperation in his voice. Uri took no pleasure in the turn of the tables. He didn't care enough to take pleasure. A Jewish Studies 101 lecture had shifted his interest from his fourth only friend to Dr. Berns.

He inhaled his new freedom from Vel deep into his lungs, unhooking himself from the last link of the invisible chain that had bound him to Vel. With his next breath, he closed the clasp on a new chain, one that bound him to the Professor.

He remembered Ernie saying in rehab that Professor Berns invited some students to off-campus seminars. If he had an invitation, it would be a sure sign of the acceptance he had longed for since the death of his mother and for his whole sad life. Vel was weak, he now knew, unable to keep what he wanted, only attracting other weaklings. If Dr. Berns invited Uri, he would become cool, one of the strong ones, extraordinary, a member of an elite inner circle educated about the true nature of God.

CHAPTER 16

Uri was finishing another aggravating hour in the synagogue with Adan when the boy surprised him.

"My mom wants you to come over for dinner. Beats me why. She's invited a guy she's been dating, and she says she wants you to be the, like, chaperone or whatever."

"When?"

He guessed Flora wasn't angry at him, if she ever was, for taking Adan to the party and then burning down the house when they cancelled the wedding.

"Friday for *Shabbat* dinner. And get this. The guy she's dating? He's the spitting fucking image of fucking Simon."

Uri wondered if he would forever date the spitting image of Jenny or another girl who would pay him to make another guy jealous. He thought of science fiction stories of people caught in time loops, in which the same situation was repeated. But any middle-aged guy Flora dated might resemble Simon. Even Dr. Berns resembled Simon. They all looked alike to him and no doubt to Adan, too.

Somewhat curious, he rang Flora's doorbell on the next *Shabbat*. Adan opened the door.

"The fucker's already here," he stage-whispered.

"Are you going to ruin this one for your mother, like last time?"

"If I do, it won't be the same way. Not that I admit anything. Just saying."

Flora came to greet him, wearing a red dress a lot like one Uri remembered his mother wearing.

"So glad you could make it, Uri. Adan was very eager to have you over. He lets me know indirectly, of course. It's his way. Come to the dining room and meet my friend. Then I'll light the candles."

The boy gave Uri a repugnant glare.

A shock even greater than Flora's invitation awaited. Her friend was Dr. Berns. *The* Dr. Berns. The same one who taught Jewish Studies 101. Uri had to hold a chair to keep from collapsing. He hovered over his body again. If he had the Feeling Chart, he would have pointed to the emoji with two wide circles for eyes and a circle of equal size for the mouth.

"David, this is Adan's *bar mitzvah* tutor, Uri. Uri, this is Dr. Berns," Flora said.

The Professor held out his hand, something few did when eyeing Uri's artificial one. He responded by offering his good hand. The Professor held it, giving it a slight squeeze. Uri's hovering self lifted further upwards.

After the candle-lighting, they sat.

"You look familiar," Dr. Berns said.

Uri was sitting opposite him. His scar blazed as he tried to both engage and avoid the Professor's stare.

"I'm in your class."

"Yes. Of course. One of my students."

"You wouldn't forget a monster like him in a hurry," Adan said.

"Adan! Manners!" Flora said, moving the candles to the center of the table.

"You are unusual." The Professor smiled at him, looking only at him, including him, excluding Adan. The boy noticed.

"Tell him about how you got the scar and the hand and the limp. Tell him what you did to get yourself in prison. Tell him all about your *unusual* self."

Adan's voice was a near shout, as if a rise in volume would turn the Professor's interest away from Uri.

"Oh, Adan. You shouldn't be rude. Come into the kitchen and help me bring in the food," Flora said.

Adan stomped after her.

"It's from a burn. And a truck hit me."

"You've had misfortune."

The Professor knew. He hadn't stopped looking at him. Uri wanted to tell him everything—setting fire to two houses, killing his mother and her fiancee's son, trying to die himself, his incarceration, what he owed Don, working for Tough Talk, his friendship with Vel. But it was important that Dr. Berns believe misfortune strengthened him, not that his three words brought Uri a swallow away from tears.

"You... You look like my foster father. He died."

"May his memory be a blessing."

Simon would have given him a kind smile. The Professor's stare was sharp, inquisitive, yet encouraging.

Flora and Adan appeared, carrying platters. During the meal, Dr. Berns addressed Flora and Uri, excluding Adan no matter what attention-seeking behavior the boy exhibited.

"Which *Torah* portion are you tutoring?"

Dr. Berns savored a bite of roasted chicken, closing his delighted eyes and smiling at Flora.

"Delicious."

"Thank you, David. Do you like the rosemary?"

"It's divine."

"Yuk." Everyone ignored Adan's interjection.

"It's *Vayishlach*. The verses where Jacob struggles all night with someone."

"Ah." Dr. Berns set down his fork. "A profound portion. The most important part is the end of the wrestling match, when Jacob won't let go of his opponent until his opponent blesses him."

"Jacob doesn't win. He's weak." Adan's interruption didn't merit a response.

"The passage suggests that struggles contain blessings. Have your misfortunes led to blessings, Uri?"

"Oh, my. What a hard question," Flora said.

Uri thought she was trying to help him. Then he realized Simon's death brought her the "blessing" of this new, more prominent boyfriend. And everything that happened to him—the fires, the scar, prison—brought him the "blessing" of this moment, sitting at a dinner table with the Professor, who showed an interest in him, who asked the hardest of questions. He had to think of an answer that wouldn't shame him.

"My misfortunes haven't stopped yet, so I don't know the outcome."

The Professor nodded. Uri exhaled. What he said was okay.

"You may need someone's guidance through your misfortunes to discover all the blessings."

There was a crash.

"Uh, oh. My plate just fell on the floor," Adan said. "It must have been from the excitement of this boring discussion of my *bar mitzvah* portion. I thought I only had to learn it on Sundays with that one, *el creepo*."

"That's enough, Adan. Please go to your room."

It was the first time Uri heard Flora discipline her son, as mild as it was.

"If I can take dessert with me."

"It's in the kitchen."

Dr. Berns raised his eyebrows at Uri. They were in agreement regarding the boy. Flora picked up the pieces of the shattered plate while Adan skipped up the stairs, carrying a large piece of cake. His cheeks bulged with a chunk already in his mouth.

"Let me help you," Uri said, rising from his seat.

Dr. Berns continued to eat, oblivious of the drama. When Flora returned to her seat, he patted her hand, signaling his pleasure in the evening despite the antics of a naughty child. He punctuated his point by turning his attention to his date. Uri understood it was time for him to leave. Flora gave him a slice of cake to take with him.

When he returned to the dorm, Jenny was waiting. He wasn't in the mood for acrobatic sex with her, but he needed the twenty dollars. Soon he would have enough for a good laptop. He no longer had the cheap desktop the foster agency provided. It perished in the fire, and the agency would have reclaimed it anyway, now that he had aged out of the system. He had been using the library's computers in order to do his class assignments.

He had grown another inch and filled out. The agency had helped him sign up for disability income. A lump sum arrived. He could buy clothing that fit, new shoes, and get a professional haircut instead of cutting his hair himself. If he could save several thousand dollars, he could purchase a well-made prosthetic hand and cosmetic surgery for his ear. He would never appear normal, but he could look better.

Meanwhile, in the Jewish Studies class, the Professor's interest in his students centered on the three girls from Youth Group, Zhong and Uri. He ignored Vel, who wound up in the back of the lecture hall with Sam, relegated to insignificance. Unlike Adan, who fought to get the Professor's attention, Vel lapsed into obscurity. In the dorm, he said little, lying on his bunk playing games or just staring, no longer keeping his hands on Uri. How quickly he had given up after his glory years in high school. Most of the time, Uri didn't even notice the once promising leader who had sputtered out at eighteen.

Before long, Uri received an email inviting him to the Professor's off-campus Wednesday night seminar, held in his home for a select group of students, pizza and soft drinks provided. There was also an email from Zhong.

You get invitation? Want to go together?

Dr. Berns' house was in walking-distance of the dorm, in the neighborhood where much of the faculty lived. His was an imposing two-story colonial, with white columns in the front and black shuttered windows. A note on the front door read "Wednesday seminar students: Please enter." Uri and Zhong hesitated for a moment, wondering if they should ring or obey the sign, then entered. They found themselves in a foyer with hooks on the walls for coats. A wide staircase stood opposite the door. Two large rooms branched from the left and right. The one on the left was brighter. Uri followed his second only friend into that room, lined with bookshelves and print books. A handful of other students were already seated in scattered chairs. Don was among them. He was the only one Uri knew, aside from the invited members of Youth Group. Only four of the seminar attendees were male. The rest were girls, all attractive. Jenny peeled herself away from her two friends and approached Uri.

"Remember, no matter what went down between us, I'm not your girlfriend. In fact, I'm not in love with Vel anymore, so I won't be coming over."

"Are you in love with someone else?" It seems strange that her love ended so abruptly. Two days earlier, they had vigorous sex while Vel was in the room.

"I'm going to fall in love with Dr. Berns. I can tell."

"But he's old."

She shrugged, then rejoined the others.

A few minutes later, an attractive woman in her late twenties entered with five pizza boxes. She put them on a coffee-table.

"Help yourselves," she said.

She left the room, returning with boxes of soft-drinks. She put some in a large ice chest on the floor next to the coffee table. The rest remained on the floor.

Don, who was nearby, sidled up to Uri when she left the room.

"That's the Professor's wife, Rachel. She's not his first."

"His wife? But he's dating my foster father's former fiancee, Flora."

"They have an open arrangement."

"What's that?"

"They can fuck other people."

Uri realized he was in a scene where the rules differed from any he had experienced before, even in a place as different as prison.

"Let's get the room organized," Rachel said. "Those of you who aren't new know the Professor enjoys having you adoring young women at his feet. He'll be sitting in this chair. We call it his throne. A couple of you can get the floor pillows from the corner and arrange them in a semi-circle around the throne. Then some chairs in back for the guys."

She took a seat in a chair to the side of the group. It was a smaller version of the throne. Ten minutes later, Dr. Berns strolled in and sat. He looked around the room and started speaking with no preamble.

"One of you is studying the verses in *Vayishlach* in which Jacob struggles all night with an ambiguous man. Who is this man? The sages thought he was the 'Guardian Angel of Esau'— Esau is Jacob's brother, his enemy. The Guardian Angel of Esau is linked to Satan, the representative of evil.

"If an angel, a messenger from God, is evil, does Jacob wrestle with a dark force that is part of God? If so, God is terrifying, insisting on our absolute obedience, delivering long, harsh punishment—like the breaking of a hip bone—for any transgression.

"Are any of you wrestling with your own evil nature? Do you crave a long, harsh punishment you think you deserve? Or are you seeking the one guardian angel who can protect you in return for giving him your complete loyalty?"

Uri thought of Simon, who was always kind and gentle, and his double, Dr. Berns, who was unsettling, even unprincipled, dating Flora while committed to another woman. Was it Uri's own dark side that drew him to the Professor? Anything was better than being as weak as his foster dad.

CHAPTER 17

After the next class, Dr. Berns motioned Uri down to the cone's point.

"I wonder if you would be interested in becoming my amanuensis."

Uri's eyebrows knitted.

"The word originated in ancient Rome, where it meant a slave who copied what his master dictated. It was a top position for a slave. Now they use it in academic circles to mean 'assistant.' Sometimes unpaid."

The Professor looked straight at Uri, not hesitating or excusing the word 'slave,' suggesting it was an honor he offered, even if it still had the Roman meaning. It reminded Uri of the slavery laws in *Leviticus*. Owners must treat slaves well and free them after a time. Uri couldn't imagine wanting the Professor to free him.

"I have high expectations. There wouldn't be time for other employment or activities, besides your course assignments. You'd need the finances to take this position, since it's unpaid, a private position. If I had to go through campus channels, it would be a needless waste of time. All the tax forms and such."

Uri nodded his head, smiling, scared the Professor didn't mean it or would take back his offer. Being the Professor's slave would be the best thing that ever happened to him. He had forgotten the five-syllable word Dr. Berns used—*aman-*

something. He'd just call it 'slave' to himself and 'assistant' to anyone who asked.

"I'd need you to be available night and day. Sometimes, I can't sleep and think of an errand I need accomplished, like a book from the library at 3 a.m."

He would give up his paid role in Tough Talk to have every minute ready for the Professor. He'd tell Don he wouldn't put him to sleep anymore, deal or no deal. Jenny already fired him. Rabbi Shapiro would need to find someone else to do yard work at the synagogue. His only other commitment was tutoring Adan, and there were just six tutoring sessions left. These he would have to fulfill because of Simon's will.

"You have Flora to thank. She suggested you."

Uri pictured Flora in the red dress, looking just like his mother, helping him get ahead the way his mother would have. He owed her. He had to ask the Professor about her before accepting.

"Uh… About Flora. There's Rachel, and I…"

"I call Rachel my wife because she is my heart's wife, not my legal wife. We have an understanding. Rachel knows my work needs funding, and Flora is comfortable."

He winked at Uri.

"My mother's name was Lora. She looked like Flora. So I guess I'm, like, protective of her or something."

"That's admirable. Flora, Lora, Leah. Remember, Jacob had to marry Leah first, then wait seven years before marrying Rachel, the one he loved best. The Bible exaggerates time, so I'm guessing it was seven months before he took Rachel as his head wife."

The Professor stared hard at Uri, daring him to object.

"Okay, I understand. It's fine with me. I accept." Uri spoke fast, in case the Professor had second thoughts because of an impudent question about a matter that was none of Uri's business.

The Professor patted Uri's arm the way he had patted Flora's hand.

"What about Adan?"

"Adan is a variant of the name Adam. God locked him out of the Garden of Eden. Why? A woman encouraged his insolence."

The Professor turned to gather his papers on the lectern. The matter was settled. There was nothing more to discuss.

When Uri left the classroom, he understood what the expression "walking on air" meant. He floated across campus toward his dorm, lifted above his body, unaware of his feet touching the ground. For the first time, he knew what total happiness was. The Professor trusted him. The Professor needed him. He might have asked anyone, but he chose Uri. A cloak of specialness had descended on a mere student, a deformed one at that.

Vel was in their room, lying on his bed as usual. He looked unkempt, unshaven, with greasy hair splayed on his pillow. He may not have moved in days. Uri knew he should show concern, but he couldn't take on his third only friend's problems now that he needed all his spare time and energy for Dr. Berns. He went straight to his desk to complete his assignments so that he would be ready for any text that came to him from the Professor.

A text arrived from him an hour later.

I'm out of Zatarain's Creole Mustard. Get me a jar. No substitutions.

Uri had never heard of that kind of mustard. He rushed to the international grocery, which had it in stock, then to the Professor's house, ringing the bell. To his surprise, Jenny opened the door, took the item from him, then closed the door again without asking him in. There was no offer to pay him, but it was only four dollars. Uri had a little money left from his disability check.

That night, at one a.m., another text arrived.

Get me Tylenol. There's a 24-hour CVS on Third Street.

Uri had just gone to bed. But the Professor needed something. He bought the Tylenol and took it to his house. Jenny didn't open the door this time. The Professor did, in his bathrobe, accepting the medication with a grunt, not offering to pay. Perhaps he would once a week? It might be petty to ask him for money, Uri thought. He didn't want to let the Professor down.

There was no text until 3 p.m. the next day.

You must pick my laundry up from the Campus Cleaners on 10th Street.

This was a major expense for Uri. Eighteen dollars. He wondered what he should do.

Meanwhile, he had to talk to Rabbi Shapiro about the mowing. After handing the Professor the dry cleaning, he stopped at the synagogue. The Rabbi was in his office, typing on his laptop. He looked up through rimless glasses when Uri entered.

"Did you come to talk about Adan's *bar mitzvah*? I hope his essay is near completion."

"He's having difficulty because the struggle between Jacob and the man ends in a draw. He thinks it means Jacob is weak."

"Ask him to read the verse with more care. *He said, 'Let me go, for dawn is breaking.' But he answered, 'I will not let you go, unless you bless me.'* Jacob is the victor. His opponent cannot break his hold. Jacob only lets go when the angel blesses him."

"Adan has this thing about strength and weakness."

The Rabbi saved his work and closed his laptop.

"Many boys his age do. They understand fights with winners and losers, but not struggles that may be ongoing, with no obvious outcome. You must help him understand ambiguity. The struggle with darkness never ends."

"That's not why I stopped by. I have a full-time job now and can't do yard work anymore."

"Oh?"

"Yes, I'm an assistant to Dr. Berns."

Uri wanted to brag about the Professor choosing him until he noticed that the Rabbi's expression changed. He looked at Uri with worried eyes.

"I know of Dr. Berns. Many college students fall under his spell. Be careful, Uri. He may not be what he seems."

"Like how?"

"It would be the transgression of *lashon hara*—gossip—for me to speak without proof."

"Is it because he teaches about humans inventing a frightening God with no compassion?"

"It's not about his evolutionary views. God's compassion is everywhere in the Torah. Take Psalm 86: *But you, Lord, are a compassionate and gracious God, slow to anger, abounding in love and faithfulness.* Even if we view God as a human invention, what humans invented is a compassionate God. Ask yourself why, Uri."

It was the same old dull Rabbi, spouting teachings that lacked excitement, that he had heard a thousand times over the years. If God is so compassionate, why is the Torah filled with war and bloodshed? Why make Jacob exhaust himself struggling all night instead of giving him a blessing at sunset instead of sunrise.

The Professor was right. Blessings come from struggle and misfortune, not from God's so-called 'love.' Without knowing why, the Rabbi enraged Uri. On the way back, he kicked stones, garbage cans, anything in his way. Let the Rabbi whine about love. It is better if someone high up favors you than if some low down person loves you.

He soothed himself with a daydream. The Professor had him bring a book to his house. When the door opened, he was shirtless and muscular, like a younger man. He invited Uri into the room to the right of the foyer. Uri had never been there before. There was no furniture, just a mat on the floor. He threw Uri onto the mat, saying nothing, and got him into a full-body hold. Unlike Jacob, Uri didn't struggle, instead resting in the Professor's arms until dawn broke. Then the Professor let him go.

When the daydream ended, he found himself at the upperclassmen's dorm without having planned to go there. Ernie wasn't there, but his fourth only friend was.

"What's up, man?"

"I'm the Professor's new assistant."

"The fuck! That's what I was for about two weeks."

"Two weeks? What happened?"

Don turned away so Uri couldn't see his face.

"Nothing happened. I had too much classwork. The Professor expected too much. Even with my Tough Talk funds, it cost me more than I could afford. The Professor gets too distracted to ask what he owes. That's all."

"I won't be doing SteelSpine anymore. Ernie might want the role again."

"I'll ask him."

Adan's *bar mitzvah* was five weeks away. Uri became a regular guest of Flora's at *Shabbat* meals, along with the Professor. The next time Uri came, he arrived before Dr. Berns while Adan was still upstairs in his room. Flora excused herself to see to the meal in the kitchen. Uri was alone in the living room. He noticed Flora's purse, left wide open. With no one watching, he lifted out her wallet. There were three twenties and two singles inside. He took them, knowing she would blame her son, then excuse him. Now Uri could afford the Professor's errands for a while. When he was out of funds, he would have to steal again. There was no other way.

CHAPTER 18

An email came from the Professor.

"This is a two-part communication. The first part will go to everyone in the Wednesday seminar. The second part, dear Uri, is for your eyes only, since you are my trusted amanuensis."

The first part followed.

"To Wednesday night seminar students: No one can expect a scholar in my position to give of himself for free or there would be endless requests for appearances. Therefore, I am requiring a fee of two hundred dollars per semester for all those who wish to continue studying with me off-campus."

Then came the second part.

"For your eyes only. I will soon announce the formation of a second off-campus seminar to be held on Tuesday evenings. There will be ten spots, each having a fee of two hundred dollars, the same as for the seminar on Wednesdays. I'm offering you the eleventh spot at no cost if you fill two of the remaining spots. Have those interested contact me, and have them mention your name so you can get credit."

It elated Uri that the Professor called him "dear," trusting him with the private second part of the email. He would get Ernie and Sam to enroll. Vel would be the backup, although his depression might bring everyone down.

It made sense that the seminar would have a fee, and it was generous of the Professor to charge less than for a course at

State. The remaining amount of Uri's disability check and the money he stole from Flora would cover the cost of the Wednesday seminar. It was lucky he had blown none of the rest after buying new clothing and paying the expenses racked up by errands for the Professor.

At the next *Shabbat* dinner, all the talk concerned Adan's upcoming *bar mitzvah*, a week and a day away. Flora rattled on about the catered luncheon, held at the country club after the service at the synagogue, for the entire congregation and for the out-of-town guests. A smaller group would attend a dinner there, followed by dancing. Uri suspected the Professor was right about Flora. She had to be "comfortable" to afford two receptions costing thousands. Had she inherited money from Simon?

At their last Sunday tutoring session, Adan, who behaved better than usual, came with the completed essay—his sermon—that he would read to the congregation. It reminded Uri of the essay he had prepared for his own bar mitzvah before they canceled it. Adan read his aloud.

"Jacob's name means 'trickster' because he tricked his brother Esau out of his birthright. Esau was hunting him down when Jacob and a man struggled all night. There are many ideas about who the man was. He refused to tell Jacob when Jacob asked his name at the end of the struggle."

So far so good.

"The man is the dark part of Jacob's own mind. Jacob had to struggle with this part of himself to become a good person who asks his brother's forgiveness. I intend to struggle with whatever darkness is in my mind so I can be a good Jew. I want to be like Dr. Berns, who is the best man I ever met. Thank you, Dr. Berns, for helping me understand the story of Jacob."

Uri was taken aback. Did Adan mean what he had written, or did he intend to add sarcastic embellishments to shock the congregation? There was no law against ad libbing. It was no use asking the boy. He would lie if he was going to sabotage the event. Uri would have to wait and see.

Meanwhile, the Professor demanded that he run more expensive errands, like takeouts from pricey restaurants and out-of-print books ordered from local rare book dealers.

Uri decided he would dare to ask the Professor to pay what he owed, and he received an encouraging response.

"Haven't I paid you back? My bad. Tally up what I owe you and bring me the figure next Wednesday."

Full of hope, Uri did as he was told, putting the folded paper with the figures on the coffee table in the Professor's house after the seminar. But the following Wednesday, he saw that the paper was untouched, in the same place he had left it the previous week. The Professor had loftier things to consider than what he owed his *aman*-something, his slave. Uri didn't dare bother him again about it. He would have to come up with another way to finance the errands.

Dr. Berns couldn't attend the *Shabbat* dinner at Flora's home the evening before the *bar mitzvah*. Adan was quiet, staring at his dinner plate without eating. He seemed different. Uri wondered if it had something to do with the Professor.

"Would you like to take your plate to your room?" Flora asked him.

He left saying nothing. Uri had a sense of foreboding.

"The poor boy is very nervous about tomorrow. I can tell. I think he wants to prepare every minute he can. Is he overdoing it?"

Uri felt awkward, trying to make conversation without the Professor there to lead a discussion.

"It isn't easy," he managed.

"I have some good news to share. David is organizing a second seminar on Tuesdays. He will allow a few post-graduates, like me, to attend, as long as I bring two others along. There's a fee, but it isn't much. I'm going to ask two of the girls at work."

She shook her head, smiling and chuckling.

"David can be so amusing. He wants the women I invite to be attractive. He likes to have adoring girls at his feet during seminars. What a jokester he is."

Uri had heard Rachel say something very similar. If Flora came to the Tuesday seminar, Rachel would be there. He wondered if Flora knew about Rachel. He realized he wasn't the only one who the Professor told about the new seminar.

The morning of the *bar mitzvah* arrived. At the service, Adan read the *Torah* verses in passable Hebrew, and then gave the sermon with no changes to what he had written. Everything went smoothly. This was a surprise.

Uri stood in the back, next to the table where congregants and guests placed envelopes containing gifts for Adan. There were many, and Uri realized that if he took a few, no one would miss them. When he didn't see anyone looking, he took some fat envelopes and stuffed them in his backpack. Later, when he opened them, there was enough cash to pay for the Professor's errands for several weeks.

Before the luncheon, Uri approached the Professor, asking him if he noticed a difference in Adan.

"I minded for Adan a couple of weeks ago when Flora had to attend a conference required by her job. That night, I taught the boy the meaning of '*painful toil*,' God's curse after expelling Adam from the Garden of Eden. Let's just say we came to an understanding."

Uri shuddered to think what the teaching method might have been, while wishing the Professor used it on him. It was the same wish he had for punishment ever since he was Adan's age. But he doubted the boy craved any type of suffering.

At the luncheon, Don sat next to him.

"I saw what you did. You took envelopes."

"And?"

Uri was shaken. He didn't think anyone observed him.

"I won't tell if you help me sleep again. I haven't had a good night since you stopped."

A server arrived with plates for those at the table. Uri's stomach twisted, balking at the sight of food. He dreaded being caught, arrested, sent to prison, and losing the Professor. Don tucked into the baked salmon.

"Are you blackmailing me?"

"It's more like—you scratch my back, and I'll scratch yours."

Uri remembered Don saying he was in prison for something to do with money he owed. He wondered if Don got into debt for doing unpaid errands for the Professor. He said he had assisted him for a mere two weeks, but there could have been high expenses even during that short time. They might have arrested Don for getting funds by illegal means.

He would have to do what Don wanted. The Professor's middle-of-the-night calls and early morning classes exhausted Uri. If he had to be at Don's room every midnight, he would get even less sleep. He would drop out of classes if it weren't for Simon's will.

His mind swirled with this dilemma for the rest of the luncheon and through the dinner. During the dance, Lois approached him. She had an attractive, shorter haircut. Her sad green eyes contrasted with her bouncing red curls.

"Hey. Remember when we were in high school, and I used to ask you if Vel ever mentioned me?"

Her voice had a melancholy note, as if she were ready to weep.

"It's funny how in love I was with him back then. Now I don't think of him at all."

"I know what you mean."

"Don't you room with him?"

"Yeah, but we don't talk much."

"Now I'm… attached to someone else."

"Who?"

Her eyes seemed about to brim over.

"With Dr. Berns."

"No kidding!"

That's what Jenny had said. Maybe all the seminar girls adored the Professor.

"I know you're close to him, his assistant or something."

"Something like that. Yeah."

"Could I hang out with you and be your, like, friend? No one outside the seminars understands what's so great about the Professor, and why we'd do anything for him."

"I can see that."

Her lashes moistened.

"Only some things he wants…"

She didn't finish her sentence. Just then a *Hora* line passed her. Someone grabbed her hand and pulled her in. She looked back at Uri, mouthing something he didn't understand. Did the Professor want something Lois was reluctant to give? Was that what she was trying to tell him?

He didn't have a chance to ask her before the evening was over. Don wanted him in his room to resume his nightly duty. Ernie was there, and as usual, they spent a few minutes talking in whispers after Don was asleep.

"Dr. Berns let you in his Tuesday seminar. You said you've been wanting an invitation. He wants you there."

"Bullshit. I'm enrolling, but you're making up the part about him wanting me. He doesn't know me from Adam."

"You'll see."

"Besides, I already know everything he'll say. I took his Jewish Studies 101 class. God is scary *blah, blah, blah*."

Ernie's arrogance still annoyed Uri. He let him prattle on.

"It's not what he says. It's his charisma. There's a mystery to it I'd like to find out more about, seeing how I'm going to be a businessperson and all. I'd make a fortune if I could awe people the way he does."

"No one's ever going to be like the Professor. He's one of a kind."

"Could be."

Uri thought the Professor was more extraordinary than the four figures on Mount Rushmore and should be made the fifth.

Dr. Berns might not be President—yet—but he, more than anyone, was a towering figure. Uri wished, as Adan had said, to be as good a man, or half as good a man, as the Professor, if that were only possible for someone who had killed his mother and first only friend.

CHAPTER 19

Thanksgiving break coincided with the *bar mitzvah*. A week later, classes resumed, and a week after that, Uri realized he hadn't seen Vel in a long time. Soon after, Vel showed up. He had cleaned himself up, wearing laundered clothing, without the clouded eyes or greenish complexion he had for most of the semester. Right away, he attacked Uri without explaining his absence.

"So, man. Are you still the assistant or whatever for Dr. Berns?"

"Yeah. I am."

Vel shook his head.

"Dude. You've drunk the Kool-Aid."

"If I have, I'm doing just great."

"Pathetic!"

He wanted to be civil to Vel, who had a rough time with depression during the first part of the semester, but his inferences about the Professor were insulting and ungrounded.

"You know what? You're jealous."

"Jealous? Of that scammer?"

"Everyone used to follow you, the popular one in high school. Guess what. That's finished. And I'm glad I found a brilliant man who can teach me things you'll never learn about."

"The college is full of brilliant professors. Dr. Berns is just one of them. It's his job to be brilliant. You're letting him brainwash you."

"It's his job to make me an educated person and a better human being. If that's brainwashing, fine with me."

"Not by accepting his fucking opinions as yours. That doesn't help your mind grow."

"Unless his fucking opinions are the truth."

Vel moved closer. He stood inches from Uri's face.

"He's a bullshitter, and you fall for it. You're falling for bullshit, man."

Uri felt his spittle shower his skin. No one was going to spit on him. He gave his former third only friend a hard shove. Vel landed on his bed in a sitting position.

"Don't you ever disrespect the Professor again or I'll give you worse."

Vel stood and gave Uri a swift punch in the face.

"Ow! My nose. You made it bleed. Shit head."

"Fuck you, stupid ass."

"Fuck you back."

Vel threw Uri a box of tissues from his night table. They both sat on their beds, breathing hard, Uri holding tissues to his nose.

"You're mad because you aren't what you used to be in high school."

"And what did I used to be in high school, huh?"

"The popular kid in Youth Group."

Both calmed down. Uri's nose stopped dripping.

"And you think I miss that? Every one of you wanted something from me back then. I didn't have a clue what it was or how to give it. None of you were ever satisfied. It was miserable."

Uri stared at Vel as if seeing him for the first time. It astonished him that Vel had been miserable. He imagined he was the only one.

"Everyone wanted to be your friend. I wanted to be your friend. When you rejected me, I wanted to die, man."

Uri tried to end it by walking into traffic, but it would go too far to say that to Vel.

"Don't put that on me. I never rejected you. That's a dumb ass thing to say. I searched for what I didn't know I needed, going from one kid to another to see if they had it."

"Had what?"

"Whatever the fuck you think you've found with the Professor. Only if he's your answer, you're worse off than I ever was."

Uri paused, fishing for a response.

"But I have found it. I just can't explain what to you. It's a vibe or something."

Vel walked to the bathroom and inspected his face in the mirror for any damage after the near fist fight. It was Uri's face that got the worst of it.

"I'm taking Freshman Psych. A lot of it's about how humans need parents for an extended time, even into their twenties, because they aren't born self-sufficient like animals and fish and things."

Uri dabbed his nose, looking for any trace of blood.

"Yeah? So?"

"You're an orphan, right? And your foster father died, right? You want this Dr. Berns to be, like, a father to you."

Uri's gaze floated to the wall. A nature calendar hung there with a picture of a fat seal with her white-furred baby.

"Fuck that! You could say the same thing about any student who works for a professor. One's older, one's younger. It's only optics to call it a father and son-like relationship."

Vel returned to his bed and sat.

"Sorry about your face, man."

"You threw a hard punch. It hurt."

"I got mad. That's all."

"You got an anger problem there, dude. Did you learn about that in Psych?"

Both stayed quiet for a couple of minutes. Then Uri started again. It was the only honest conversation he ever had.

"Why did you, like, pick Zhong for your first friend in Youth Group?"

"That's another dumb ass question. It's obvious. Because he's Chinese."

"So?"

"He's different. I thought he might have what I was looking for."

"And why did you pick me second?"

Vel's eyebrows raised at this self-evident question.

"*Geez*. With your scar and eye and hand, you're not normal, dude. I was looking for not-normal."

Uri's scar reddened. He hated anyone referring to his appearance.

"I'm more worried about the girls from Youth Group—Jenny, Sylvia, and Lois—than I am about you. You're a dickhead, but they could get hurt."

"What do you mean?"

"Have you noticed that the Professor only invites ugly guys like you to his special seminars, but all the girls are hot?"

"No."

"I bet he fucks the girls."

Now it was Vel who was going too far.

"He likes to have adoring girls in his seminars. It gives him enjoyment, and it's also a kind of joke. Besides, his wife Rachel is always there. She keeps close tabs on him."

"Just saying. The 'optics,' as you called them, say he's fucking them."

"Well, optics are just optics, not truth."

"Unless they are the truth."

"You always talked about fucking the girls."

"I never touched them. I didn't want to get any of them pregnant or whatever and be stuck with them. Not when none of them were, like, the love of my life."

Uri reddened. Neither mentioned his fantasy Remedial Math sex partner or his having sex with Jenny in the dorm room. He hoped Vel wasn't aware of his lies or of his getting paid. They exhausted the subject for the time being. Uri resented the entire conversation. He wouldn't let anyone make him doubt the Professor.

"Anyway, where've you been? You've been gone since break."

Vel turned away.

"If you must know, my parents checked me into a psych hospital. They were scared I'd commit suicide. I guess you tried when you walked onto the highway, and all you got from it was a bad limp. That made me reconsider. If I had a gun or something, I'd be out of it by now."

"Man! I didn't know."

"The hospital wasn't bad. I didn't care at first. Then they pumped me with drugs, and I started caring. After that, I learned how to handle stress better in the therapy groups."

Uri recalled Dr. Rubin with his Feeling Chart and his Lexapro after a truck hit him. Only surgery and rehab saved Uri from a stint in a psych hospital, too. Maybe if he had learned to handle stress, he wouldn't have set the second fire and landed in prison.

That night, he pondered the things Vel brought up. What struck him was that Vel had been wretched while making others wretched. Uri always considered being popular the same as being happy. It puzzled him that Vel didn't see it that way. He didn't understand the effect he had on others. They all wanted something from him, and he couldn't figure out what. It wasn't rocket science. Everyone wanted to be his one and only special friend forever—his BFF.

None of the other students had the extra chance to be close to the Professor that Uri had on *Shabbat*. Flora still invited him to the Friday night dinners, even though he no longer tutored her son. Adan and a whole new crew of high school students were in the Youth Group now. During the meals, Adan was polite and quiet when Dr. Berns attended. But Uri saw the boy look at the Professor with a malicious glint when no one else was paying attention. Adan was biding his time, Uri realized.

Vel might do the same, intending to expose the Professor, lie about him, get even for taking his former friends away. The

Professor was too high-minded to realize he had two enemies. He thought he had subdued the boy and thrown Vel into college limbo by ignoring him. It was up to Uri, who knew better, to protect the Professor from those who wished to harm him. It was up to Uri to save the Professor in order to save himself. If the Professor went down, Uri would be lost.

CHAPTER 20

It was the first session of the new Tuesday off-campus seminar. Rachel was there to greet the students, most of whom had never been to a professor's house before. They scanned the room with its bookshelves, framed paintings of Jerusalem, artistic *menorahs*, a piano, and the "throne."

The absence of a television did not surprise them. Professors were supposed to be erudite, learned, above tv offerings.

Flora came with two attractive women from her workplace, both younger than her. Ernie and his brother Sam showed up. Zhong brought two Jewish students from Asia, one from India and the other from Singapore. The remaining two were good-looking coeds Uri had never met. As usual, the Professor wouldn't appear until Rachel made all the arrangements, collecting the fee, having floor pillows brought out for the younger women and chairs for Flora and the guys.

Rachel didn't say who she was. Uri wondered if Flora thought she only assisted the Professor's seminars. There was no sign of jealousy from either woman. Rachel had greeted her in the same manner that she greeted all the attendees. She made the same joke about the adoring women on the floor pillows she made during the first Wednesday night meeting. She brought in the boxes of pizza and soft drinks, urging everyone to help themselves.

At the sound of footsteps descending the staircase, everyone hushed. The Professor entered and went straight to the throne. After sitting, he took his time, glancing at each student, longer at the women, ignoring Rachel, perhaps for the sake of Flora. He began to speak as he always did, without preamble.

"I've been considering the *V'ahavta*, the prayer observant Jews recite morning and evening after the *Sh'ma*. What interests me is the passage in the second verse about what happens to those who don't obey God's commandments. *'God's wrath will flare up against you.'*

"How would God punish idol worshippers? Not with a flood, as He did in the time of Noah. *He will close the heavens so that there will be no rain.* In other words, with a flood's opposite—drought. Instead of excess, absence, loss, death by starvation. In modern times, we can interpret the drought as psychological—loneliness, shame, alienation, a lack of connection with others."

His sharp gaze cut into each of them.

"I sense many of you are in a drought—thirsty for someone to end your isolation, your abandonment, and offer you the relationship you desire, to treat you as the special person you never knew you were."

When the Professor concluded his remarks, he closed his eyes. No one knew what to do. Rachel took over from her smaller throne, still off to the side.

"Do any of you recognize yourselves in this interpretation?"

This prompted a discussion. At first, a few students offered timid opinions, looking toward the Professor for approval. He kept his eyes closed.

"Like, sometimes I think I'm behind a window, watching everyone having fun on the other side."

"All I ever wanted was for someone to give me approval."

At Rachel's urging, the debate grew more animated, each participant hoping for some sign of Dr. Berns' recognition. His eyes remained closed.

"Love is the way we connect with each other. There's nothing more miserable than not being loved, but it may not be because you've done something wrong or disobeyed God. The other person's just not into you."

The Professor's eyes stayed shut.

Zhong spoke up.

"*V'ahavta* is God's punishment for entire people, Israelites, now Jewish people, for disobedience. Someone needs show how to obey. Someone strong, special, like Professor."

The Professor's eyes snapped open. He shifted on the throne and gave Zhong a long look, saying nothing. Uri felt the sting of his third only friend's rise in the Professor's estimation. Everyone else looked at Zhong with parted lips. They all understood he was the seminar favorite. They all envied him.

I could've said that, Uri thought. He suspected everyone felt the same way. As he reflected on the seminar, he wondered if the Professor punished the way God did, by withdrawing, withholding himself, firing his assistant. An icy knife pierced Uri's heart as he imagined himself being cast out as he had been by Vel in high school, even if Vel denied it. It had unnerved him when the Professor kept his eyes shut, excluding all those whose remarks disinterested him. If that one gesture rattled Uri, how much worse would it be to hear the words, "I don't need you anymore" or "You've disappointed me. Leave!"

That made Uri obsess about money, again. He was running out and needed more. He would have to sell his laptop and use the library computers. The next day, he visited a local pawnshop. It was his first time in such an establishment. It amazed him to see the array of items—clothing, musical instruments, kitchen appliances, jewelry. Anyone could pawn anything, unless it had a serial number in the police database of stolen items.

The adults had stuffed Adan's half of the room with gaming devices and all the latest teen gadgets. He owed Uri for not returning Uri's possessions when they bunked together. Uri could claim they were his. It would be easy to get in there while the house was empty. Flora seldom locked the back door. The next day, he entered that way. If anyone noticed, he would say he was returning a pen he borrowed. It was lame, but it was all he could dream up.

After pawning a bag full of Adan's belongings, with no questions asked by the pawnbroker, he had enough cash for a few more weeks of errands. At *Shabbat* dinner two days later, Adan said nothing about the items missing from his room. He stared at Uri, his eyebrows lowered with suspicion.

Flora was exhilarated.

"David, you were so enlightening on Tuesday. I've said the *V'ahavta* all my life, although not every day, just at services. But it was just words. You made me think about it in a deeper way."

The Professor was busy being praised by Flora and didn't notice Adan's expression. He gave her an amused smile while appearing to revel in her praise. Yet, Uri knew the Professor didn't need praise from anyone. He humored his hostess.

"Your remarks on drought, as they meant it in the *Torah* and now in the twenty-first century—so insightful and rich." Flora passed the wine to him for uncorking.

She was wearing the same red dress that always made Uri want to protect her. She might make a fool of herself. Yet, she risked making the Professor suffer from the embarrassment of being admired in excess. It was intolerable that either should have any discomfort. If Uri provided a distraction, he might save the situation for both.

"Ow! Oh. Oh." He winced, holding his arm.

"What's the matter?" Flora rose from her seat while the Professor untwisted the cork with a few adroit turns of the opener.

"I get muscle spasms above the prosthetic hand. It's like my brain doesn't accept the amputation. That's what the physical therapists told me." He rubbed his arm.

"What can I do?"

"Nothing. It'll go away."

While he was looking down at his arm, he heard her voice.

"Just don't burn yourself."

He looked up. Flora was seated again with a concerned look. Neither the Professor nor Adan reacted to what Uri thought she said. Did she say something, or was it another hallucination?

Losing of his mother was a kind of drought. Being haunted by her, if that's what was happening, was no solace when her ghost kept reminding him of the fire that killed her. He didn't understand what the ghost wanted or what his mind wanted if he was imagining things. It wasn't to kill himself, as his suicide attempt proved. Both his mother and his mind seemed to want him to stay alive and eat himself up with guilt. Only the Professor's acceptance of him brought any relief.

After the *Shabbat* meal, Flora and the Professor always attended services. They dragged Adan with them. Uri often attended, too. Members of the old Youth Group, who were now in the seminars, divided their attendance between Hillel and the synagogue. The high school teens in theYouth Group were there, sitting together, joking and teasing before Rabbi Shapiro began. Adan, who joined them, appeared to have Vel's former role, attending to some and ignoring others.

It was unfortunate that the Rabbi used the *V'ahavta* for his sermon so soon after the Professor's lecture. It highlighted the difference between them, to the Rabbi's disadvantage.

"The *V'ahavta* is a prayer about love. It instructs us to love God with all our heart, soul, and might. It asks us to teach our children to love God. The *Torah* commands us to love God, our neighbors, and strangers. How? With acts of kindness and caring. Why? So that 'you shall eat and be full.' Full of food and contentment."

Uri imagined the scorn the Professor must experience hearing such empty words about love. How high school, how weak and dull, how simple-minded the Rabbi sounded. Contentment didn't come from a childish emotion. It came from being singled out as special by someone better than yourself. God singled out Abraham, Jacob, and Moses, not for "love," but for leading the Israelites on a journey to "the land which I will show you"—Jerusalem.

After services, Lois caught up with him on his walk back to the dorm.

"What did you think of the service tonight?"

She sounded ready to cry.

"Feeble, after the Professor's seminars this week."

"Such a coincidence that both focused on the same prayer. Although each chose a different verse to emphasize—the Rabbi on the first about the commandment to love God, and the Professor on the second about what happens if you don't."

"That's the point, isn't it? You're commanded to love, which no one can command anyway, since it's an emotion, then told what will happen if you fail."

She glanced at him with eyes so wet they seemed about to melt.

"I don't think the *V'ahavta* is about the emotion called love. It's about acting in a loving way. But I agree with you that the seminar was more interesting. The Professor says new, startling things. With Rabbi Shapiro, it's same old, same old."

"It's the difference between a brilliant mind and an ordinary one."

"It's not fair to the Rabbi, but I prefer the Professor. I'm so… in awe of him. I'm just one of his adoring girls, as Rachel says, sitting at his feet and drinking in every word, nothing more to him than that, but I don't care as long as he lets me adore him."

"Some of us love Dr. Berns with all our heart, our soul, and our might. He is a god to us."

She was the only one who might understand.

"Yes, we give Dr. Berns what we should give God. I can't help it. I don't know how to be any different."

"Sometimes I think the Professor is, like, the *Messiah.* I'm being extreme, but that's what I think, sometimes," he said.

"Me, too," she said.

Now Lois was weeping into her palms as she walked.

"Why are you crying?"

She stopped and turned to him.

"I have no control, that's why."

Uri had the same problem, no control over his fear of not meeting the Professor's demands and no control over what he had to do to meet them. Lois' sadness was contagious. Tears spilled from his eyes, too. They stood on a street corner, hugging and crying, unaware of all the reasons.

CHAPTER 21

Flora sent him a text.

Come here tonight at 7 p.m. Important.

When he showed up, she led him to the dining room without her usual warm greeting. There, on the table were all the possessions he had stolen from Adan. Uri's lungs refused air.

"The police brought these from a pawnshop. Your name is on the merchant copy of the receipt. You stole these, Uri. We reported the theft to the police. Adan is good about recording serial numbers, and they were entered in the database pawnshops use. They urged me to press charges. The only reason I refused is for Adan's sake."

Adan stood in back of his mother, peering at Uri with a spiteful grin.

"If Adan didn't look up to you and love you, I'd let the police arrest you. As it is, I paid back the pawnshop and the costs of confiscation and storage. You have some explaining to do, young man."

Before Uri said anything, Flora told her son to collect the items on the table and go to his room.

"I need to talk to Uri alone," she said.

When Adan's bedroom door closed, she continued.

"I didn't want Adan to think you needed money for drugs or gambling. He'd be so disillusioned."

Uri started sobbing. Before he was able to stop it, the entire story tumbled out of his mouth. The honor of being chosen as the Professor's assistant. The expense of the errands that weren't reimbursed. The Professor's lack of attention to detail, like the tally Uri left on his coffee table. Uri's desperation when he thought he might disappoint the Professor. The only thing he left out were the items Adan refused to return when Uri didn't die.

"Why didn't you come to me? You didn't before your suicide attempt, and you didn't when you ran out of money."

He glanced at her. She shimmered through his tears.

"How could I ask you for anything after killing you?"

"What?"

There was the sound of a crash from upstairs. The door opened.

"That was my Nintendo. I dropped it, and it broke. It's Uri's fault for stealing it and making me have to move it."

"Close your door, Adan. We're not finished."

The door slammed closed.

"Please don't tell the Professor... *Sob*... He'll fire me."

"I won't tell him you stole, but I will talk to him about giving you enough for his errands. Whether you have money is not the point. Reimbursement isn't the answer either. He should provide the money you need in advance."

"He'll fire me for telling you."

"I won't let him."

Why was she so nice to him? Maybe she was his mother, after all.

"There's one more thing."

"Anything."

"Stop being so cold to Adan."

She caught Uri off guard. Cold to Adan? The little brat had been trying to torture him every chance he got.

"He wants you to be a big brother to him. Spend time with him. Take him places. Show him things a boy his age would like."

"Are you sure that's what he wants?"

"Of course. He may not say so, but I can tell."

Uri felt like his eyes crossed.

"I'll call him down so you can make plans with him."

When Adan was in the room, Uri forced himself to suggest a time to hang out. Adan turned to his mother.

"Do I have to?"

"You know you want to."

The boy stamped his foot.

"I'd rather rake leaves—and I hate doing that—the spend time with *el creepo*."

Flora smiled, as if her son was being entertaining.

"Adan will be happy to hang out with you, Uri. He'll be ready when you knock on the door."

That night, Uri told Don what happened.

"You're lucky, dude. That's what landed me in prison. You keep thinking the Professor will pay you back. When he doesn't, you get desperate and do something that gets you in trouble. You do it anyway in order to keep pleasing the Professor so he won't throw you out of his inner circle."

"Flora promised to get him to pay."

"Ha! She'll wind up paying you herself. The Professor is a master at getting others to finance him."

A torrent of stress-related problems afflicted Uri—insomnia, nausea, diarrhea, weight loss, stomach pain, trouble swallowing, headaches, muscle tension. His grades were abysmal—a D+" in Remedial Math, D" in Remedial Biology, C+" in Remedial English only because he could parse sentences. He didn't have his Jewish Studies grade yet, which he had taken pass-fail. If he failed, he'd take it again. He hoped to take a course with the Professor every semester, whether new or repeated.

A few days later, the time arrived for him to hangout with Adan.

"Want to shoot some hoops?"

"Jewish boys don't do sports."

"The library?"

"*Boooring.*"

"Okay. So you tell me what you want to do."

"Shoplift."

"The fuck!"

"You asked, shit for brains."

Finally, Adan made a suggestion that wasn't wholesome or politically correct, but at least wasn't illegal. They would walk around town rating women for hotness on a scale from one to five, with "one" meaning a dog and "five" meaning super hot. Uri made the boy keep his voice down so the victims couldn't hear. He let Adan do all the rating, refusing to be more than an observer. When the boy got tired of doing it all by himself, he changed the game.

"Now let's rate the girls who used to be in your Youth Group. I think their names are Jenny, Sylvia, and Lois, right?"

Uri didn't know if Adan had a warped sense of humor or if he was trying to rattle him.

"That's their names, but we will not rate them."

"It's not like they'll hear. C'mon. My mom wants me to have fun. Want me to tell her you didn't try?"

Uri's bowels shifted. Flora had to believe he was making it up to her son for stealing his things, or she might not tell the Professor to keep him on as his assistant. She might not ask him to pay for the errands.

"Okay, okay. Who first."

"Jenny."

"Five."

"Explain why."

Uri wasn't about to reveal that Jenny had been his sex partner.

"She's pretty." He hoped that would satisfy the boy.

"You know what? You're a fag. What about her tits or her ass? Anyone who doesn't think those are what makes a girl hot is a fag."

"Not true. Even gay guys understand what makes a girl hot. Most fashion designers are gay. They can understand without being attracted, Adan."

"So you're admitting you're a fag."

"I'm admitting nothing, but what's it to you, what I am?"

"My mom would sure like to know if she made me hang out with a gay guy who might molest me. Should I tell her you touched my dick?"

Uri realized Adan could blackmail him with any lie.

"What do you want from me?"

"A cut of whatever cash my mom gets from the Professor for you."

After hanging out with Adan, Uri realized he hadn't kept his promise to hang out with Sam. The next day, he met Sam at a campus coffee shop. When they took off their jackets, all Sam was wearing was a sleeveless t-shirt. On his right upper arm was a tattoo of a six-pointed star with the letters D" and B" in the middle.

"What's that?"

"Some of us who are in the Professor's off-campus seminars and who admire him had this done. The letters are for his initials—David Berns. It helps recognize other admirers, like we're all members of the same club."

"Why didn't anyone tell me about this?"

"There's a tattoo place on Walnut Street that does everyone. I'll give you the address."

"Thanks. I'd like that. I want one, too."

"Consider it a return for the favor you did, inviting me to the Tuesday seminar. My brother, too."

As soon as they parted, Uri headed for the Walnut Street tattoo parlor. That night, he showed his new purchase to Don and Ernie.

"I've had mine since the time I was his assistant for a couple of weeks. He called me his amanuensis, but I say 'assistant.' It's easier on the mouth."

"Sometimes, I call myself his 'slave'."

"It can seem like that at night, if you are sleeping, and he wakes you up to get him a donut or whatever."

"Sam and I got our tattoos right after the first Tuesday seminar." Ernie pulled up his sleeve to show them.

It shocked Uri that anyone as cynical as Ernie respected the Professor or anyone beside himself. And that Don wouldn't change the tattoo after the cause landed him in prison. When he showed Lois, he had another shock. She had one as well.

"All the girls do. It started with an older girl in one of the Professor's senior-level classes. Jenny knows her. When Jenny saw it, she had to have the same one. She talked the rest of us girls into getting them."

Uri was so proud of his tattoo that the next time he had to hang out with Adan, he made the mistake of showing him.

"You got yourself branded with that phony's initials? Like you're his property or something? I always knew you're an idiot, but now you're an idiot times two."

"It's not a brand. It's a tattoo."

"Same difference."

They were in Adan's room, playing one of his games.

"What do you have against the Professor, anyway?"

"For one, he's a bully. For another, he's screwing my mother when it's obvious he just wants the money Simon left her. She either dates losers, or she dates con artists. I wish she would listen to me, for once."

"The Professor isn't a con artist."

Adan responded in a voice laced with sarcasm.

"*Ooooh.* He loves her with all his heart, all his soul, all his might. So much that he'll sign a prenup before marrying her. Because he wants her, not her money. And not because he wants to be a father to her bratty son."

"You are a brat. Who'd want to be your father?"

"I'm a reformed brat with him. I keep my mouth shut."

"How did he reform you?"

"With fucking cruelty."

Adan stuck his lower lip out. Despite Uri's urging, he wouldn't say more. Uri figured that whatever went down between the boy and the Professor, Adan deserved it.

In both the Tuesday and Wednesday seminars, everyone showed up with the tattoo, except for Flora. She discussed her reasons with Uri.

"God created us in His image, Uri. Our bodies are temples. We should care for our bodies the way we would temples."

"Temples have decorations."

"The decorations are like clothing. They can be removed. Tattoos are permanent."

He didn't want to say that permanence was the point. It signaled a commitment to the Professor, like a covenant.

"Look. I'm very fond of David and delighted to be a guest in his seminar. I might accept a ring from him if he'd accept one from me as an equal. But he won't be getting a tattoo with my initials or yours or anyone else's."

"If you mean I'm not the Professor's equal, you're right. I'm a student. A freshman. He's a professor. He outranks me."

"Not forever, Uri. Not when you graduate."

"Even then."

He remembered when his mother was alive and unable to understand his desire for a fierce superhero father. Now her double, Flora, couldn't be expected to understand his yearning for a master to worship. It wasn't anything the Professor asked of him. It was voluntary on Uri's part, and that assured him he wasn't dedicating himself to a con artist. He needed the Professor. But the Professor didn't need him.

CHAPTER 22

Uri heard it from the Professor himself.

"I'm planning a Sunday evening seminar for the synagogue Youth Group. Adan will do the recruiting. There will be an introductory fee the first year of a hundred dollars, just to get things rolling. I won't charge Adan if he gets the others interested."

It seemed like a good idea. High school students would get an early exposure to the Professor's brilliance.

"What about Rabbi Shapiro?"

"The Sunday afternoon Youth Group will still be his. It's part of the synagogue's religious school program. Parents decide whether adolescents attend. I won't interfere, and I won't expect the Rabbi to have a say in what happens on Sunday evenings."

It seemed a lot to assume that kids would want two *Torah* sessions in one day every week. Yet Uri knew they were likely to protest going to the Rabbi's and show eagerness for the Professor's. Many parents would see the benefit of having their children taught by a renowned scholar and agree that they had enough years of the Rabbi's influence. The number of Youth Group attendees was sure to shrink.

The genuine surprise was that Adan would cooperate, unless he was being forced. Uri brought it up the next time they met.

"The Professor may be growing on me a bit. Not that I'm giving up my suspicions. He's a *goniff*, as my *bubba* used to say, a thief and a scammer. But I'm kinda curious to see what goes on in the fucking seminars, since my mom goes to one of them. It's a way for me to check them out."

Meanwhile, in the Tuesday night seminar, there were signs of tension between Rachel and Flora. The Professor spoke about the two wives of Jacob, the sisters Leah and Rachel. Their father, Laban, compelled Jacob to marry Leah first. When the Professor finished, he sat with his eyes closed, as he always did, while the students debated.

Flora seldom took part, but this time she surprised everyone.

"Jacob must have loved Leah, since he had so many children with her."

Rachel defended her namesake.

"Only because of God's blessing. *'Be fruitful and multiply; a nation and a company of nations shall be of thee.'* He had children with both wives and with their hand maidens to fulfill the blessing. It had nothing to do with love."

Flora frowned.

"Leah had six sons and a daughter before Rachael had any pregnancy. When Rachel complained to Jacob, his *'anger was kindled against Rachel.'* He's never angry at Leah."

"He doesn't care enough about her to get angry," Rachel said.

Flora swiveled in her chair, facing the smaller throne. Rachel sat up straighter. The throne and the power it signified were hers.

"I have a son the Professor is helping me raise. You have no children and wouldn't understand the way a child binds a man and woman to each other," Flora said.

"It doesn't mean what binds them is love and not just obligation."

Flora shouted, "You know nothing about it!"

"Don't raise your voice at me, Flora. I'm the Professor's assistant in this seminar."

Flora stood and took a step closer to Rachel.

"And what else are you? His whore?"

A gasp arose from someone in the group. Others looked down, and all were silent. The Professor's eyes remained shut. Flora looked at the door, perhaps considering leaving, then sat again. Rachel looked away, ignoring everyone. After a few quiet minutes, the Professor spoke.

"The patriarchs had wives and concubines. Rivalry must have seemed inevitable, as it was among their many children. It had nothing to do with romantic love. It was about favoritism, rank, and inheritance. There's a lesson in that for moderns, who tie love to monogamy. Sisters can share a husband and still have affection for each other. The same is true for women who are not sisters. Sharing a special man is part of the natural order."

The young women on the floor pillows were smiling and nodding their heads. Only Flora and Rachel had pursed lips.

Later, Uri asked the tearful Lois for her opinion.

"I didn't expect Flora to lose it. She's, like, a mom, older, more mature. We girls get jealous, sometimes, but the Professor says it's because of how we've been raised to believe in true love and soul mates and all that stuff."

"It's good it didn't happen in the new high school group."

"I'm worried about those kids. The Professor's thinking can be very unorthodox. They may be too young for it."

Uri considered.

"I can't remember anything he said that would harm a high schooler."

"Not even his denial of the importance of love?"

"You loved Vel in high school. We all did. We'd have been better off if someone had turned off that spigot."

Tears rolled down her cheeks.

"I can't deny that," she said.

"What we have for the Professor is admiration, wonder, and, speaking for myself, need."

The tears were dropping off the edge of her jaw.

"You say that because he chose you as his assistant. You're already favored. I'm in love with him, and I'm not ashamed to admit it or use the 'L' word. It's much more than I ever felt for

Vel. I'm beside myself with love for the Professor. And I want like crazy to be the one he loves best. If he's unable to love, I still want to be his first choice."

"What about Rachel and Flora?"

"From what I saw tonight, they feel the same way I do. Rachel loves him, but she's generous with us girls. Flora's still new at this."

"What the fuck do you mean by 'this'?"

"You know…"

"I don't know."

But Lois didn't say more.

It was Vel who spread criticisms of the seminars when he heard about them from others.

"What the Professor's running is a cult."

"That's bullshit," Uri said. "If it was a cult, no one could leave. They would isolate people who joined, separate them from their families. Everyone would have to give up their possessions and work for the leader."

"That's where those seminars are heading. Look at you. You're brainwashed. You'll do anything the Professor asks."

"He never asks for anything I don't want to give."

"He fucks with minds. Everyone in cults believes they have choices. It's part of the brain fuck to think you have choices when you don't. What do you think would happen if you did something the Professor didn't like?"

At these words, Uri's chest pounded.

"Nothing would happen."

The next day, as if he had overheard, the Professor asked Uri to come to his campus office.

"Close the door," the Professor said when Uri arrived.

He sat at his desk. All the while he spoke, he looked down at a book that was open, his eyes moving from left to right over the pages. Every so often, he turned one of them.

"There's a problem concerning the student you room with. He's committing the transgression of *lashon hara*, gossiping, most of it untrue. I don't want him going to the college administration. There may be some foolish rule forbidding faculty from giving seminars off campus."

He paused, taking a highlighter and using it on several lines in the book. Then he looked up, straight at Uri.

"Would you take care of the matter for me?"

Uri's answer was immediate, even though he wasn't clear about what he was agreeing to do.

"Of course."

The Professor looked down, continuing to read.

"Good. That's all for now. You can leave."

Uri walked through campus, trying to figure out how to accomplish the Professor's task. It would be no use just asking Vel to cool his criticisms. He wouldn't listen. When an idea finally came to Uri, he went into town to the Walmart, where he purchased a hooded sweatshirt and a gorilla mask. That night, he followed Vel. When they were in a quiet part of the campus, he slipped on the mask and caught up with his roommate. Without saying a word, he punched Vel in the face, knocking him down. Then he kicked him in the ribs several times. He finished with a thick branch that lay nearby. Then he bent down and whispered in his ear.

"Keep your mouth shut."

He walked away from his groaning friend, throwing the mask and the shirt in the closest trash can. Vel did not come back to the dorm that night. Had he guessed it was Uri who had beaten him? No one could prove anything without a witness. If campus security asked him about it, he would say he was in his room studying at the time.

He remembered having the daydream in high school that Vel and Zhong beat him after a Youth Group meeting. Somehow, that made Uri suppose he was justified in what he had done. *An eye for an eye.* In a dim way, he realized a fantasy was not the same as reality, but he forced himself to dismiss that recognition. Besides, Vel could harm the Professor, and harming the Professor was the same thing as harming himself. That's what devotion meant. He would protect the Professor the way he would protect himself.

The Professor hadn't asked him to do anything in particular, just take care of the matter. Uri thought of the method himself, with no guidance, and he did what he did voluntarily. That proved it wasn't brainwashing, didn't it?

Vel stayed away for a week. When he showed up, there were yellowing bruises on his face. His breathing was shallow and pained. His torso was bandaged.

"What happened to you?" Uri asked.

Vel gave him a long look.

"I fell."

"*Geez*. You better be careful."

He hoped Vel understood the double meaning of his warning.

"You don't want to fall again." Uri emphasized his point.

"Don't worry."

"Do I have anything to worry about?"

"Not from me."

Vel wouldn't talk to the administration. If the Professor knew, he'd be pleased. Uri smiled.

That night, trying to sleep, he had a fantasy. He was standing in the back of an auditorium, like the cone-shaped one where the Professor held classes. At the bottom were the Professor, the man who wrestled Jacob holding a large wooden box, and Adan holding a tiny box. The Professor scanned the room. When he spotted Uri, he motioned for him to join them. Uri descended the stairs. He passed all the members of the seminars and both Flora and his mother Lora, seated together. A man who looked even more like Simon than the Professor did sat near the two women.

When Uri reached the bottom, the Professor asked him to get down on one knee. Adan stepped forward, opening the smaller box and handing a key to the Professor, who turned toward the man and unlocked the box he held. Inside was a medal on a red sash.

"For your exemplary service to me," the Professor said, putting it around Uri's neck.

Uri looked at the medal. It was decorated with a six-pointed star with the initials "D" and "B" in the center. With tears in his eyes, he looked up at the Professor who gently raised him by the elbow, then put his hand on Uri's shoulder. A sensation of warmth at the place the Professor touched coursed through Uri's body. It was his proudest moment.

CHAPTER 23

The Professor held a series of executive meetings, inviting Rachel and Uri to attend. During the first one, he explained his goal.

"If I can acquire as much money as State pays in salary and benefits, I can leave academia and devote myself to an independent educational enterprise. The petty requirements of State and the Religious Studies Department that I publish in peer journals don't interest me. My concern is teaching, not research. Imagine courses on *Torah* topics for the public, taught by the three of us, with no university or synagogue association looking over our shoulders."

Uri was astounded to be included. Rachel seemed startled as well.

"The two of you and others we choose would conduct the introductory level seminars. I would do the advanced ones."

Uri and Rachel glanced at each other. Was the Professor under the impression that they were ready?

"The fee would have to be higher than a couple of hundred dollars a semester. I'm considering two or three thousand for the beginning courses and upwards of five thousand for those I lead. There could be levels as students complete courses, signified by different color *yarmulkes*. Something like yellow for high school students, orange for college freshmen, blue for post-graduates, and so on."

"Where would the money come from?" Rachel asked.

"From wealthier students and their parents. We need more Floras. And Rachel—isn't your father well-off?"

"He is, but he gives to the Jewish Federation. He won't give to any cause that doesn't support Israel the way he does."

The Professor shook his head.

"Our organization won't take a position on Israel. We'll be an educational, *Torah* study enterprise. Our business will be with the Bible, not contemporary politics or which commandments to observe or how anyone should live their lives. We would take no position on circumcision, keeping kosher, celebrating Jewish holidays, antisemitism, ultra-orthodoxy, or even the Holocaust. Instead, our involvement would be with the text for those who don't know religious history or Hebrew or Aramaic, the language in which the *Torah* was written. It would interpret the text for non-academics, considering my theories, which I would teach."

"I'm still a freshman," said Uri. "I haven't learned enough to teach."

"You tutored Adan. You've proved you can handle the youngest high school students. Besides, I'd train you."

He closed his eyes. Was the meeting over? Then he opened them again, scrutinizing Uri and Rachel.

"We're just dreaming at this stage. We're seeing what's feasible. Rachel, talk to your father. I'm putting you in charge of fundraising."

"Okay. I'll try." Her voice quavered.

"I don't have parents. And I'm broke. I wouldn't know how to fundraise," Uri said.

The Professor smiled.

"You're in charge of security."

"Security?"

"Yes. We'll have enemies, both at State and outside the campus walls. You'll have an invaluable role keeping us safe."

Uri left in a daze. It was exciting to be on the ground floor of the Professor's project and to observe the Professor's theories reaching a wider audience. It overjoyed him to be trusted with such an important part. Imagine, being a teacher, being in charge of security, two roles that would have seemed out of reach when he entered State. He wasn't even in his second year, his courses were still remedial, yet the Professor chose him for this distinctive work.

On his walk back to the dorm, he wondered if his fantasy the night before of being honored had been true. He could almost sense the coolness of the medal against his chest. Never had he seemed to matter to anyone. He was a felon, an arsonist, and an orphan, yet he felt important, special. If his head was in the clouds, he meant it to stay there.

Then a dark idea floated into his mind. If he was the project's security, he might have to be aggressive more often. He had always had the pleasurable dream of being beaten. Now, he would do the beating. That was another kind of pleasure. The power of it was a fresh sensation, another first. It amazed him how easy it could be. Vel went down after a single punch. He hadn't even resisted. Uri didn't have many talents, but security was something he could be good at. He would only do it for the Professor. He was no thug who would beat people for money or for the sport of it. Protection, like self-defense, made it ethical. Why shouldn't fun and ethics mix?

Back in the dorm, he looked at Vel with disdain. To think he once admired such a weakling. His own shoulders no longer rounded. He would go to the campus gym, work out, lift weights, ready himself for security work. If his biological father was the superhero Uri once imagined as a boy, he would become his heir, a powerful man, muscular, masculine, frightening to those like Vel who deserved to be frightened.

The Professor called another executive meeting to report on progress to date.

"Flora is about to make a sizable donation. She is one of the core believers in my work, and she will convince other middle-class widows and divorcees to contribute. What about your father, Rachel?"

"He listened to me, but he's not convinced yet. He's afraid you have me under a spell."

"Bring him to a seminar so he can judge for himself. Then introduce us. A private chat with me may allay his doubts."

"That's an excellent idea, Professor."

It was Uri's turn next.

"Tell me what you want, and I'll do it."

The Professor peered at him with cagey eyes

"You would benefit from having a girlfriend who attends the seminars."

Uri was prepared to do security. This was unexpected. It made little sense, but this was what the Professor wanted.

"I'm not attractive with my scar and the rest."

"You and Lois are already friends. You would be good for each other. Outsiders, who might convince those in seminars to leave, are a danger to our cause. Boyfriends and girlfriends, spouses, lovers, parents."

Lois? His mind shifted. He hadn't allowed himself to think of her that way before.

"But she says she's in love with... someone else."

"Leave it to me. I'll arrange it."

The Professor took an interest in Uri's personal life. It was the closest thing to being his son. He did more than give advice. He took the action that gave Uri what every young man needed. It overwhelmed him. It was wonderful.

After the next Wednesday seminar, he walked out with Lois as usual. She put an arm around his waist, and he followed by putting his arm around hers. She smiled up at him. He broached the topic of feelings to get them out of the way.

"I know you're in love with the Professor. Is this going to be hard for you?"

Her eyes were already wet.

"Not if we take it slow. I trust the Professor to know what's best for both of us. He's pairing off others, too. Jenny with Sam, Sylvia with Zhong."

"That's crazy."

"I admit at first I didn't find you, like, appealing in that way. You're great to talk to as a friend and all. The Professor convinced me that if I acted like a girlfriend, the feelings would happen. I decided to try after his lecture on Leah and Rachel."

"Why?"

"Their father arranged their marriage to Jacob, just like the Professor is arranging things for his students. Leah and Rachel became actual wives who had actual children, no matter how they felt about it at first. Rachel became very upset when it took her so long to conceive. Marrying Jacob did not upset her. As the Professor always says, romantic love is an illusion, not in the image of a majestic God."

They walked on for a while in silence while Uri digested Lois's words.

"Will it be hard for you?" She asked.

"It'll easier for me because I'm not in love with anyone else. Besides, the Professor put me in charge of security. That's given me a lot more confidence."

"Security? Why does he need that, and what's involved?"

He wouldn't tell her everything. It might change her mind.

"Some people claim the Professor is leading a cult. My job is to convince them otherwise."

"How?"

"By telling them that our devotion is voluntary, and all the ways the seminars differ from cults."

"Sometimes, I think we are in a cult. Like everyone getting the same tattoo with the Professor's initials in the center. And the difficulty of refusing what he wants from us."

"I always take it as an honor when he asks me to do something."

"Like being my boyfriend?"

"A perfect example."

The next day, the Professor asked Uri to get him pastrami from the Jewish Deli for his lunch. Rabbi Shapiro, seated at one of the formica tables with a sandwich, motioned him over.

"Join me. My treat."

Uri spent all the money Flora gave him on the Professor, and with Adan's cut, he was always short. He had no funds for a deli meal. The offer was too good to refuse.

"What are you up to these days?"

Uri couldn't help bragging.

"Besides my courses, I'm helping Dr. Berns with his seminars and with security. He has included me in his plans to expand."

Rabbi Shapiro put down his sandwich and took a swig of his coke. He used a paper napkin from a dispenser to wipe crumbs off his beard while he finished chewing.

"I've known you since your *bris*, your entire life, and now that you are without a family, I take a special interest. It's only natural for you to search for a substitute family, but Dr. Berns may not provide one in a wholesome way."

For the second time, the Rabbi suggested there was something wrong with a close association with the Professor. It struck Uri as odd that a rabbi would find a Jewish scholar objectionable. Each had different ideas about the *Torah*, but wasn't the point of education to get different perspectives? The Rabbi was in a rut, sticking to his own point of view instead of celebrating the chance to learn another one.

"What's unwholesome about the Professor?"

"It's not his interpretation of *Torah*, although his approach is far from mainstream, it's where it could lead."

"Where is that?"

The Rabbi picked up his sandwich again, holding it without taking a bite. His brow wrinkled.

"Fascism. Autocracy. A cult."

It irritated Uri to hear another person accuse the Professor of forming a cult. No meal made it worthwhile to listen to such utter crap.

"I understand seminar students are getting tattooed. That's forbidden in the *Torah*. Why doesn't Dr. Berns say so? During the Holocaust, they tattooed Jews by force, if you need another reason not to get one."

Uri's annoyance grew.

"I have the tattoo, if you must know."

He didn't care if he was being rude.

"Anyone who directs your life in a way that serves himself is acting like an autocrat, a fascist. You have free will, Uri. You don't have to obey."

"What I do for the Professor is voluntary."

"I believe otherwise."

That was enough. Uri rose, grabbed the package of pastrami, and turned to go, saying nothing.

"Be careful, Uri."

That's all he heard the Rabbi say, although he may have said more.

PART THREE
THE CULT

CHAPTER 24

In 2010, The Struggle was in the second year of its existence as a tax-exempt organization. Besides the chapter at State, three others existed, one for high school students and two for the public. Uri would have been a senior if he hadn't dropped out to do full-time work for the Professor.

Security kept him too busy to do the Professor's everyday errands. Sam became the new amanuensis. It relieved Uri from having to ask Flora for funds, although his withdrawal from college put a halt to his share of Simon's estate. He moved from the dorm to a closet-sized room in The Struggle's leased space, a combination office and classroom. The always available pizzas, donuts, and coffee kept him fed. Sometimes Lois snuck him into the college cafeteria for a more nutritious discount meal.

The Professor consulted him often about his enemies on and off-campus. The most treacherous threatened to expose The Struggle as a cult, although without proof, that didn't go far. Still, Uri spoke to them, often parents of enrollees. For this purpose, he was well-groomed, with a haircut and a good suit paid for from The Struggle's funds. He could appear to be a clean-cut young Jewish man, adept at representing the purpose of the organization as educational.

But if the Professor needed something more persuasive, such as with other Religious Studies faculty who regarded The Struggle with derision and deep suspicion, the same way they had always regarded the Professor, all he had to ask Uri was to "see to the matter." Uri understood. He deterred without violence, which would have been imprudent. The older faculty, intolerable to the Professor, were his enemies for years before The Struggle existed, zipping ahead of him in rank, even though they were hired after him and had inferior intellects. The worst of these was Dr. Meyerson, a runt of a man, almost as small as Don, but with a swarm of publications and lunging to a deanship. He convinced the Promotions Committee to deny the Professor's bid for the upper ranks, an obvious case of jealousy. No one could ignore the Professor's popularity with students.

Uri understood what to do and how to do it. A mysterious fire broke out in Dr. Meyerson's house when no one was home. It destroyed many antiques. The investigation of the cause was inconclusive. No one suspected the former arsonist.

Two other faculty members remained on the Professor's "hate list." Dr. Barbara Cohen found her tires slashed repeatedly. And Eric Levinson had his laptop stolen. Like many technology-naïve academics, he hadn't backed up the manuscript he had spent the last ten years perfecting. When he bought a new computer, that was stolen, too.

Besides the plague that afflicted Religious Studies, Uri's security duties extended to students who bad-mouthed the Professor or The Struggle. Some lacked the funds for the seminars or weren't invited. Uri silenced them the same way he had silenced Vel. He shared no details with the Professor or with Lois, keeping his pride in his work to himself.

The only person Uri wouldn't attack, even for the Professor, was Rabbi Shapiro. In part, it was superstition. Lightning might strike. But he also had an uneasy respect for him. The Rabbi was dull, but he had always supported Uri, and he was too weak to do any harm to The Struggle. Now that the Youth Group had all but disbanded when the teens followed Adan into the high school seminar, most of the congregation was old. There was no reason to do anything about the Rabbi, no matter what he said about the Professor running a cult.

After two years of working out daily at a gym, first the one on campus and then one in town, Uri achieved the look he wanted. His reflection in the mirror resembled the appearance he had imagined of the man who wrestled Jacob—over six feet tall, well-muscled, with a gruesome scar, uneven features, and an unnerving mechanical hand. Yet, in a grim way, he now attracted women, as Vel had predicted years before. Lois was happy to be seen with him.

He planned to marry her as soon as she graduated. She was still enrolled, majoring in education and planning to teach for The Struggle. Uri already taught beginning courses for high schoolers, called the Yellow Group for the color of the *yarmulkes* they wore.

The year before, when they discovered they wanted a future together, they had a serious conversation about integrating their relationship with The Struggle. It took several of these talks for Uri to agree.

"I love you, but I can't be yours alone," Lois said.

"What do you mean?"

"As I told you when we started seeing each other, I'm in love with the Professor. That's still true, even though I'm also in love with you."

"How can you be in love with two men?"

"They're different kinds of love. I love you like a future husband, but also like a brother. I love the Professor like someone close to God, the *Messiah,* maybe an angel, and also like a father."

His next question went to the core.

"But you'd only be sexual with me, right?"

"That's possessiveness, Uri. In The Struggle, we're above that. You must've figured out by now that the Professor has sex with the girls."

It hadn't occurred to him, or he hadn't let it occur to him.

"You've had sex with the Professor?"

"Once or twice."

"But... But... But..."

"A few times, I guess."

"You'll stop if we get engaged. You'd have to."

"I can't promise that. I still love him."

"What if I had sex with, say, Rachel?"

"It's not the same at all."

"Why not?"

Her eyebrows raised. The answer was obvious.

"She's not the Professor."

He had to think this through. At least she didn't have sex with guys their own age. It was just with the Professor and him. If he was a girl, he'd have sex with the Professor. Wasn't he in love with him, too, in a way? Besides, Lois reminded him that those in the organization should be above petty feelings, like jealousy and envy. *Thou shalt not covet.* They were in an intellectual cooperative, sharing ideas, thoughts, feelings, and even possessions.

Despite the shock of learning that he was sexual with others beside Rachel and Flora, Uri knew the Professor lived on a higher plane, with more privileges than ordinary men. After several twists and turns while arguing with himself, he settled on the Professor's right to have whatever he wanted, including the girlfriends and spouses of guys in the seminars. This acceptance led to the next serious conversation with Lois.

They lay in his closet bedroom in The Struggle's leased space. No one else was in the building. Both were naked, having just finished enjoying each other.

"You know I love you, right?"

She turned to him.

"Yes, and I love you, too."

"And you know how dedicated I am to the Professor."

Uri sighed. "I'm dedicated to him, too."

"We have something to discuss."

"If this is about having sex with him, I'm okay with it."

"It's about the next step."

The hairs on the back of Uri's neck rose. Was she going to leave him for the Professor? He could take anything but that.

"What's the next step?"

"For me to get pregnant."

She rotated onto her back, staring at the ceiling. Her red curls splayed on the pillow.

"We've talked about having a family after you graduate."

"Not by you. By the Professor."

He whirled toward her.

"You want to have the Professor's baby? Not mine?"

"Of course I want yours. After the Professor's. Think about it. Neither of us are anywhere near as brilliant as the Professor. The organization started as one way to spread his views. But it's not the only way. The more children he has, the more opportunity to continue the line of the best of our people."

"You're saying you're not the only one who wants to get knocked up by him."

"Don't be coarse about it. Jenny's already there."

"The fuck! Jenny? But she's with Sam."

"That's my point. Imagine if all the girls had his children. There could be dozens. And think of all the grandchildren. *Dor v'dor*. From one generation to another. All from the Professor's seed."

"They'd be half-siblings."

"Raised *kibbutz*-style. In a cooperative."

"I don't know. Let me think it over."

It took the same arguments in his head for Uri to come around to the idea. There was logic on the one hand, feelings on the other. But feelings had to be suppressed in the name of logic. It was a basic principle of The Struggle. Could he raise another man's child? If it was the Professor's, he answered with a reluctant 'yes.'

In October, Lois stated she wanted to try with the Professor, and that they'd have to stop having sex until she conceived so they'd be sure of whose baby it was. That way, she could have the baby in the summer, right after graduation in early May. They planned to marry in June, although not with a newborn joining them under the *huppah*. By November, she was expecting. The baby was due in July, a month after the wedding date.

Uri had to talk to Rabbi Shapiro about officiating at the wedding, and if the baby was male, at the *bris*, the circumcision, when he was eight days old. He would confide in him, just to get another perspective. The Rabbi was obliged to keep their conversation confidential.

"Lois and I want you to marry us next June. We don't want a big wedding, just the minimum. She's pregnant and the due date is in July."

"Congratulations on two counts. I've officiated for three before."

"This time, you'd be officiating for four."

The Rabbi's brow furrowed.

"The baby would be from Dr. Berns. He'd be on the birth certificate, although I'd adopt it."

"Don't tell me other young women are planning pregnancies with Dr. Berns."

"I'm only telling you my circumstance. I'm not in charge of what others may tell you. As you can guess, this is difficult for me. I love Lois, and we put honesty before monogamy. She never tried to fool me. I've known about her relationship with the Professor."

"Uri, we don't live in biblical times. The Professor is not one of the Patriarchs. And I know about open marriages, although I haven't seen them work. But this is not an open marriage in the usual sense. It's a one-way ticket for the Professor to impregnate young women, if others in your group all believe the same thing."

"I believe in what we are doing."

"If Lois is already pregnant and won't get an abortion, you can't go backwards. You are both young and can have other children. Will any be yours?"

"That's my hope."

"Take care of your *nefesh*, your soul. My fear is that it is in danger, Uri."

The Rabbi said what Uri expected him to say. If he didn't have complete faith in the Professor, it would have shaken him.

CHAPTER 25

As devoted as he was to The Struggle, with a baby coming, Uri realized he would need to make money. At the gym, there was talk of an underground group called Punches, an illegal fight club. There was a purse for the winners, and a lesser one for the losers. People got paid to fight.

It was by invitation only. Uri's tough reputation among gym-goers helped him, and he soon found someone who could get him in. Punches had three rules. Keep the club secret. Keep the club secret. Keep the club secret. Other than that, the rules depended on the match. All were bare-knuckle, but some allowed bats or rackets. If the opponents were hurt, they had to agree not to go to a hospital, where doctors might question the source of their injuries.

A promoter named Wacko, a former fighter with a flattened nose and lidded eye, agreed to sponsor Uri in Punches. He set up matches.

"First, you gotta make up a persona for yourself, like pro-wrestlers do, so you'll be more interesting. Pick a name like Ogre Otto or Monster Mel."

Wacko rubbed his cauliflower ear.

"I used to be SteelSpine on 'Tough Talk.' How about that?"

"Something unique to fighting would be better."

They settled on Demon Jake. That would be his identification in Punches.

"Also, you've gotta quit eating all them carbs. Fighters need a high protein diet to build muscle and strength."

Uri stopped subsisting on food available at The Struggle. He needed money to buy quantities of beef. He began stealing again from backpacks of the seminar students. No one dared accuse the head of security.

Meanwhile, the seminar enrollment continued to grow. When Passover neared, the Professor gave a lecture to commemorate the festival.

"What is *Pesach* about? A battle between two competing gods—Pharaoh, the Egyptian sun god, and *Yahweh*, the god of the Israelites. Pharaoh shows his strength by holding the Israelites in bondage for four hundred years. *Yahweh* shows His with the ten plagues. Boils, frogs, locusts and the rest didn't make the sun god give in. But when *Yahweh* killed the firstborn of the Egyptians, the Pharaoh conceded."

It reminded Uri of Punches. Two supermen duke it out.

Flora had her head cocked.

"What kind of god kills firstborns? It's the worst of crimes to kill babies."

"A god in a competition. A god with a plan for a certain group of people who won't let other gods thwart him," the Professor said. "Sometimes, in the same way, there is a superior human who looks out for his followers by defeating his enemies. He only wins by being ruthless, like God can be."

With that, the Professor closed his eyes while the discussion continued.

Ernie was next.

"I don't buy it. Pharaoh was just a man, and a pretty powerful one not to buckle under nine of the plagues. But it was an unfair fight. A human ruler against God. When a so-called superior human defeats a weaker one, it's plain brutality, that's all."

"The point is, *Yahweh* proves his power. He wins," Rachel said.

"My point is, there is something wrong with the whole setup," Ernie said, crossing his arms. "It wasn't a battle between two gods. There's only one God, *Adonai,* who loved his people and got them out of bondage. That's what *Pesach* is about. Ask Rabbi Shapiro."

Later, the Professor asked to see Uri.

"That student, Ernie, contradicts my teaching. Perhaps you can make him understand."

Uri knew this was a security matter. For the first time, someone within The Struggle needed persuasion. Uri understood what to do. But he owed it to Ernie, who was his friend, to talk to him first. That night, he went to his dorm room. Both Don and Ernie were there.

"You know why I'm here, don't you?" Uri asked.

"To hang out?" Don lay in his bunk.

"To talk to Ernie."

"About what?" Ernie, who was at his desk, turned in his chair to face Uri.

"The way you answer the Professor is disrespectful."

"Disrespectful? Nah. I just know what he's going to say before says it. *Yahweh* isn't loving. He's cold-blooded, nasty, and into punishing. *Blah, blah, blah.*"

"No one contradicts the Professor."

"Or what?"

"Or they get slugged."

Uri raised his arm.

"Hold it! Don't slug him."

Don jumped off his bed.

"What are you going to do about it if I do?"

Uri looked down at him.

"Just don't hit me," Ernie said, his voice raised an octave.

"I don't like to, but you're making me."

"Don't hit me."

"Don't hit him."

"It's his own fault."

"Please don't."

"Don't hit me. I can't take pain. Jews don't hit each other. It's antisemitic."

"Get ready."

"Don't!"

"Please. No!"

"Hey! Hey! Hey!" Don shouted.

Ernie lay sobbing on the floor. Uri debated whether to kick him, but he seemed to have learned the lesson after a couple of hard slaps.

"After this, you'll agree with everything the Professor says."

"Okay, *sob*, just don't hit me again."

"Don't hit him anymore," Don said.

"I'm not."

"Don't hit me," Ernie said.

"I won't if I don't have to."

As he was leaving, Don had one more question.

"Why'd you do it to a friend?"

"It's my job."

Soon after, Wacko staged the first match at Punches for Demon Jake and an opponent. The location of events changed often. This time, they held it in a commercial warehouse with a large space. Seventy or eighty spectators stood around a clearing with no ropes to section it off. Demon Jake and the other man came to the middle and, without a bell or signal, pummeled each other. It didn't last long. After a few punches with his good hand, Uri's opponent gave up. They declared Demon Jake the winner and gave him a prize of three hundred dollars. He would use part of it to fill the unused freezer compartment of The Struggle's refrigerator with steaks. The rest he gave to Lois for baby clothes.

The next time he had a date to hang out with Adan, he took him to Punches to show him how real men prove themselves.

"We're going to a secret place. Don't tell your mother."

"Where?"

He gave him a doubtful look.

"It's called Punches. It's an underground fight club. You'll have to say you're my younger brother for me to get you in."

Adan's eyes widened.

"You're taking me to a fight club? For real?"

"Tell you mom we took in a movie or something."

"I've always wanted to go to a fight club. If there's lots of blood, I'll be fucking ecstatic, man."

"Don't tell anyone."

"Boy, oh boy, oh boy!"

This time, the event was in someone's cramped basement. Uri pushed to the front so Adan could see. He wasn't in any of the matches himself. It turned out to be a brutal night, even though they didn't use bats. The injuries mounted. Heads and noses bled hard to the cheers of the crowd. They passed Jim Beam around. Adan took a swig before Uri could stop him.

Afterwards, on the walk home, the boy was excited. He imitated the fighters, throwing punches into the air as they walked.

"*Pow! Pow.* That was rad, man."

Uri told him about being a fighter. Adan looked at him with something like admiration.

"You? I've got to see you fight. Take me when you do, please, man."

"Not 'til you're older. I can't watch you and fight at the same time."

"Aw."

After that, Adan arranged hang outs with Uri with enthusiasm. Flora was very pleased. Uri found that the little brat wasn't as bad as he seemed. Maybe he didn't kill Simon. It was impossible to know for sure.

Wacko placed him in more matches. Demon Jake won them all. Spectators had increasing respect for him. Some offered him security jobs. His promoter advised caution.

"Fight clubs are entertainment, Demon. Don't accept jobs. They'll turn you into a mobster, and you'll wind up in prison. I've seen it happen."

"I haven't accepted any. But the money would sure be helpful. I have a wedding and a baby to pay for. If I just took one job, it might solve my financial issues."

Many jobs paid thousands of dollars.

"Do *not* buy a gun. You'll wind up killing someone."

"It's holding me back. What if I have a job, and the person pulls a gun on me?"

"It's a slippery slope, you're on."

Uri tried to take Wacko's advice. He wished he could consult the Professor or talk to Lois, but that would mean revealing the secret of the fight club. The Professor appreciated the security work Uri did for The Struggle. He never asked questions. Lois enjoyed having more money. If she noticed bruises, Uri told her he got them sparring at the gym.

His life became a beehive of activity. He attended three or more seminars and frequent executive meetings, cleaned the leased space, worked out at the gym, hung out with Adan, did security work, spent time with Lois, and fought at Punches several evenings a week. His calendar was filled. There were also Flora's *Shabbat* dinners and Friday night services at the synagogue.

Flora invited him to a *Seder* at her house on the first night of Passover. There would be a communal one at The Struggle on the second night. Wacko, whose actual name was Mel Levy, also invited him, but Uri had to turn him down. His first commitment remained with the Professor.

As everyone expected, the Professor presided over the *Seder*, interpreting passages in the *Haggadah* to emphasize the fight between two gods. Adan, the youngest present, had the role of asking the four questions, which he did without sarcasm.

"*Why is this night different from all other nights?*"

An unspoken difference from all previous years was the many women the Professor had impregnated. Jenny had the biggest bulge, followed by Lois, who was at the end of her fourth month. Rachel was in the first trimester. Sylvia was still trying. Even Flora, who was in her late thirties, mentioned in vitro fertilization. Did she hope to get pregnant?

The babies of the younger women would all be firstborns for the mothers. This led to jokes about using the blood of a lamb on doorposts so that death would pass over, as it had in *Exodus*, and the babies would survive. Unless the jokes were serious. Only the Professor was above all doubts about the wisdom of fathering so many with responsibility for none. The women depended on their own resources and the willing participation of their men for things to work out. Uri wondered how many of the guys worked to suppress uneasiness while revering the Professor at the same time.

Since his talk with Ernie, there were fewer reasons for security work in The Struggle. Everyone behaved. Uri needed ways to relieve tension. Fights at Punches weren't enough. It was too easy for him to win matches. Only a job would give him the outlet he craved.

CHAPTER 26

Uri accepted a job in a nearby town. Because of his glass eye, he didn't have a license and made the illegal drive in a borrowed car. He didn't buy a gun. The target owed money. Uri had to persuade him to settle up, being sure not to kill the target so that there could be payment after the beating.

He discovered the pleasure of doing the job with the thoroughness of a professional. He didn't know the target and felt no need to hold back, as he did with Vel and Ernie. There was no emotional involvement. He concentrated on the task, ignoring the target's pleas and cries. It satisfied him to bring someone to the point of passing out, then find the restraint not to go overboard.

Now that he had financial security, Uri no longer stole cash from seminar students. That was another positive. But if he wanted something from someone in The Struggle, all he did was use a certain tone of voice. All the students feared him.

Other jobs followed. At first, Wacko wasn't aware of what Uri did outside of Punches. In time, word came to him. He shook his head.

"Demon, this ain't good. What yer doin' ain't right. Remember—*Tikun olam*, repair the world, social justice. That's what Jews are supposed to do."

"If I don't do these jobs, someone else will. It's security, my profession, Wacko."

"You wanna do security? Go back to college, and then get a job with the police or the FBI."

He didn't tell Wacko that he served time for a felony. That would disqualify him for any police work. Besides, he gave up the funds for college in Simon's will, and he needed money now.

Secrets lay within secrets. Few knew about his past as an arsonist. Deep down, fire still fascinated Uri. People at the Struggle never heard of Punches, and people at Punches never heard of The Struggle. Adan belonged to both, but wouldn't reveal anything about the fight club and risk being barred. Wacko found out about Uri's illegal activities, but nothing about The Struggle.

Perhaps his security work in other towns became one secret too many. The violence that kept him from splintering also pulled him apart. Who was he? The burned orphan? The Professor's closest aide? A future husband and father? A security worker-for-hire? Demon Jake?

Throughout his teens, he fantasized about violence, wrestling, bigger guys beating him, punishment for his terrible crimes. At what pointed did he switch from victim to torturer? When did the pleasure of having pain inflicted morph into inflicting it?

Lois noticed a change.

"You seem so far away," she said.

"I'm right here."

"Do you realize you don't look at me anymore?"

"That's not true."

He was looking away from her at that moment.

"Is it because of my body? Is it ugly now that I'm showing?"

"Of course not."

But the growing bulge was ugly. It wasn't his baby in there. He should be glad to raise the Professor's child, but that didn't mean he liked the evidence that his future wife fucked someone else. He tried his best not to care. Jealousy was against The Struggle's unwritten rules. Sometimes, when he fought an opponent at Punches or hit a target, a vision of Lois and the

Professor flashed before him. He wound up doing the job with more vigor than necessary.

He only took a few jobs when he was low on funds. The target had to be a person unlikely to carry a gun. He wouldn't kill anyone. If he did, he would have more guilt than he could bear. He couldn't be such a bad person if he let the target live.

Lois kept pestering him.

"You need to come to childbirth classes with me."

"Why?"

"So you can help me during the delivery."

"You mean, be in the room?"

His stomach twisted at the thought. It was one thing to bloody a target, but to watch a bleeding blob come out of his soon-to-be wife's insides wasn't for him.

"I can't do that," he said. "I'd puke."

First, there was the wedding to get through. He wasn't sure he wanted to be married anymore, or that he loved Lois like a future husband should. The only people he ever loved were his mother, Vel, and the Professor. If he didn't count his mother, those he loved had been male. He might be gay. But he enjoyed fucking women. He didn't enjoy what he had done with Don. Did that mean he wasn't gay? Or that he shouldn't marry Lois?

The dreaded day of the wedding arrived. They limited attendance in the synagogue to Lois' parents, who Uri met one time before, Lois' friends from The Struggle, Flora, Adan, a handful of senior congregants who came to everything, and the Professor. The *huppah* was a sheet thrown over four rods. Sweat beaded on Uri's brow. Lois wore a white maternity dress. Rivulets of mascara ran down her cheeks, spoiling her make-up.

After the reception at Flora's, Uri walked home with his lumbering wife. She refused sex, in case it would bring on a premature delivery.

"We're married. There are years and years of sex ahead of us," she said.

"Do you think we did the right thing?"

"Getting married? Why? Do you have doubts?"

He twisted away from her.

"No, no. It's just that… the baby. I can't get over that it isn't mine."

"It's yours, Uri."

"What do you mean?"

Was she saying she never fucked the Professor?

"You're married to me. The baby is yours."

"Not the Professor's?"

She looked at him with eyes of steel.

"It's yours."

"Wait a minute. I'm confused."

"It's yours."

"But the Professor's name will be on the birth certificate, right?"

"It's a piece of paper."

"The name of the father on that piece of paper is the father."

"It's your baby."

No matter how often Uri brought up the topic, Lois never wavered. It was the one thing that didn't make her cry. She both acknowledged and didn't acknowledge that he wasn't the father. He couldn't tell her real thoughts.

Nothing seemed solid except the punches he threw, the cracking sound of a jaw breaking, the thud of his fist against an eye socket. The rest was fluid, slipping through his fingers, evading his grasp.

The Professor stifled yawns at the wedding and never cast an interested eye on Lois after she became pregnant. He didn't say a word about the pregnant women in the adult seminars. Uri, too, expressed no concern about the baby that was due in less than a month, despite his wife's hounding.

"Don't you want me to tell you if it's a boy or a girl?"

"Surprise me when it is born."

"Let's pick out a name together."

"You pick it out."

When Lois went into labor, he drove her to the hospital. He didn't park and go in. Instead, he drove home to wait. She would call him when they discharged her, after a night in the obstetrics unit. When he returned to the hospital, she was waiting by the curb in a wheelchair, with a wrapped bundle in her arms. He said nothing when she got into the passenger seat.

"It's a boy, Uri. You have a son. I named him Jacob."

He drove without looking at either of them. Lois didn't know that his Punches name was Demon Jake. Everyone there just called him Demon, so it didn't matter. On the way home, Lois said she had done some thinking.

"I've got my degree, and there's an opening for a kindergarten teacher right here in town. If I take the job, you can stay home and mind the baby."

"What? No!"

"You make a good income, but you never tell me how you get it. I'm guessing you are doing something illegal, like dealing. And all those bruises. Whatever you're into, it's got to stop. You're a father now, and you can't let yourself be arrested."

"I know nothing about babies or kids."

"I'll earn enough for both of us until you get a legal job. And you can get practice taking care of Jacob tonight. I'm exhausted from the delivery, and my milk hasn't come in yet. All you have to give him is water from a bottle."

When they arrived home, Lois asked if he wanted to hold the baby.

"I'll wait until you're ready for bed."

He dreaded the moment, longing to call Wacko to arrange a match. His shoulders tightened, with knots spasming his back. If only he had something to punch.

When the time came, Lois handed him the baby and went straight to bed without looking back. It was 9 p.m. She left no instructions. Uri looked at the bundle in his arms for the first time. It had a scrunched-up face and an open, roaming mouth. He had never seen anything so ugly. And the sound it made—a loud, insistent squawking. He scanned its monkey face to see if it resembled the Professor. But the immediate necessity was to stop the thing's ear-splitting shrieks.

Bouncing it on his lap did nothing. He tried the rocking chair and pushed it back and forth in its stroller. Water helped for a few seconds before it figured out it wasn't what it wanted and started screaming again. The only thing that quieted it was walking with it in his arms or against his shoulder. It would fall asleep, but when he put it in the bassinet, it would awaken right away and wail again. For hours, Uri walked round and round the apartment he had rented with the money from his jobs, until he was familiar with every corner. He dragged his aching hip from the kitchen to the living room to the closed bedroom door and back again, in a circuit. When he looked at his phone, only an hour had gone by. It was 10 p.m. He was desperate for rest, but the baby wouldn't give in. Perhaps it was in pain from being born and having to breathe.

When its diaper needed changing, Uri faced another hurdle—Pampers. He unwrapped the baby, and during Uri's anger and confusion about what to do, the baby's helpless fingers and toes seemed to reach out for him, asking to be put in a hold, or to be held. But holding Jacob put Uri in a hold, since he didn't dare put the infant down except for diapering. He was never so tired. Why didn't Lois wake up and take over? At that moment, he hated his wife.

Again, he walked the circuit with the infant in his arms. The hours passed. Midnight, 2 a.m. 3. By the first light of dawn, the baby settled into a proper sleep. Uri thought he better keep him in his arms, so he could sit at least. Now that Jacob's face relaxed, he looked better and still not a bit like the Professor. That was a relief. He lay nestled against Uri's chest. If he had named him, it wouldn't be Jacob. Perhaps something else from the Bible, like Isaiah. He would call him Izzy.

When Lois awoke, she found Uri asleep on the couch with Izzy cradled in his arms. She took a photo with her phone. Her giant of a husband cuddling a seven pound newborn. Later, when they discussed the night, she had difficulty accepting the name Izzy.

"It's too Yiddish."

But Uri kept right on calling him Izzy, and the name stuck. Meanwhile, for the first month, they alternated between waking and sleeping, each one taking care of Izzy. By the *bris*, on the boy's eighth day, Uri was an expert in newborn care. Lois nursed and pumped, and Izzy slept a couple of hours at a time once they appeased his hunger.

It wasn't long before Uri felt the full weight of fatherhood. Lois was right. He had to give up Punches and his illegal activities. His only security work would be for the Professor, and that was light security work. He never had to do more than he did with Ernie. There was no payment, so Lois accepted the kindergarten job. She would miss being home with Izzy, although she loved teaching.

Uri had sex with Lois again after she healed from the delivery. She was thirty pounds heavier, with a rounder face and the hint of a double chin. He didn't find her as attractive as before, but he enjoyed having sex with her. Would he enjoy it as much with any woman?

But Izzy wasn't any baby. He was Izzy, unique, special, the only baby Uri could care for and, he had to admit, love. Lois said he had Uri's eyes. The baby still didn't look like the Professor.

CHAPTER 27

Uri taught the teen seminar that met on Sunday evenings. It was early September. *Rosh Hashanah*, the Jewish New Year, was around the corner. Following the Professor's instructions, Uri focused on the fates of individuals for the next year, sealed on *Yom Kippur* the next week. There were a few days left to atone in order to avoid an unhappy destiny.

"What are examples of behaviors in your age group that need *Teshuva*, atonement?" Uri asked.

The boys answered. Lying. Drugs. Shoplifting. Back talk to parents.

One of the girls, Megan, burst into tears, running from the room. Another girl, Sheila, ran after her. When class finished, Uri asked Adan what was up with the girls.

"Abortions," he said.

"Abortions, plural?"

"Yeah. Both of them. Don't say I told you."

When he arrived home, he asked Lois if she heard. The girls were only fourteen. Tears dropped when she answered.

"Yes. They grow up fast in The Struggle."

"How so?"

"It's not rocket science, Uri. Figure it out."

"They're fucking the boys."

Izzy was nursing. Uri needed to clean up his language before the baby was old enough to understand.

"That's one possibility."

Meanwhile, now that he was a father, Uri decided to repent for what he did to Ernie and Vel by apologizing to them. He couldn't do the same with the out-of-town targets without being arrested. If that happened, he couldn't take care of Izzy. Then he had an idea. He'd apologize to Wacko, who told him not to take jobs. The next day, he went to the gym.

"Hey, man. I need to tell you something."

"Yeah?" Wacko wiped down a treadmill.

"You were right. I shouldn't have taken those jobs. I didn't listen to you, and I'm sorry."

"I'm not the one you put in the emergency room. Tell the police you're sorry. The judge might go easy on you."

"I can't. Lois and Izzy need me. I can't go to prison. I just can't."

"Then I can't help you, Demon."

He hoped for a better outcome with Ernie. Don wasn't there when he showed up. Ernie backed up when he saw him.

"Chill, man. Are you here to slug me again?"

"I'm here to apologize. I'm sorry."

"You're a motherfucker. I'm not your friend anymore."

"I said I'm sorry, didn't I?"

"My grandmother used to slap me like that and whip me, too. It hurt like hell. But you hurt me ten times worse. You don't know your own strength."

"I guess not. Dude, I'm sorry."

"I could understand if you were mad at me. But the Professor was mad at me, not you. What you did made no sense."

"I'm the Professor's security. I protect him."

"From me? A student? Like I'm such a big fucking danger?"

Vel, when he found him, was no better.

"Just stay the fuck away from me. I've nothing to say to you."

Uri realized he didn't have a single friend left, except Adan, who was just a kid. And the boy didn't ask to hang out with him that often now that Uri dropped out of Punches. He suspected

Adan of hooking up with other spectators, who didn't mind taking him along.

The day came when the Professor called him for another security assignment. It was a shock to hear it was a woman who needed persuading—Jenny, the mother of a baby two months older than Izzy. He wouldn't tell Uri the specific nature of Jenny's offense. Just that she should think twice before speaking. Uri didn't recall her contradicting the Professor in a seminar. Maybe he hadn't been paying enough attention.

He visited her and conveyed the message in a dark tone. He wouldn't slug a mother or any woman. She didn't seem fazed.

"You worship the Professor. I used to, too. Look, I even had one of his babies. That's how much I adored him."

"You're using the past tense."

"Because I've realized that although he has a brilliant mind, the Professor is a flawed human like the rest of us."

"You're wrong, Jenny. He's special. He lives on a higher plane."

"Grow up. A higher plane? That's science fiction, Uri. We're parents now. It's time to act like adults."

After that, he had a strained conversation with Lois.

"I'm thinking of leaving The Struggle," she said.

Tears splashed onto her shirt. There was loud agitation from the washing machine on its spin cycle.

"What! You can't. It's a commitment."

"A one-sided one. Who is the Professor committed to?"

"All of us."

Uri stared at her as if she was an alien being.

"Let me rephrase. How does he show his commitment? By asking for more money from us for every ten-week seminar? Money we can't afford?"

"It's not so much if we recruit others."

"I've asked everyone I know, and you haven't had friends since you took on security for the Professor."

"That's not true," he said, even though it was true.

The washing machine rattled to a stop and signaled its completion with a chime.

"I'll get it."

Loading the clothes in the dryer would give him a chance to collect his thoughts.

Did Lois have postpartum depression or something? Leaving The Struggle, if she was serious, was crazy talk. He considered phoning her doctor to ask for Lexapro for her. Or an antipsychotic. The reason she gave him was so flimsy that Jenny or some other complainer must have influenced her. A few hours later, she brought the subject up again.

"I've given my relationship with the Professor a lot of thought, Uri. My brain is scrambled. I still love him. Don't worry. We haven't had sex in almost a year. But I'm also disappointed in him."

"Why?"

"He has no boundaries with sex, money, or what to ask of students."

She irritated him with her usual vague way of speaking.

"I don't have the foggiest idea of what you're getting at."

"I know you don't." She was in full crying mode now. "I'm skipping the seminar Wednesday to see what it's like not to go."

"The Professor won't approve."

"You can say I'm sick."

She was sobbing.

"Everyone shows up, healthy or sick."

"Don't you see? That's part of the problem. They're afraid not to show up."

The Professor expected full attendance in his classes at State. He passed a sign-in sheet around and docked truant students a grade. Absences were noted in the seminars, too. What would happen if he asked Uri about Lois? The only solution was to lie, saying Izzy was also sick. It annoyed the Professor when babies fussed during his lectures.

But lying to the Professor would be so upsetting, it might cause Uri to vomit. He would become the sick one. If the

Professor caught him in a lie, if he no longer trusted him, it would break Uri. He remembered the time in high school when he felt so low that he walked into traffic. Now that he had a family, he no longer had that option. Lois might be crazy, and Izzy was a helpless infant. Uri had to take care of both of them and protect the Professor. His wife wasn't the only one with a scrambling brain.

Unless he could talk her out of skipping.

"If you don't go on Wednesday, it'll be hard on me."

"It's a test to see if I can stay away from the Professor. He has some sort of hold on me—and you. I'll never be free if I can't walk away for a single evening."

"What about me?"

"It's not about you. It's about whether the Professor is running a cult. Because if no one can leave, that's what it is."

"Don't say the word 'cult' to me. I won't listen."

He held his hands over his ears.

Not long after that, he had a surprise visit from Zhong. They had little to do with each other in the past two years, since Uri dropped out of State. Zhong was busy with advanced classes. He was planning to do graduate work in one of the top out-of-state universities. The only thing they had in common was the seminars.

"Sylvia's been talking to me about leaving The Struggle. I don't know what to think." He sat with slouched shoulders, his hands clasped between his legs.

"You, too? Lois said the same to me. The girls must influence each other."

"She says he's done bad things. She doesn't say what."

"Oh, C'mon, man. He's the Professor, a brilliant man. What bad things?"

"His way of interpreting *Torah* doesn't inspire moral behavior, Sylvia says. It justifies the opposite."

"That's bullshit, Zhong."

Zhong looked straight at Uri.

"I know what you did to Vel and Ernie. You broke three of Vel's ribs. He's still in pain."

"Are you hanging out with that loser again?"

"He's no loser. He got into Harvard for graduate work."

"Big fucking deal."

"If you believe you're created in the image of a cruel God, as the Professor teaches, you will be cruel, Uri. You are cruel. If I decide to leave The Struggle, it will be in part because of what you've become."

"Is that what you've come here to tell me? It'll be my fault?"

"Yes. That is why."

After Zhong left, Uri was in a state of fury. *I should've crippled the little gook.* Instead, he took out his anger on a punching bag at the gym. His control pleased him. He hadn't hurt Zhong. If he had done some cruel things in the past, he was proving he had moved on from that now, hadn't he?

On *Yom Kippur*, the Day of Atonement, everyone in The Struggle went to the synagogue. It was a full house. Rabbi Shapiro led in his usual dull way, except for the sermon he gave on *Kol Nidre* on the first night. He looked at the Professor as he spoke, without using notes.

"The *Torah* is a gift to the Jews from God. It has given us the prayers we chant that replaced the animal sacrifices Israelites practiced at the time before invaders in Jerusalem destroyed the temple. Even then, animal sacrifice was a substitute for the human sacrifice practiced by pagan religions. That was an early example of our religion's moral compass. True Judaism is ethical, obedient to the principle *Do not unto others that which you hate done unto yourself.* That sums up all you have to observe to be a good Jew. Treat others like you want to be treated. Judaism is the opposite of a cult because Jews have the free will to decide for themselves how they wish to be treated. Who would take that from them?"

Zhong was the first person in a long time who Uri treated as he wished to be treated by someone mad at him. Neither was violent nor even yelled. But Uri did not feel respected, either. He had been defensive instead of admitting the truth, that he had acted with cruelty, beating Vel beyond necessity, slapping Ernie hard more than once.

How would he have wanted to be treated if he had disrespected the Professor? Would a word of warning be enough, or was a single slap in order? What would be too much— a savage beating—and what wouldn't be enough? In his own case, one sharp look from the Professor would make him wretched. He'd rather someone slug him.

Lois, Jenny, Zhong, Ernie, Vel all hinted that the Professor had some sort of unethical streak. Uri needed perspective. He would talk to Flora.

When he called, she invited him over that evening. Adan would be at a friend's house studying, unless he was sneaking to Punches behind his mother's back. They sat in the kitchen. Flora poured them both a whiskey.

"Now that you are no longer a minor, this is legal. I'm so glad you're coming to me with a problem. Is it about Lois?"

She sounded even more like his mother than usual. She pulled her hair into a ponytail, just as his mother did when she lounged at home.

"In part. She and several others are doubting The Struggle, even thinking about leaving it. They say the Professor lacks boundaries and justifies his behavior with his interpretations of *Torah*. And on *Kol Nidre*, Rabbi Shapiro seemed to say the same thing without naming the Professor or The Struggle."

Flora took a long swallow of her drink, taking her time to respond.

CHAPTER 28

Right after leaving Flora, Uri called Wacko.

"I need you to arrange a match tonight."

There was a pause.

"Tonight? That's difficult, Demon. They've already booked the matches."

Uri paced outside of his car. He kept running his hand across his shaved head.

"It's urgent, Wacko. I'm so antsy, I don't know what to do with myself."

A second pause followed.

"The only way is if you take on two of the opponents. They'd both fight you instead of each other. And without the mechanical hand. You ready for that?"

"Sounds perfect. Set it up."

There was great interest at Punches as word spread about the match—one-handed Demon Jake against two. The location moved to a larger arena, in a private back room of a gym. It had enough space for almost two hundred spectators to jam in. Excitement ran high, aided by alcohol and drugs. Large bets were being made. No one had beaten Demon Jake in one-to-one combat.

As soon as the capacity crowd assembled, Demon and the other two walked into the open space in the middle of the room, and the fight began. Wacko stood up front, yelling instructions and encouragement to Demon. The two other promoters did the same.

"Watch out! Behind you."

"Close in. Close in. That's right."

"To your left."

The crowd chanted.

"Fuck him up! Fuck him up!"

The energy zapping Uri's arms and legs landed powerful kicks and punches on his opponents. In a blind rage, he struck out, egged on by the crowd and the robust feel of his one hard fist connecting with soft muscle. At the first sight of blood splattering, the exhilaration of the crowd grew. When one of his opponents circled Uri, a spectator jumped on his back.

"Rumble," someone yelled.

At that signal, everyone rushed to the center. The spectators joined the fight, pummeling the three opponents and each other. Wacko and the promoters tried to gain control.

"Stop," they screamed. "Everyone get back."

No one listened. A whirlwind of zeal kept the melee going. Those still standing stepped on and stomped the crumpled bodies lying on the floor. Groans, grunts, screams and loud thwacks of bats that some used added to the din. A slippery rink of pooling blood lay underfoot.

A whistle pierced the air.

"Raid!"

A voice sounded through a megaphone.

"Police. Put your hands up and stand back. Everyone line up facing the walls."

The sirens of ambulances and back-up police vans approached from a distance.

Wacko had called 911.

After Lois bailed him out, Uri realized it was time to stop hiding the now obvious truth.

"I've been a member of a secret fight club. Punches. It's how I've been controlling my aggression. When I told you my injuries came from the gym, I lied."

"You're a mess. Let's get you home and patch you up, then we'll talk about it."

At home, he told her how Flora had stoked his anger with her shocking revelation. He didn't know what to think.

"As much as you revere the Professor, I understood you needed to figure it out yourself," she said.

"It would've been better if you had told me."

"You wouldn't have believed me."

"Tomorrow, I'll talk to the Professor before I believe anything."

Despite the purple bruises covering his face, Uri met with the Professor the next morning in his office in the leased space.

"I need you to tell me—did you have sex with underage girls in the teen class? Did two of them get pregnant by you so they had to get abortions?"

The Professor had been typing on a laptop. He looked up at Uri.

"What happened to you? You look terrible."

"Never mind that. Just answer my questions."

"There are nasty rumors being spread about me. My enemies want to destroy The Struggle and everything I've worked so hard to build."

"But are the rumors true?"

The Professor began typing again.

"I've never had sex that wasn't consensual."

"What about with underage girls?"

With his fingers still on the keyboard, the Professor snapped his eyes upward to meet Uri's.

"Who would say that about me? Who is the one most likely to want to get me in trouble? That's the security matter I need you to handle."

"There's several people saying that about you. There's even talk of leaving The Struggle."

He wouldn't say that Lois was one of them.

"Yes, but there's someone who started the rumors."

"That doesn't make the rumors false. Just tell me the truth."

The Professor closed his laptop and clasped his hands on top of it.

"Now is the time for you to decide for yourself whether you believe in me. It's not about my answer to your questions. It's about what's inside you, whether you are committed enough to me and The Struggle to accept what you see with your own eyes, not what others tell you."

Uri stared at the Professor, trying to make sense of his words.

"Remember Jacob's struggle with the man. When Jacob asked the man his name, the man wouldn't answer. Jacob had to decide for himself who his opponent was—an angel, a devil, or a part of himself. Your doubts are part of yourself, Uri, not a part of me."

"But there's such a thing as objective facts. You either fucked the girls or you didn't."

"I'm giving you two jobs. Handle the rumor mongers and figure out where you stand—with me or against me. That's all I have to say."

He opened his laptop and typed without looking up again.

In-between taking care of Izzy, he had a conversation with Lois that lasted for days. She remained calm, having processed the rumors weeks earlier. Uri swirled in a vortex of emotion, weeping, yelling, sometimes leaving the house to walk the streets for hours. Each stuck to their position. Lois accepted the rumors; Uri didn't without proof.

"Why don't you just talk to the girls in the Teen Seminar," Lois said after they had exhausted the topic.

"I can't do that. I don't see how."

Lois threw up her hands.

"Then I can't tell you what to do."

On another of his long walks, Uri went back-and-forth in a two-sided conversation in his mind.

If the Professor fucked fourteen-year-old girls, he's a criminal. If he didn't, someone is slandering him, and he's a victim.

He fucked college girls thirty years younger than him. It's plausible he could as easily fuck girls thirty-five years younger.

Why would he fuck teens when he might get caught, and when college freshmen, a couple of years older, are available to him?

While the purple bruises yellowed, then faded to pink, he obsessed, not sleeping, not able to eat, his body wracked with bouts of diarrhea and vomiting. He had a low-grade fever and muscle aches. Lois stayed home from work, caring for Izzy and making Uri drink Gatorade. For several days, he lay in bed, throwing off the blankets, then chilling and pulling them back on.

He had another courtroom daydream that might have been an actual dream. This time, he was the judge, and the Professor was the accused.

"How do you plead?" He asked.

"Neither innocent nor guilty."

"You must choose one."

"Then you figure it out."

"That's not possible."

"Sometimes the judge is the guilty one."

When he was well enough to get out of bed, it was the day of the teen seminar. He stumbled into the shower. When he was dry, he shaved and put on fresh clothing. Lois would drive him to the leased space while he was still recovering. He would talk to the girls after class, although the prospect threatened to revive his nausea.

The verses for that day came from the Garden of Eden story. Uri repeated the question asked in the adult seminars with none of the Professor's charismatic spark.

"Eve gives Adam the apple before either of them knows right from wrong. They only understood morality after eating the apple. Does God blame them for disobedience when they are still innocent, before they swallow the apple?"

He gave the class time to answer, without prompting, just as the Professor did.

"Maybe Adam understood after one bite, yet went ahead and, like, ate the whole apple anyway."

"You don't have to know what's right and what's wrong to understand you should obey."

"They could have thought that God would be mad, but not kick them out of their home."

"Or that they wouldn't be caught."

When the time was up, Uri asked Megan and Sheila to stay behind. The girls looked at each other, then stared down at the floor. Uri had rehearsed his question.

"Someone told me something disturbing about you two. That you had sex with the Professor and had to have abortions."

In the silence that followed, they heard the printer pounding in another room. Someone was making a lot of copies.

Megan whispered something.

"I couldn't hear you. Say it louder," Uri said.

"Not the Professor."

"Not the Professor?"

"No."

Uri smiled. Not the Professor. He inhaled deeply for the first time in days.

"The Professor didn't make either of you pregnant?"

Both girls shook their heads.

"Who did?"

There was more silence.

"C'mon, girls."

"Dunno."

"Of course you do. You must. Tell me, or I'll talk to your parents."

The girls glanced at each other again, communicating in silence.

"They know we were, like, pregnant. They had to sign for us to get abortions."

He was aware of how young they were. Still children. A little more than a decade older than Izzy. They were both small, not yet grown into womanly bodies, quiet girls, shy girls, not like the types who would consent to sex with the Professor or any older man.

"Did you want to have sex with whoever did this to you?"

After another silent stare, they both nodded yes.

"You did? Why?"

"Love."

"What?"

They looked up into Uri's eyes.

"We were in love."

"With who?"

"Don't tell our parents."

"That depends."

They were frustrating him by now.

"We'll sit here all night if we must until you tell me."

They both sighed before answering.

"Adan."

CHAPTER 29

While Lois drove him home, Uri was ecstatic. He kept turning to smile at Izzy in his car seat in the back, while saying nothing to Lois about the source of his glee. The baby, now five months old, gave him wide smiles and coos in return. His chubby arms waved and his legs kicked in his puffer snowsuit.

"Are you my boy? Are you my baby boy?"

"You're in a good mood," Lois said.

After they put Izzy to sleep, he told Lois about his evening.

"I took your suggestion and talked to the two girls, Megan and Sheila. Guess what? It wasn't the Professor who fucked them. He's in the clear. That little shit Adan did it."

Lois pinched her lips.

"That's what they told you? Adan had sex with them?"

"Yes. Adan."

"They're covering up."

"No way. I had to drag it out of them."

"The Professor is very skilled at seducing young women and girls, making them think it's what they want. Then swearing them to secrecy."

"Bullshit. It's no secret that he's the father of a half dozen babies in The Struggle."

Without planning it, Uri violated the unwritten rule in their marriage—never naming the biological father of Izzy. When Uri brought it up during Lois's pregnancy, her response was always the same.

"You're the father, Uri."

Was that what the other mothers told their boyfriends or husbands?

"The only reason some of us revealed the Professor made us pregnant was to tell the world we were spreading his seed. His descendants would advance the Jewish people. Anyway, that's the theory."

It was the only time since their original discussion before their wedding Lois acknowledged that the Professor fathered Izzy.

"Now I realize we were practicing eugenics, an immoral science. The Professor had clever ways of putting ideas in our minds, saying no words that might implicate him."

This was true. The Professor asked him to "handle matters." He left how this could be done to Uri's imagination, never telling him to use violence. No one would blame the scholar for what his assistant did. The same thing happened when Uri asked him if he fucked Megan and Sheila. Somehow, the Professor turned the question back on Uri. It was up to Uri to figure out where he stood.

Adan, a junior in high school by now, was another Vel. The girls in his class might fall in love with him and compete to have sex with him. It was very possible, more possible than the Professor molesting them. The Professor didn't even teach the teen seminar, although he put in an appearance from time to time so parents would think they were getting their money's worth.

While Uri remained unconvinced that the girls had covered up for the Professor by blaming Adan, his buried feelings about Izzy's paternity surfaced again. He scrutinized the baby's face for signs of resemblance to the Professor. But he looked just like Lois, with red fuzz growing on the top of his head and tearful eyes, even when smiling. Uri would distance himself if he hadn't already opened his heart to Izzy, loving him more than he had ever loved anyone. If he had any joy in his life, it was because of Izzy.

He became haunted by new ideas—that Izzy would want to connect with his actual father, the Professor, at some point and that he would love his father more than the man who raised him. Or that the Professor might take an interest in his son, taking him away from Uri to be raised "the right way." Or that the Professor might become attracted to Lois again, even though she hadn't lost the thirty pounds, and convince her to divorce Uri, taking her and Izzy to live with him.

Uri spun in two directions at once—toward the Professor, unable to believe he molested the girls, and away from the Professor for fear he would steal Izzy. He fell into jagged pieces. Without Punches, which had disbanded since the raid, he didn't have an outlet for his feelings. They festered and smoldered inside him as the days wore on.

That's when Izzy spoke to him like an adult would, in complete sentences, when they were alone. Uri thrilled at the boy's precociousness.

At first, the baby was pleasant.

"You take good care of me, Uri."

Why did he call him by his first name?

"I'm your dad. Call me Daddy."

After a few rounds of this, the pleasantness disappeared.

"You aren't my true father. You're nothing to me."

"I'm raising you as my own, Izzy."

Tears welled in Uri's eyes. Izzy's nose flared. The sharp tone of his baby voice was cutting.

"You are just some felon my mother married. Go burn yourself like the piece of dead meat you are."

This made Uri weep.

"I love you, Izzy."

"I love my true father, the Professor."

At other times, in Lois's presence, Izzy's sweetness returned. He reached out for Uri, babbling in baby language. Uri tried to tell Lois.

"Izzy doesn't love me anymore. He loves the Professor."

"Nonsense. He doesn't know the Professor."

Despite his wife's reassurances, Uri couldn't be certain. Izzy repeated his insults more often, even when he slept, in the middle of the night while Uri lay awake trying to make sense of all that had happened—the melee at Punches, the seduction of the teen girls, the Professor's apparent denial, the girls' blaming Adan, and the awful things Izzy said to him.

After a few nights, Izzy shortened his comments to three words, which he repeated during the day and at night.

"Go burn yourself."

When Uri looked in the mirror, he saw the scar on his face glow. Smoke arose from it, curling toward the ceiling. Was he on fire? He slapped cold water on his cheek to reduce the burning sensation. The pain, which he hadn't felt in years, returned. He visualized fire again with fascination. Images barged into his mind from the distant past. The small blazes in the dry grass in his backyard. The match game with Adam. The dance of the curtains when they caught. The race of flames across his bedroom ceiling. Cigarette burns on his arms.

"Go burn yourself."

Before his *bar mitzvah*, he shoved the lit end of cigarettes into himself to prove his toughness. Now, the same act drew him for a different reason. His son, who was not his son, wanted him to hurt himself. He wanted to prove his love to Izzy. He would do what the Professor hadn't done.

There were no cigarettes in the house. Second hand smoke harmed children, and Lois wouldn't permit it. Uri bought a pack on the sly. He waited until Lois left for work, and Izzy napped. In the back garden, he lit one, took a couple of drags, then rammed the burning end into his upper arm. The pain was excruciating. He suppressed a scream. A few seconds later, he was as calm as he had been after a fight at Punches. He lay down on the grass and stared at the clouds. They formed what looked like a benevolent face, perhaps Simon's, smiling down at him.

The good feeling and happy cloud face lasted a few minutes. Uri took a deep breath, contented, enjoying the soft nest of grass, the fresh air, the sunshine, until a sudden breeze changed the cloud shape. Simon's face transformed into the Professor's. Instead of a smile, he bared his teeth. Words hurtled down.

"Are you with me or against me?"

Uri yelled back up.

"Don't steal Izzy. Promise me that."

"What would Jacob do?"

Uri answered without thinking.

"Steal a birthright."

"It's you who stole from me. You took what is mine. Give me your wife and my son."

"No, no, no, no."

Uri cried hard with loud hiccups. The agony of losing his family would be worse than the burn. He wouldn't survive without Lois and Izzy.

He must've fallen asleep. The next thing he knew, Lois stood over him.

"What's the matter? Why are you lying on the ground? Are you ill? Where's Izzy?"

He tried to think.

"The Professor took him."

"What?"

She ran into the house and emerged minutes later with the baby wrapped in a blanket.

"He's fine. It's freezing out here. Get up and come into the house. I'll make you soup to warm you up."

Back in the house, Lois instructed him to take a hot shower. In a daze, he let the water run over him until it was no longer warm. Once dry, he crawled into bed under the quilts. In another part of the house, Izzy fussed. When he quieted, Lois came into the bedroom with a thermos of soup. She wasn't friendly.

"What got into you? You went to the backyard and left Izzy on his own in his crib in a wet diaper. If he gets a rash, it'll be your fault."

"He told me to burn myself."

She took a step back.

"That's ridiculous. You blame anyone except the people who are at fault. Adan, who's a boy and now a five-month-old baby. You're being a jerk, Uri."

She stormed out.

He hated it when his wife was mad at him. It scared him to think she might leave him. The Professor would be there for her. They could have planned to wait until Uri made a mistake, like he did that day, not staying in the house with Izzy. He was an unfit father. If Lois divorced him, she would get custody. A judge could deny Uri visitation. He might never see Izzy again.

With these thoughts cycling in his brain, he dozed off. When he awoke, he heard the voices of Izzy and Lois co-mingling.

"You're ridiculous."

"Go burn yourself."

The most urgent thing was to apologize to Lois. He struggled out of bed, dragging the quilt with him, and stumbled into the kitchen where she was feeding pureed green food to Izzy. He opened his mouth like a young bird as the spoon came toward him. With Lois, he acted just like a baby.

Uri sank to his knees. Because of his height, he was level with Lois's face.

"I'm so sorry. I don't understand what happened. Please don't leave me. Please," he burbled.

"Leave you? The only thing I'm leaving is The Struggle."

Izzy grunted when the spoon didn't come fast enough. Uri paused, digesting her words.

"You've decided?"

"Yes. The Struggle is a cult, and the Professor is a sexual molester, a rapist. Did you know that everyone in the teen seminar has the tattoo? They somehow got it without their parents' permission. What does that tell you?"

"How could it be a cult if we joined voluntarily?"

Lois stopped feeding Izzy to stare at her husband. Izzy squawked.

"It's not voluntary if he's brainwashed you."

He didn't know what to say. Serious charges were being made against the Professor—rape and brainwashing. Even if rape was a slander and untrue, brainwashing had to be considered. It was possible that Lois had been the one brainwashed by whoever spread nasty rumors about The Struggle. If she could leave, didn't that prove it wasn't a cult?

But he couldn't bear it if she left without him. He was sure that would lead to divorce. Either way, his marriage was in trouble. If she stayed in The Struggle, she might wind up leaving him for the Professor. If she left without him, she might not want to stay with a man connected with what she considered a corrupt and criminal organization.

Uri's phone vibrated. It was a text from the Professor.

I need you for security work. The Struggle is under siege. I'm under siege. Don't let me down. Come to an executive meeting at the leased space right after tonight's seminar.

Without replying, Uri went back to bed, pulling the quilt with him. This time, he fell into a sound sleep, missing the Wednesday night seminar. Lois stayed home, too. He awakened early enough to get to the executive meeting. The Professor would be angry at him for his absence. Lois might be angry that he was going to the meeting. That was a risk he would have to take. She knew he was on the fence.

CHAPTER 30

Rachel came to the meeting with her newborn son. They were the only ones attending besides the Professor and Uri.

"His name is Jesse, after the father of King David," she said.

"You have a special interest in Jacob," the Professor said to Uri. "David was descended from Judah, one of the twelve sons of Jacob. He was only ten generations removed from Jacob."

With that, the Professor closed his eyes, leaving the rest of the meeting in the hands of Rachel.

Did he mean that Izzy, whose actual name was Jacob, was his favorite, and he had nine other children in descending order of preference before Jesse? Or was Jesse his favorite because he was only one generation away from David, the Professor's namesake? If Jesse was the Professor's favorite, Uri had less cause to worry about losing Izzy. Yet, the Professor paid no attention to the infant and didn't ask about Uri's wife or son.

Rachel put the baby down and embraced Uri. She never hugged him before. He wasn't sure what was happening.

"We love you, Uri. You're important to us, more important than anyone else in The Struggle."

"You do? I am?"

"Never doubt it."

How he had longed to hear such words. It would have been a dream come true if the Professor said them. But Rachel said, "*we* love you." We. That included the Professor, didn't it?

"I'm glad you came tonight to stand with us, when so many haven't. It concerned me when you didn't show up for the seminar. Never mind. You're here now. That's what's important."

"I fell asleep. I'm sorry."

"It happens. Don't worry about it."

"It's the first time I missed."

Uri hoped to be neutral at the meeting, but the embrace, endearments, and lack of criticism for his absence drew him in. He wanted to belong, be accepted despite his scar, and nurtured by the Professor even if it meant being punished and excluded on occasion. He whizzed into his desire never to disappoint the Professor, ignoring his fears about Izzy.

"Dear Uri. We need your help. The fake news from the teen group is a threat to The Struggle and the Professor. Child Protective Services is investigating. The Professor is a 'person of interest.' I am as well."

"You are?"

"Yes. They're trying to say I procured the girls for the Professor. Such crap. Why would I do that?"

A prickle of fear ran through him. This was more serious than losing members or rumors spreading. This was legal trouble. There could be arrests. Even if nothing came of it, the publicity would be ruinous.

"We've had to refund seminar fees. The Struggle is broke. There isn't enough money to pay for next month's leased space. The seminars may have to be cancelled because of drop-outs."

Jesse fussed. Without a trace of modesty, Rachel pulled up her shirt, lingering to give Uri a good look at her engorged breast before picking up the infant and nursing him. She treated Uri like a family member, unless she was being seductive. Uri couldn't tell which. When it was time to put the baby on her shoulder to burp him, she left her breast exposed.

"What can I do?"

He did his best to avert his eyes.

Out the window, traffic slowed and car horns blared. Pedestrians turned their heads toward the window, although it was uncertain they saw more than their reflections.

"Perhaps you could convince the teens to tell the truth."

"How?"

"We rely on you to find a way, dear Uri. You're our only hope."

Uri left the meeting with Rachel's voice added to the chorus he heard every waking minute.

"Our only hope."

"You're ridiculous."

Before going into his house, he stopped in the backyard to give himself his only relief. Cigarette burns and scabs covered his arms and legs. Pain gave him a pause to think without confusion tangling his mind.

When he entered the house, Lois had news.

"Two men knocked on the door when you left. They had FBI badges. They asked to come in and talk to me. So I let them in."

"What did they want?" Uri sat.

He was too light-headed to remain standing.

"They asked me questions about The Struggle and the Professor."

"Such as?"

It had been awhile since Lois cried every time she spoke. Her personality had toughened. Waves of bitterness spewed from her once baleful eyes.

"The payment schedule for the seminars. The babies. What I knew about the Professor and the teen girls."

"What did you tell them?"

"The truth! Why would I cover up for The Professor? I don't love him anymore. I hate him."

This should have given Uri some peace. If Lois hated the Professor, she was unlikely to take Izzy and run off with him.

She sat next to Uri, holding his arm.

"It's time to let go of the Professor. He's no good. Walk away with me. We need to start over. Let's cooperate with the authorities and get this behind us."

"I'm not sure."

"Hurry and make up your mind. I won't wait forever."

She meant she would leave him if he didn't leave the Professor and help with the investigation. It dawned on him that he might be in trouble, too, if they interviewed Ernie or Vel. Wacko, if they questioned him, might reveal information about the jobs Uri did in nearby towns.

But Uri had no personal knowledge of the Professor seducing underage girls. Adan was the one the girls blamed when he asked them. He would lose Flora if he said Adan was the perp. Lois said the girls named Adan to cover-up. The boy might be innocent, unless he was guilty.

He decided to talk to Adan to see if he could wring the truth from him.

It had been several months since he attended one of Flora's *Shabbat* dinners without Lois and Izzy. He asked if he could come alone. Flora hadn't invited the Professor since she broke up with him. Adan was there, with a smug smile not seen since Simon's death. It was just the three of them.

After the candle lighting, Flora said she had something to tell Uri. She already told Adan.

"I'm pregnant. I didn't realize it could happen so easily at my age, thirty-six. The father is David, of course. I'm trying to decide whether to get an abortion, like the Sheila and Megan did. Adan wants me to. He doesn't want a sibling related to a child molester. I haven't decided what to do."

"Is that what you think the Professor is?"

"Yes. Adan convinced me. I didn't want to believe it at first. David explained about Rachel and his other women. That was hard enough. But having sex with young girls crosses a line."

"The FBI questioned Lois."

"They've come to the house and talked to both of us. It was hard for Adan. He was a great admirer of the Professor, even if he never used those exact words."

Flora went to the kitchen to get dinner. She returned with a large pot, setting it on the table. While she ladled the stew into the bowls, she continued.

"I just can't believe I had such faith in a monster like David. I'm crushed." She sobbed. "How does a person overlook so much in someone they love?"

She sat weeping into her palms. Adan reached over and patted her shoulder.

"If I didn't have my son, I don't know what I'd do. He's my rock."

"You're better off without him," Adan said.

Uri had nothing to say. He still had some faith left in the Professor. Adan might have slandered him to persuade Flora to break up with him.

After dinner, he accompanied Flora and Adan to services. He hadn't been to the synagogue for a while. He noticed some former members of The Struggle were there, including the kids in the teen seminar. Their parents must have pulled them out after hearing the rumors. The Youth Group would flourish again.

Rabbi Shapiro's sermon seemed to address the situation as he always had without mentioning the Professor.

"The *V'ahavta*, which is recited at every service, commands us to *love Adonai your God with all your heart, with all your soul, and with all your might*. This is unconditional love, which we are to give to no other authority. To do so would be idol worship, a serious transgression. The *Torah* instructs us to love our neighbors, our families, our children. But the word 'all' in the *V'ahavta*, repeated three times, reserves the kind of love described for God alone."

After services, Uri asked Adan to walk with him instead of riding in the car with Flora. They hadn't hung out much since Punches was raided.

"I want to talk to you about the Professor. Someone has accused him of having sex with the girls in the teen group. I'm guessing that person was you."

"That's for me to know and you to find out," Adan said.

"Okay. I'll straight out ask you. Did you start the rumor about the Professor fucking the girls?"

"What if it isn't a rumor? If it's true, whoever told the truth is a hero."

"And if it isn't true?"

"Then whoever tells is a lying snitch."

This was the old Adan, a little weasel capable of anything.

"You're a lying snitch."

"If I am, I got my mother to break up with that *schmuck*."

Now Uri felt like he was getting somewhere. Adan admitted his motivation.

"You arranged the same thing with Simon. You killed him so your mother wouldn't marry him."

Adan stopped walking. He stared at Uri with raised eyebrows.

"I didn't kill Simon. He had a heart condition. He told my mother he was seeing a heart doctor for chest pains. *Geez*."

"You bought X at the senior party and put it in the juice or coffee at the wedding breakfast. It killed Simon."

"No way. Yeah, I bought drugs. I used most of them myself. The tiny amount I put in the juice wouldn't have killed a frog. Simon only had a couple of sips. I watched. He had a heart attack on his own, that's fucking all."

Uri stepped toward him.

"I don't believe you."

"What are you going to do, hit me?"

He was almost daring him to.

"And you're the one who fucked the girls. They told me."

"Flora knows we're together. If you hit me, she'll know you did it."

He grabbed Adan by the shoulders. The boy remained calm, smirking at Uri.

"Tell me the truth. Did you fuck the girls?"

"You tell the truth about all the people you beat up for money. Everyone at Punches knew about you. You better take your hands off me, or I'll go to the police and tell them everything they said about you."

Uri released him. He walked away, fuming. How he would have enjoyed hurting the kid, not just for avoiding the truth that night, but for all the years of insults, starting the moment they met when Simon was still alive.

But he was done with violence, unless he did it to himself. If he didn't have cigarettes, he cut himself with razor blades he kept on a top shelf in the garden shed. He had to hide his body from Lois, only undressing when the lights were off and not letting her touch him. Their sex life dwindled away. As long as he was loyal to the Professor, she didn't care.

CHAPTER 31

Lois invited Jenny and Sam to the house to talk about leaving The Struggle. It was clear to Uri that she hoped their friends would convince him. Lois was the only one of the four who missed Rabbi Shapiro's sermon.

"When the Rabbi said loving an authority is idol worship, he referred to the way we felt about the Professor," Sam said.

Izzy slept in his crib in his bedroom. Jenny sat in the rocking chair, soothing her baby, Abe, with the gentle motion. Lois, Sam, and Uri sat next to her in the living room, wine glasses in their hands. A bowl of chips and a pacifier lay on the coffee table.

"If I sit here rocking for our entire visit, he'll let me take part," Jenny said.

"Did the Rabbi call our admiration for the Professor 'idol worship?' Like the golden calf in the Bible?" Lois asked.

"He did," Sam said. "I esteemed the man more than anyone. He's brilliant. The thing is—I don't miss the Professor, but I miss the esteeming, being connected to someone stellar, on a higher plane than me."

"Yeah," Jenny said. "I fell so in love with him. I'll never be in love that way again. Oh, I love Sam, and it's a comfortable love. But it's not that head-over-heels, I'll-sacrifice-my-life-for-you thing I had for the Professor. Not that he ever returned even one percent of it.".

"Loving the Professor is a one-way street. He gives nothing back. I've had a wake-up call since he fucked the teen girls, but Uri's still hanging on," Lois said.

"You're worshipping an idol, Uri, an evil one," Sam said.

When he met Sam, he had been ugly, and Sam was an attractive lifeguard. Now Sam had a pale, flabby appearance. But if the others saw Uri's cigarette burns, they would have considered him uglier than ever. The healing wounds itched. Uri listened, scratching absentmindedly.

"What if the Professor is innocent? I believe Adan seduced the girls, then blamed the Professor," he said.

"Are you saying The Struggle is not about idol worship? That our feelings for the Professor were normal?" Jenny asked.

"If Adan is the perp, all the rest is *lashon hara*, gossip. It's a transgression to bear false witness, too. I'm being careful. The Professor is innocent until proven guilty in Jewish law and American law."

Lois spoke up.

"You want proof of a crime. This is about loving the Professor to the point of worshipping him like a god. That's what you've been doing, Uri. Even if the Professor molested no one, he seduces in other ways, gets others to work for him without pay, buy things for him without ever getting repaid, have sex with him, choose who we should marry, have his babies."

The talk continued, interrupted by the needs of Izzy and Abe for feeding, diaper changing, and baby admiring. The uninvited couple, Sylvia and Zhong, were absent because Sylvia's failure to conceive set them apart. In the past, the others pitied them for not having one of the Professor's children. This also had caused jealousy in the complex relationship everyone associated with The Struggle had with their leader.

"I wish Abe didn't have the Professor's genes. But deep down, I'm proud that he does. I want him to be brilliant without being immoral," Jenny said.

"That's how I feel about Izzy," Lois said.

This surprised Uri, who wished Izzy was his biological son. Lois never discussed her mixed feelings with him. Neither knew what to do with their shame for wanting to raise the Professor's child. It kept them from being close. Lois offered a repair if he left the Professor and moved away with her. And the Professor offered the love Uri wanted, if Rachel could be believed, if Uri didn't follow Lois.

The evening ended with Uri still split down the middle, undecided, wanting what he couldn't have, Lois and Izzy and the Professor. Now he knew why the Professor was a problem for Lois, Sam, and Jenny, even if he hadn't molested the teen girls.

The next day, Jenny phoned. She told them to look at the digital edition of the local newspaper.

"Professor of Religious Studies Under Investigation for Tax Fraud," the headline read.

The Struggle had a not-for-profit status with the IRS, even though the Professor charged fees that more than covered expenses. Uri remembered thinking the Professor was too lofty to be concerned about money when he didn't repay Uri. His mind scrambled to find an excuse. The Professor signed IRS tax returns without reading them. Rachel handled tax issues, and she committed the fraud. The profits supported The Struggle, but carelessness with accounting kept that hidden.

Messy business with the IRS didn't seem so bad compared with child sexual abuse. It wouldn't be a good enough reason to abandon the Professor. It occurred to Uri that he wouldn't care if Lois left him, if she would give him custody of Izzy. He wasn't sure he loved her the way a husband should love his wife. Not anymore. But his name was not on Izzy's birth certificate. If he didn't stay with Lois, he would have no legal right to his son.

If he chose Lois, they would have to start their relationship over, find a love that wasn't determined by the Professor's requests. Were they capable of doing that? If not, the only thing binding them together would be Izzy. If they had other children, Uri wondered if they would love them more than Izzy, who would always be tainted by the Professor's genes, although he couldn't imagine loving anyone more than the baby.

But if he chose the Professor, his life would be simpler. There would be only one person to love. There would be nothing for him to decide. He would just continue to do whatever the Professor asked of him.

He went to the baby's bedroom to watch him sleep in his crib. How beautiful he looked. The red fuzz on his head grew into curls. He had his mother's fair complexion, so pale he saw the blue veins under his skin near his temples. His heart-shaped lips, the pink blush of his cheeks, his curlicued ears were precious.

A stuffed bunny lay in the crib's corner, near the baby's head. In another age, this might have been an idol, a household god, placed there to protect Izzy. Uri picked it up, turning it over in his hands. Idol worship was a sin, yet for centuries most of the world engaged in it. It must have been a comfort to parents to believe their children were safe. Uri looked at the top of the dresser. The baby monitor stood there, its little green light blinking. Modern parents used it instead of an idol.

That night, as Uri tried to fall asleep, the story in the *Torah* of Jacob's ladder floated into his mind. Jacob dreams of angels ascending and descending a ladder connecting heaven and earth. He remembered Rabbi Shapiro suggesting an interpretation, which bored him. He and some of the other Youth Group students rolled their eyes, as they did at almost everything the Rabbi said. The ladder represented moral choices, and like the angels, humans climbed up and down over the course of a lifetime. Uri realized he was on the ladder, going downward if he was idol-worshiping the Professor, as his friends from The Struggle said.

Although he was only twenty-three years old, he had been going downward most of his life. The match game that killed Adam and his mother. His lack of gratitude to Simon, who had the generosity to foster him. Almost losing his life when he walked onto the highway on purpose. Meanness to Zhong. Jealousy of Vel's other friendships. Violence toward the

Professor's 'enemies,' at Punches, and while on jobs in other towns.

The only upward movement was his care for his beloved baby boy. He fell asleep with the image of Izzy in his arms.

The next day, he had another conversation with Lois about The Struggle.

"How do you know when your love for another human being crosses over to idol worship?"

Lois didn't answer. She loaded the dishwasher and finished the job first.

"I can only answer for myself. It was when I gave up free will with the Professor. After he invited me to the Tuesday Seminar, I was so flattered I fell in love with him. I craved being near him. Sex was a way of being close and—for a brief time—being his only one."

She added detergent and started the machine. It began the serious business of cleaning dishes.

"I didn't have to think about anything else. Not the times I had been inconsiderate or bitchy. Not my sadness about my grandmother's death or my guilt about not visiting her enough in her nursing home. Not about who I should date after the Professor said we'd be a good match. It solved all my problems except for the biggest one."

"Which was?"

"How to get the Professor to love me and only me."

"I get that one."

"I thought having his baby would make us closer. But the Professor doesn't like pregnant women or babies or children. He ignored me as soon as the doctor confirmed my pregnancy, and he didn't even look at the ultrasound. That was so painful. He couldn't have cared less."

The dishwasher surged.

"That was the turning point. He hurt me and hurt Izzy. I was so mad I hated him. And then I heard he fucked the teen girls. They had to get abortions. I had been in love with a monster. You, too, Uri. Break loose, or you'll be lost."

Uri was being convinced, but didn't know how to detach from someone he adored. He imagined using an ax to break the tie with one swift blow. It would cause intolerable pain. It meant never seeing the Professor again starting that minute. What would he do with the hole in his life if the Professor didn't fill it?

Or he could wean himself from the Professor slowly, like using a razor blade to cut the cord a little each day. The pain wouldn't be any more intolerable than the cigarette burns or the cuts he made on his arms and legs. But it would take forever to cut all the way through, and each cut would heal a bit before the next one happened.

It would be a start. Instead of a daily contact in person or by text, he could reduce his contact with the Professor by one day a week. By the seventh week, the relationship would end. He would make himself accountable to Lois.

"Seven weeks from today, I'll leave with you."

The dishwasher gurgled, sounding like Izzy did when he laughed.

CHAPTER 32

Before he started the weaning process, Uri received a voicemail from the FBI.

Please come to our office for an interview this afternoon at 3 p.m.

This wasn't good. It would have to concern The Struggle. When he told Lois, she agreed.

"Cooperate with them. Promise me you'll do that."

"I can't promise until I find out the details. I guess they want to ask me about the Professor, but who knows? It might be about something different."

"Like what?"

She twisted her skeptical lips.

In his bones, he realized he was about to encounter something unpleasant that would put him between a rock and a hard place. He paced around the apartment, wringing his hands, scratching the burns, running his hands through his hair, sensing his scar blaze.

He showed up for the interview right on time. The office was a small local branch in a strip mall, placed between a furniture store and a dry cleaner. A receptionist asked him to wait on one of three chairs in the small, bare-walled area. Forty-five minutes later, a man came into the room from the interior, looking just like FBI agents in tv shows, tall, lean, in his thirties, with short brown hair, a grey suit, navy blue necktie, and brogues. As he introduced himself, Uri stood.

"I'm Agent Myers."

He didn't extend his hand.

"Follow me, please."

He led Uri to a tiny interview room with a metal table and two chairs. Agent Myers gestured for him to sit.

"Would you like water?"

Uri shook his head.

Agent Myers opened a laptop he carried in with him. He spent several minutes staring at the screen, hitting a few keys several times. Uri watched his eyes move from left to right.

Finally, he spoke, looking at Uri when he did.

"Your name is Uri, correct?"

"Yes."

"Are you a member of an organization called The Struggle?"

"Yes."

Whenever Uri answered, the agent looked back at the screen and typed.

"How would you characterize The Struggle?"

Uri had memorized a response in the days when he convinced parents to enroll their high schoolers in the teen seminar.

"It's an unaffiliated Jewish educational organization dedicated to *Torah* study from the perspective of Professor David Berns, an eminent scholar who is on the Religious Studies faculty at State."

"How would you characterize Professor Berns' perspective?"

He had a ready answer for this question, too.

"God is *Elohim*, a Lord to be feared and obeyed. Certain humans, created in God's image, are to be feared and obeyed by the rest of us, too."

"Is Professor Berns one of those humans?"

"Yes."

Agent Myers tapped on his keyboard.

"And what happens to those who don't obey Professor Berns?"

"Until recent times, that was rare. If someone who disrespected the Professor didn't see reason, we excluded them or dismissed them from The Struggle."

Uri rose to the challenge of the agent's questions, so far.

"Is it true that you provided security for the Professor?"

The agent would have known this only if the FBI had interviewed others before Uri. He shifted in his chair, wondering how much information Agent Myers had about him.

"Yes."

"What did security work involve?"

Uri guessed it would look bad if he mentioned beating anyone.

"If a member disrupted the seminars, I talked to them."

"Talked to them?"

"Yes."

The agent paused to read the screen. Several seconds passed. Uri's underarms perspired, wetting his shirt.

"What can you tell me about the Professor's relationships with female members?"

"What do you mean?"

"Did he have sex with female members?"

"Some of them, I guess. I wasn't privy to all of it."

"Which females did he have sex with to your knowledge?"

It would be safe to name the names of women who admitted having sex with the Professor. The FBI would have known about them.

"Flora. Rachel. Jenny. Sylvia."

"And your wife?"

"Yes."

Agent Myers looked up from the screen at Uri.

"What can you tell me about the Professor's sexual relationships with underage girls?"

"Nothing."

"Nothing?"

"Nothing."

"You taught the teen seminar in its first year. Two of your students became pregnant and had abortions. And you had no awareness of this?"

Agent Myers gave him a sharper stare.

"Only afterwards. But I believe the Professor was not the one who got them pregnant."

"What convinced you?"

"The girls told me it someone else had sex with them."

Agent Myers surprised him by not asking who the "someone else" was. Instead, he returned to his screen and tapped some keys. The FBI knew about the teen girls' abortions.

"We have been informed that your security work involved assaulting several students enrolled at State. One suffered serious injuries. You belonged to an underground fight club, Punches. You made connections there with men who hired you to assault others in nearby towns. Some of those required medical attention."

Uri was astounded. The FBI must have interviewed Wacko, who told them about the jobs. No one else knew. His neck prickled. He swallowed hard.

"If you are charged for any of the assaults and are found guilty, the court will sentence you to a prison term of five years, perhaps more."

Something in Uri's chest collapsed. His bones seemed to cave in. He sagged toward the tabletop, heaving and crying. Minutes passed until Uri controlled his sobbing. Prison. The FBI knew what he did. He might never see Izzy again.

The agent just sat, waiting. When Uri calmed, he spoke again.

"No charges have been pressed yet. If you cooperate with us, we may be able to help."

"What do you mean?"

A fresh bout of tears spilled down his face.

"We believe the Professor had sex with underage girls. We need someone to say so in court, on the witness stand, under oath. If you did that, the potential charges might disappear."

"How can I say that under oath if I don't know for sure?"

"That would be up to you to figure out. We can't speak for the consequences if you don't or won't."

While walking home, Uri tried to recall everything the agent said. Some of it was muddled. Did he ask Uri to lie about the Professor having sex with the teen girls? Or did he expect Uri to discover the Professor's possible crime on his own, then reveal it in court? He was being blackmailed into betraying the Professor. If they blackmailed others, a raft of witnesses would insure a guilty sentence. Or he could be the only one, a last resort after all the others refused, because the FBI had the goods on Uri, the only true criminal among all the student members.

Wacko had informed on him. Maybe Vel and Ernie, even though Uri had apologized to them. Adan? Rachel? Anyone in The Struggle, perhaps everyone, had given him up. Now the agent asked him to give the Professor up. There would be no slow weaning process if he wanted to see Izzy again. He had to decide right away. It was unbearable. His shoulders curled under the colossal weight of it as he walked, a giant hunched over.

His thoughts strayed to the time he had crossed the highway. He wished he had died. If he tried again, it would be the only way to hurt no one—not the Professor, not Lois or Izzy. It was a way out. Suicide. But walking into traffic wasn't a sure thing and might cause others to die, as cars crashed into each other to avoid him. His mind grasped at other methods. He could apply to buy a gun, but it would be days before they completed the background check. And he had a felony conviction. Did the application go to the FBI? Would they stall it to get him on the witness stand?

He could throw himself off the roof of a building taller than five or six stories. Surely, he wouldn't survive. He imagined stepping off the edge and falling in slow motion, floating to the street below, people craning their necks at windows to watch his drawn-out tumble, the blackness catching up with him a split second before the end, before the thwack of his skull hitting the ground.

An office tower stood across the street. He counted—nine stories. That should do it. He entered the glass doors and stood with a group of people waiting for the elevator. They must have known his intentions because he heard their thoughts.

"It'll be over in seconds."

"It's the only way out."

"It's like Jacob's ladder—first you go up, then you go down."

No one looked at him, but that had to be deliberate. When the elevator door opened, they all piled in. Uri was last. He turned to face the door. The others whispered about him behind his back.

"He won't have the nerve."

"Agent Myers guessed he was a coward."

"Prison is too good for him."

He stepped aside to let others on or off at each floor. When the elevator reached the ninth, he got out with two others, who veered away to their offices. Uri found a staircase that would take him to the roof. The door leading outside wasn't locked.

On the rooftop, he was aware of a loud humming. It had to be the collective thoughts of all the people below, urging him on, telling him to finish what he started. There was considerable wind. His jacket didn't keep him warm enough. He hugged his arms across his chest. It was colder than he expected it to be.

A low wall ran around the perimeter of the roof. He would have to step onto it before jumping off, but he was exhausted, too worn out to lift his foot for the climb. He needed to rest before trying. A concrete block sat in the middle of the expanse. Using it for a pillow, he lay down. The tarry smell of roofer's glue near the surface stung his breath. At least the wind was more subdued closer to the ground. If he just had a few minutes' sleep.

He awoke in the furry half-light before dawn. He must have slept for hours. His cell phone rattled in his pocket. No need to look. It would be Lois texting him, frantic to know where he was. There might be scores of texts and voicemails from her. He wasn't ready to reply.

Soot covered his skin and clothing, blown onto him by the wind. The ground was hard and rough, and the concrete pillow crumbled on the edges, leaving its residue in his hair. The place was filthy. Trash he hadn't noticed the day before littered the rooftop. His hip ached from sleeping on the hard surface.

He sat up, looking around in the gloom of early morning, before sunrise. If *Eloheim* existed, He was surely not in this barren place. He imagined the Professor's God in a palace, sitting on a gold throne. This wasn't even a place for Rabbi Shapiro's kindlier God. It was a desert in the middle of town, lifeless, junk everywhere, cans, plastic, rubble, with nothing to see but other rooftops and a dull, overcast sky, with no sound except the continuous humming. Uri snorted.

If God existed, He had abandoned Uri long ago. Uri spent years trying to fill the emptiness within, with Vel, then the Professor. All it did was lead him to this rooftop, to this moment of darkness. He felt nothing. It was time to end it. He rose, walked to the low wall, and stepped up. He put his hand over his eyes and recited.

Shma Yisrael, Adonai Eloheinu, Adonai echad

Loud and clear, Adan's voice sounded.

"Die, fag. Do it."

Just then, two men came onto the roof. If Uri insulted them, they might give him the push he needed.

"Hey. What are you doing?"

"Fuck you!"

"Get off there."

"Fuck you."

They came closer. Uri reached his hand in his pocket. Matches. He lit as many as possible at once and held the flame to the bottom of his jacket. It ignited fast.

The last thing he heard was screaming. He couldn't tell if it came from him or from the two running men.

PART FOUR
THE STRUGGLE

CHAPTER 33

The scar on the left side of Uri's face matched the one on the right, except for the brighter color, typical of a newer burn. Only good fortune left his eye uninjured. He already had a glass one on the right side. The previous fire he set deformed his ear. This time, it spared his left hand.

Prison required an adjustment, but that was his choice. The FBI had been prepared to spare him incarceration if he fulfilled his end of the bargain. He had a lot of time to unravel what happened to him in court. After all his daydreams over the years about court, the real thing was nothing like what he imagined. No giant of a man showed up to administer a beating right after sentencing.

In real court, every seat was taken inside, and the media was present outside. The case against the Professor attracted national interest. A charismatic Jewish leader. A cult. A theology that encouraged crime. Polyamorous behaviors and sex with underage girls. Secret abortions. Even drugs, although that surprised Uri.

The judge, a severe older woman with graying hair pinned into an old-fashioned bun on top of her head, was determined to maintain order, slamming the gavel down at the slightest distraction from the spectators. The prosecutor and his assistant sat at a table on the left side of the room, and the

Professor sat with his legal team, paid for by those of his few supporters who remained loyal, on the right.

There were several charges involving child sexual abuse, child sexual exploitation, tax fraud, drug possession, distributing drugs to minors, and identity theft. The Professor wasn't a professor after all. He wasn't even Jewish. He didn't have an academic degree, and he never attended a *Yeshiva*. The real David Berns died years earlier. The accused perpetrated an elaborate hoax on State and the Jewish community. Uri had been just one of many young people he had roped in.

Yet, when the prosecutor called Uri to the witness stand, the Professor never opened his eyes, sitting with them closed ever since the opening remarks by the prosecutor, unless the judge addressed him. It hurt Uri when the Professor continued to ignore him despite Uri's refusal to betray him. Uri hoped for a sign of gratitude, but the Professor disregarded him along with everyone else in court.

Rachel testified against the Professor to avoid prison. She had her baby to think of. Uri didn't blame her. He wondered why the Professor didn't look at her with disgust and him with approval. The accused didn't differentiate between them. Everyone in the room was beneath his contempt. That's how Uri interpreted his expression.

The trial ran for several days, longer than expected. Half the time, the legal team and the prosecutor approached the bar to confer with the judge on some legal point. Illustrators, sitting up front, shaded in their drawings with charcoal. The spectators coughed, whispered, and shuffled in their seats when the judge didn't pay attention, only to be startled by the gavel's blow, like a hard slap in the face.

After each day's session, the gauntlet of microphones and cameras waited just outside the courthouse. The reporters ignored Uri until his testimony. Then they screamed their questions at him as he fought his way to the car, idling at the curb with Lois in the driver's seat.

"Why did you change your story?"

"Did you commit perjury?"

"Who paid you off?"

Before the trial date, Uri told Agent Myers he would testify that the Professor had sex with underage girls. He made the agreement to remain free to be a parent to Izzy. The FBI agent suggested the Professor would be convicted of at least one charge, most likely more than one, relieving Uri of his fear of Izzy being taken from him by his biological father. But testifying would be another wrong thing to do, added to the pile of wrongs Uri already committed. He didn't know with absolute certainty, enough to say under oath, that the Professor had sex with the teen girls or advised them to have abortions. If he gave them drugs to aid in his seductions, Uri didn't know that, either. He still thought Adan might have done what they accused the Professor of doing with the teen girls. If he lied under oath, it would be another crime.

After they persuaded Rachel to testify on behalf of the prosecution, the FBI showed less interest in Uri. She had the real goods on the Professor, and she had much more to lose. Uri remained on the witness list as a back-up, but they still expected him to say whatever the FBI determined the truth to be.

Everyone used Uri. Both the Professor and the FBI. Yet, Uri couldn't bring himself to hate the Professor. Not even if he would "rot in prison," as Lois put it. When he was called to testify, he entered the witness box with certainty. He knew what he had to say. Lois coached him.

"What do you know about the accused's sexual relationships with the teen girls?"

"He sexually exploited all the women in The Struggle, including the teen girls."

"How did you know about the girls?"

"I asked them. They blamed one of their classmates, but that just covered up the truth."

A lawyer for the defense cross-examined him.

"Did you ever see the accused having sex with the girls?"

"I never saw him have sex with anyone."

"Did he tell you he had sex with the girls?"

"No. He never told me things like that."

"Did you have sex with the girls, then lie to make it seem it was the accused?"

But that's not what happened.

Between the time Uri took the oath and when the prosecutor asked him the first question, he gazed at the Professor. The yearning that was always present overtook him. If he could stretch out his hand, palm up, toward the accused, supplicating, begging for crumbs, he would have done so. His shoulder ached from being restrained. He wanted to be seen, to be looked at, to be loved by the man, whoever he was. It was wrong to lie about him. Disappointing him was impossible.

"What do you know about the accused's sexual relationships with the teen girls?"

"Nothing. I know nothing about that."

When the Professor's eyes remained closed, Uri understood he had thrown his life away more thoroughly than he would have if he walked into traffic or jumped off the office building. It didn't matter. If he didn't exist for the Professor, he didn't exist. He was nothing, a zero, whether in prison or free. He felt something drain out of him on the witness stand. Was it his soul or just defeat?

The next time he appeared in court, it was for his own sentencing for battery charges. The prosecutor offered him a deal. Wacko would testify against him, as well as the men he battered. If he went to trial, he would have no alibi. His lawyer would be a public defender in a crumpled suit, who would meet with him for five minutes before the proceedings began. Uri took the deal. The one thing he wouldn't agree to do was give up the names of the men who hired him. The victims would press charges against them, anyway.

In minutes, the sentencing was over. Again, no giant showed up to administer punishment right in the courtroom. Instead, the same stern woman judge sent him to a medium security prison for a three-year term. There were no mitigating circumstances. Uri broke the law, and the judge handed down a consequence.

It appalled Lois that he hadn't lied about the Professor—a lie that would have been the truth.

"What would it take for you to realize that the Professor is a narcissistic predator?"

They talked by phone through a window during her only visit to the prison. She didn't bring Izzy.

"If I had proof beyond a reasonable doubt, it would make no difference. That's what I've learned about myself. I can't stop loving a person because he isn't worthy of my love. His not having any interest in me just makes me love him more, want him more."

"You could have had me and Izzy, two people who care for you. Instead, you've chosen someone who wouldn't give you the dust off his shoes."

"I know."

"You've tossed us aside for him."

"I know."

Soon after, he was served with a notice that Lois was divorcing him. He would never see her or Izzy again. It broke his heart, but not as much as seeing the Professor's eyes remain shut during his testimony in court.

This was Uri's second time inside, and his size and monstrous appearance brought him unearned respect among the others in his block. He never had to prove himself. He arrived with a reputation from the jobs he took and from his victories at Punches. Many inmates had attended his fights there. He could have been the leader of a gang, but he did his time quietly, by himself.

Several months into his incarceration, Uri learned that the Professor, whose actual name was Larry Jones, was in the same facility, in the Sexual Deviant's block. It made sense that he would be there, although it surprised Uri, who never thought they would wind up in the same institution.

Some months after that, a trustee smuggled a letter from the Professor, written on the back of a list of prison rules, the kind distributed to all new inmates.

Hello Uri

Through my contacts in the administration here, they have given me permission to organize a bible study group. It will be nondenominational this time, although I will miss the opportunity to instruct intelligent Jewish youth, like yourself. Would you like to be my amanuensis again? You understand what's involved.

We can communicate through the trustee who brought you this letter.

Larry

Uri imagined buying items from the commissary, smuggling them to the Professor, and never being repaid. The demands would grow over time, and they would force Uri to steal from others. In frustration, he would become violent again, beat inmates, lose it with guards, and add years to his sentence. He could not let that happen. He didn't reply to the letter.

A week later, another letter came.

I haven't heard from you. The amanuensis position awaits you. You are the only one I am considering.

Three days later, another.

Who else can I trust but you? Please don't abandon me in my hour of need.

Please don't abandon him? Was the Professor pleading? With a mixture of wonder and revulsion, Uri crumpled the flyer, then straightened it, attempting to smooth the creases with strokes of his hand, then tore it up only to repair it again with borrowed tape.

Other letters followed in quick succession, some only a sentence long, some covering the page. They cited the terrible conditions in the Sexual Deviant's unit, the vermin, the filth, the nastiness of his cell-mates, his fear of rape or worse. Or they were exaggerated reminders of their former friendship in The Struggle, of the Professor's love and reliance on Uri, their closeness, how inseparable they had been. It wasn't how Uri remembered their relationship.

Uri continued to let the letters go unanswered. After another week, the Professor's became more frantic, more self-pitying.

Where are you, my son? Have you forgotten me already?

I cannot survive here without you. My heart breaks.

These weren't the communications of a powerful man. They didn't threaten or discipline. Uri's disgust increased, erasing any desire to be in servitude to the Professor. During the years since the fire that killed his mother, he attached himself to Vel and the Professor, doing whatever they commanded. Neither had anything to give him, not even the harshness he once craved. Was that why he enslaved himself to them? So he could be a slave? Never a master?

That was over now. He was free, at last, in prison. A bitter taste coated the back of his tongue.

CHAPTER 34

During the two years before his parole, just before his twenty-fifth birthday, the only regular visitor he had was Flora. She always came with her younger son, Adam, the biological child of the Professor. Adan didn't accompany them.

"He would love to see you, but not in prison. I can almost read his mind," she said through the visiting-room telephone.

As Adam grew from infancy to a toddler, he resembled the Adam who died in the fire that also killed Uri's mother, as Adan had when Uri first met him. Adam had a cute, freckled face and, unlike Adan, always smiled, as his namesake did. Clones of Uri's mother and first only friend had returned the originals to him, in a way.

"Adam and Adan may appear similar, as brothers or half-brothers often do, but their personalities are very different. Adam wears his heart on his sleeve. No one has to guess what he thinks."

"I love you, Ri," he said in his baby voice

"I love you, too."

At first, Uri said this because that's what's said to a toddler. With every visit, Uri meant it more. No one substituted for Izzy, but Flora's son was a near-brother to him, if not a near-son because of their age difference.

Flora and Uri had many discussions about the Professor.

"He's an imposter, responsible for so much damage. All he wanted from me was money, my inheritance from Simon. Well, that's gone now."

"How do you live?"

She smiled.

"Adan supports us. He works with Max Levy in the entertainment business. Max is training him. When he retires, Adan will take over Max's share of the business."

Wacko was Adan's business partner? The "entertainment business" must be other underground fight clubs, now that the police had shut down Punches. Flora didn't seem aware of the true nature of Adan's work.

"They travel a lot. It seems they're setting up venues in other towns."

"It must be a relief to you that Adan doesn't stay in touch with the Professor, or does he?"

"No, no. He was on to that scumbag from the beginning. I would say I have regrets if I didn't get my precious Adam out of the relationship."

"The Professor is in another unit of this prison."

It made little sense to keep this from her, if she didn't already know it.

"I come here to see you, not him. I'm through with him."

Her lips pressed into a thin line.

"Why do you think we fell for him?" He asked.

She paused before answering, her eyes shifting to the left, as if the Professor sat nearby, on that side.

"I can only answer for myself, Uri. You'll have to figure out your reasons. I met him on the rebound from Simon. David charmed me. He came along when I was very vulnerable, thinking my life was over, that I'd never have a romantic relationship again. He swept me off my feet, as they say. When I became jealous of Rachel, calling her his wife, he never hid his affair with her. Instead, he convinced me that having sex with others didn't matter. It didn't interfere with our commitment, he said."

Adam, sensing his mother's pain, stroked her face, trying to please her in his own sweet way.

"Don't cry, Mommy."

"I'm sad, but I won't cry. You make me too happy to cry."

Uri had a sudden vivid memory, brought up by the sight of Adam comforting Flora. He was a small child, about four-years-old, sitting on his mother's lap. Lora. She was crying, and he stroked her face.

"Why are you crying, Mommy?"

"Because you don't have a daddy to love us. My boyfriend was mean. Mommy had to make him go away."

"Tell him to come back. I don't care if he's mean if he makes you happy."

The tears spilled down his mother's face, reminding him of Lois while he remembered.

"My boyfriend hurt you. That's why I made him go away."

"I don't care. He can hurt me. He can come back if he doesn't hurt you."

His mother's boyfriend seemed huge to Uri at that age. He didn't remember being hurt by him, but he resembled Uri's fantasy image of the giant who would beat him in court. It didn't matter that he grew into a giant himself. In his imagination, he remained a small child waiting for a big man to hurt him.

"After David, I fell into the same hole I was in after Simon died, thinking no one would ever want me again. Guess what? Someone came along who wants me."

"Who?"

Now Flora smiled. Her eyes sparked.

"Max Levy. He's my new boyfriend. I met him through Adan. He's a good man, Uri."

Wacko was Flora's boyfriend?

"I love Max," Adam said.

"He's a wonderful father to both my boys."

"I know Max from the gym. You're right. He's a good man."

Uri wondered what Adan would do to prevent this relationship from going too far.

"Max wants to see you. I can bring him next time, if you like."

"I would."

Uri remembered Wacko encouraging him to pay for his crimes. Now that he was doing time, perhaps they'd be friends again, even though it was Wacko's testimony that was responsible for Uri's conviction. He wanted Wacko to want to see him, not just to please Flora.

If everything happens for a reason, as Rabbi Shapiro might say if Uri asked him, Flora had come into his life to be a second mother and to give him three very different father-figures: Simon, the Professor, and now Wacko. It was his own stupid fault for rejecting Simon, the best of them, and instead craving a relationship with the Professor, the worst of the three. He hoped he had another chance with Wacko, who was as generous as Simon, but who encouraged Uri's aggressive streak. The fighting in Punches had not been illegal. The raid happened because of betting. Wacko disapproved of Uri's taking jobs involving battery and predicted he would end up in prison. Uri liked the fight promoter, but had to avoid being talked into fighting again. There had to be another way of venting his frustrations.

That is what Flora taught him. He calmed himself by talking to her during the visits and on the phone. Lois had listened to him, too, when they were together, but her involvement with the Professor and her decision to have the Professor's child destroyed his trust in her. His choosing loyalty to the Professor over their marriage destroyed her trust in him. There was no such baggage with Flora. He talked to her about anything, with one exception—Adan.

They steered their conversation back to the Professor.

"I love Max and hope our relationship will progress, maybe even to marriage. But I was *in* love with the Professor. Let me tell you a secret," she said. She shifted Adam and moved closer to the glass panel that separated them.

"There's still part of me that loves David. There's another part of me that hates him. The part that loves him waits for a phone call, a text, something. I don't trust myself a hundred percent. If I heard from him, he might tempt me to answer. I'm depending on Max and Adan to stop me. I don't have the self-control I need yet."

As soon as Flora said that, Uri realized the same was true of him.

"I get what you mean. It's, like, even though thick walls separate me from the Professor, knowing he is here is always on my mind. He reached out to me. I didn't respond because... he was so not himself, I couldn't believe it was him."

Adam stared at him with wide, curious eyes, even though he didn't hear what Uri said into the phone receiver and wouldn't understand if he did.

"He had this poor-pity-me attitude that seemed unlike the man I admired. It disgusted me. He's starting a bible study group for the inmates. I'm not interested. But if he was the man he used to be, I might be the first to sign up."

Flora's eyebrows raised.

"Don't. He'd draw you into his orbit again."

"I won't."

"There's this thing. It's called post-cult syndrome. Those who leave a cult feel lost. Decision making is hard. In The Struggle, David decided everything for us. Now we have to decide for ourselves, and we don't know how. Especially someone as young as you, Uri."

"It's like being in prison. I don't have to decide anything—what to eat, when to sleep, what to wear."

"When you're released, it'll be extra hard for you."

"All my life, I've either been in institutions, like hospitals and jail, or in a cult, or under someone's thumb. Or so depressed, I didn't care what happened, like I was when you met me. Sometimes I think I don't exist. I'm just a zombie or something."

His conversations with Flora were deeper than any he had ever had. He had some deep ones with Lois when they were being honest with each other. With Flora, he could be honest about himself. It helped that she had been in The Struggle and that she looked like his mother. She understood him and what he had been through.

"You're not a zombie. No zombie would say what you said. A zombie wouldn't have your awareness."

"Yeah. They're dead. Sometimes I feel dead inside, this empty sensation. But you're right. Zombies don't have sensations. I used to be a zombie. I'm coming back to life right here in prison."

They both laughed. Adam laughed, too, bouncing on his mother's lap.

When Flora brought Max, he never mentioned Punches or asked Uri to fight.

"I guess I shouldn't call you Demon anymore."

"And I shouldn't call you Wacko."

Flora shot them a puzzled look.

"We called each other by those names when we used to meet at the gym."

Punches had been like a gym, sort of. It was a harmless white lie that both of them told Flora. If she knew about the fight club, it could lead to an uncomfortable conversation about Adan. Both Wacko and Uri understood this.

"Is it true you're working with Adan?" Uri asked.

"Yes. He's an interesting young man. I'm mentoring him."

"Like you did with me at the gym?"

Wacko hesitated.

"Mmm. It's different. I'm teaching him the promotion business. Not how to work out."

"Adan'll be good at that."

Unless he gets into the illegal side of things, Uri thought.

Flora gave them an innocent smile. Adam babbled something that sounded like "Watch out for Adan."

The toddler spoke the truth, if it wasn't Uri's imagination. Adan couldn't be trusted.

"Look, kid," Wacko said. "I'm staying with Flora, now. When you get out, how about you stay with us?"

"If you've got post-cult syndrome, it'll be easier if you start with our support," Flora said.

"For real?" Uri swallowed.

He was touched, but he didn't want to cry.

"Of course. Adan would love to have you room with him again. And Adam adores you."

"Just till you get on yer feet," Wacko said.

Loneliness after his release terrified Uri. All he would get was a bus ticket to a homeless shelter and a few dollars from what he earned in the prison laundry, most of which he spent in the commissary. The leased space The Struggle had rented was gone. He couldn't stay there.

"I don't know what to say."

He meant he had no words to express his gratitude.

"Just say 'Yes,'" Flora said.

Adam babbled. "I love you, Ri."

Uri didn't imagine it this time.

CHAPTER 35

Uri spent his first week after release playing with Adam at Flora's house and looking for a job. Adan, who was nineteen and a high school graduate, ignored him. Uri, who towered over him and knew how to fight, may have been too intimidating.The little weasel kept secrets while working with Wacko, and, Uri suspected, made connections with gangsters associated with the fight clubs.

Wacko seemed to be on to his apprentice. He said nothing to Flora, but dropped Uri an occasional hint.

"Adan does things behind my back. He has too much cash. I pay him the minimum wage since he's still learning. Yet, he has fancy clothes, a nice car, and money for Flora."

"Don't trust him, Wacko. He'll hurt you without thinking twice."

"Yer right."

Uri struggled to find employment because of his appearance and the felonies on his record.

"I'll promote you, if you want to fight."

Wacko meant well, but fighting would lead Uri down the wrong path. Instead, he took his old job back doing yard work for the synagogue. It was part time and paid little, but it was honest. He took care to control his feelings for Wacko and the Rabbi, keeping any admiration low-key, letting himself like them without being dazzled. Neither man was dazzling.

He missed being dazzled. He missed the Professor and The Struggle. He missed Izzy and Lois. As Flora suggested, he had post-cult syndrome, meaning he very much wanted someone to tell him what to do, very much wanted to be controlled. The hollow space inside him grew. He risked trying to find another Professor, another Vel, if he didn't figure out how to fill his inner hole—with what?

After the first week of being paroled, he became agitated when not working, pacing around his room when alone, yanking his hair, dreaming of fires, wishing to burn himself with cigarettes. He lit matches and blew them out seconds before they seared his fingers. If only he had drugs. But weed made him paranoid, and everything else made him hallucinate. He didn't need another addiction to complicate his problems. He had already been addicted to the Professor. Besides, he had no money for drugs. He gave the little he earned to Flora for room and board.

"Consider it like withdrawal," Flora said. "I went through it after David's arrest. It's very rough at first, but every day you get a bit more used to being without."

"What replaces it?"

"For me, it was Adam, then Max. As I told you, I still have cravings for David when something reminds me of him. Max knows. I don't think that will ever go away, not for years, anyway."

"I don't have what you have."

"You'll have to find something or someone else. A hobby or a new girlfriend."

That sounded lame. It's what people said when romantic relationships ended. Exercise. Get a dog. Find someone else. There are other fish in the sea. As if one fish was the same as another, when in reality, a few are exquisite and the rest are dull gray.

Never did he feel so lost. He had been lost since his mother died, alone, lonely, without connection to anyone. It wasn't like the depression that made him not care enough to live. It was the desperation of someone who had what he wanted, then lost it. What was he supposed to do in an empty world, a vacuum without a stellar personality to suck him into its orbit? He drifted in deep space with oxygen soon to be used up. Then what?

He just finished pruning some bushes at the synagogue when Rabbi Shapiro came out in his black coat and motioned to him to a bench.

"Sit with me," he said.

"Okay."

Uri hoped the Rabbi would not lay him off.

"I make a point of remembering each boy's *bar mitzvah* verses so I can refer to them when we meet as adults. I suppose I'm superstitious, but I believe the verses remain meaningful for life. Yours was Jacob wrestling with the man, right?"

It surprised Uri that anyone remembered anything about him, except the awful stuff—how he became scarred, his prison sentence, his divorce. At least he still had his job, it seemed.

"Thats true, Rabbi."

"It's November, the month we read that verse again."

"The best month for pruning."

The Rabbi nodded, as if figuring out a way to use the gardening metaphor to make his point.

"Jacob is an example of how difficult it is to 'prune' away the past. His parents each had a favorite son. For Isaac, it was Esau. For Rebekah, it was Jacob. Jacob tricks Esau out of their father's blessing with Rebekah's help. After Jacob struggles with the man, he asks Esau to forgive him."

The Rabbi looked into Uri's eyes.

"We think Jacob has changed. But when his twelve sons are born, he favors Joseph. He continues the mistake his parents made, favoring one child over another."

"Uh huh." Uri didn't understand why he was being told this familiar *Torah* story. Until he was sure still had his job, he couldn't relax.

"Joseph is the one who changes. At first, he's arrogant. But then, he forgives his brothers, who sold him into slavery. Sometimes change takes more than one generation. The *Torah* suggests that progress happens after a period of wandering in the desert or a spell in slavery."

"I guess you're saying I've had to go through all I've been through to get to a better place."

"Something like that."

"It's just that I'm still going through it. When does it end?"

"If it doesn't end in your generation, you do what you can to make it end in the next one."

"But I never see Izzy."

"Jacob couldn't foretell that he would have a son who would change himself and the Jewish people. Like most of us, he was just trying to survive."

The Rabbi said nothing about Uri's employment. He still had his job. Their conversation reminded him of Izzy. If the Professor's absence paralyzed him, Izzy's made him ache with sadness, even after over two years. He missed Lois, too, her soft, warm body curled next to his, and her efforts to save him from The Struggle. When he thought of their marriage, it didn't seem all bad, even if the bad outweighed the good when they were together. If she saw him now that fire scarred both sides of his face, he might repulse her.

When his four hours of work at the synagogue finished for the day, it was only noon. There were many hours left until bedtime, if he slept at all, with nothing to do. His period of slavery was over now that The Struggle collapsed, and his wandering in the desert had begun. If he stayed in his room, he would have to deal with Adan, who slept until the early afternoon. Instead, he walked for hours through the derelict part of town, trying to snuff out his painful thoughts.

He walked past weed-filled lots, abandoned factories, shuttered houses, small shopping strips with auto-supply stores—reminding him he couldn't drive with his bad eye and hip, Chinese takeout—he couldn't afford the cheapest restaurant, and gloomy neighborhood bars—he had no friends to invite for a drink. His future stretched before him, undefined, without hope of a decent job, a girlfriend, or a place of his own if Flora kicked him out. He might live another fifty years, if he lived a normal lifespan, shoveling snow off the synagogue walkway and sleeping in a homeless shelter. Even if he scraped together enough money for a fast-food order, he would eat in a food pantry rather than have to decide for himself what he wanted from the many items on a menu.

Life was full of choices he avoided making. Flora fed him. He wore whichever of his few items of clothing was cleanest each day. As long as the Rabbi employed him, he didn't look for a better-paying job. Anyone who wanted to date a scarred man would have to ask him out. He didn't know how to approach a woman someone else didn't choose for him, like the Professor did when matching him with Lois.

When he encountered other people during his walks, they either gawked at him, turned away, crossed the street, or called out the familiar insults.

"Leather face."

"Monster-man."

"Fuck off away from here."

He never responded. His size was enough to prevent physical attacks.

At the dinner table, Flora and Wacko tried to coach him.

"Goodwill has clothing for men. You can find things that were never worn, with the price tag still attached, sometimes. Or almost new," Wacko said.

"The synagogue has social events for young singles. You should try them out. It's a way to meet people," Flora said.

"I don't know."

Adan continued to ignore him. That was one of the good things about living in Flora's house. He didn't want a friendship with the brat who grew up to be the thug Uri used to be. It was improbable that Adan beat people with bare fists, or even with sticks. He was too slight for that. But it wasn't beyond possibility for Adan to possess a handgun. A small young man who might do security for the unsavory characters met at illegal fight clubs required a weapon.

Uri asked him when they were alone in the room they shared.

"So. Do you own a piece?"

"Maybe. Why?"

"Can I see?"

Adan reached under his bed for a box. Inside was a Glock. It must have been a recent purchase, if its owner's proud smile was any sign.

"What are you going to use it for?"

"Scare people. Shoot people. Whatever."

"You'd shoot someone?"

"Only if it's necessary."

"You're going to love prison," Uri said.

"I won't do some idiot fucking thing to get caught, like you did. You asked to go inside."

That had been true. Uri would have avoided prison if he cooperated with the FBI. Adan wasn't the type to take a rap for anyone. Whenever they were alone after that, Adan took out the Glock, handling it, cleaning it, taking the ammunition out and putting it back in. Nothing was said. Uri understood Adan was threatening him. His size was no protection against the cruel potential of a gun in the hands of a young *gonif*.

One day, soon after, when they were both in their shared bedroom, Flora called Uri downstairs. She and Wacko were in the living room.

"I have something to tell you," she said.

Uri guessed she and Wacko had become engaged. That was where she had announced her engagements to Simon and the Professor. This time, he would expect it.

"Better sit down." She smiled up at him.

He took a seat in the winged chair opposite them. Somewhere outside in the distance, they could hear the alarmed barking of a dog. Upstairs, Adan—who had never approved of his mother's fiancees—played with his gun. Had he already heard? Would he come down and shoot them all?

"It's time for you to know, Uri. I am your aunt."

CHAPTER 36

Flora repeated what she said several times before Uri took it in. She was his mother's younger sister. Not her ghost. He hadn't been crazy or psychotic. His mother never haunted him. Flora was his aunt, and she looked just like her sister.

Uri endured many surprises in his life, but this one stole his breath. He stared at Flora, open-mouthed, stunned, a million questions jammed onto the back of his tongue, too packed together to loosen into speech.

"What?... How?..." He stammered.

"I'll tell you everything," Flora said, leaning over to put a calming hand on his knee, then sitting back again. She wiped her eyes with the back of her hands.

"Two sisters, Lora and Flora, so alike people thought of us as twins. Our mother—your grandmother—always dressed us in the same outfits. We did everything together until high school. That's when we became different. I was the good one who obeyed our parents, made good grades, and only dated Jewish boys from the neighborhood. I commuted to college from home, and married Adan's father. Until the divorce, our parents were very pleased with me."

"Do you want a glass of water, Uri?" Wacko asked.

He shook his head.

"During our senior year, your mother became what our parents called 'boy crazy.' She dated a lot, including boys from other high schools, and some older boys. She became 'arty,' going to see foreign films, listening to jazz, reading poetry. Then, instead of staying home until she married, like I did, she left town. The next we heard, she enrolled at State, in Indiana, on an art scholarship. She modeled nude in art classes for money. To our parents, she had become a prostitute. They called her a 'whore' and a 'slut.' They said she shamed them."

Tears rolled down Flora's face. Max lent her his handkerchief.

"She was my sister. I still loved her. We kept in touch. She never lied to our parents. The last straw for them was when she told them she dated an African boy. That's when they broke off contact."

Flora paused for a few seconds to regain control. After a couple of heaves, she continued.

"She became pregnant with you without having a husband or even knowing which boy fathered you. Our parents disowned her. They never wanted to meet you until Lora invited them to your *bar mitzvah*. Just the fact that you were having a *bar mitzvah* was a turnaround for them. They changed their plans when it was cancelled."

By now, Uri and Flora were both in tears.

"I came to Indiana by myself to make arrangements for Lora's funeral and for you. No one else would come with me. That's when I met Simon. I moved here to be with both of you. Simon had already become your foster father by that point."

"Why didn't you tell me right away?"

He choked the words out.

"I didn't know if I should trust you. You set the fire. And you were such a strange boy, so... unknowable. I wanted to spend time with you first. Simon wanted you to be told, but Adan, as much as he adored you, had concerns. He worried about your mental health. He wondered if you would be in a state to handle anything else."

"You waited almost ten years."

"Don't forget all that happened in those ten years. You walked into traffic. Simon died. You set another fire and went to prison. Then we both got involved with David and The Struggle. They arrested David. They sent you to prison, again. There were a series of hardships, and Adan convinced me to wait after each one."

"Adan."

"Yes. He always put your welfare first."

"He knew all along."

"Of course. He's your first cousin."

That was the second stunner of the day. If Flora was his aunt, the brat had to be his cousin.

"Adan's my cousin."

Under his breath, he repeated Flora's words in a whisper, feeling them roll around in his mouth.

"David didn't want you to be told. While I was under his influence, I believed anything he said."

"Why?"

"He didn't want any distractions from your obligations to The Struggle."

The Professor wanted everything to revolve around him. That's what not having distractions meant. Uri had allowed someone else to control and manipulate him for goals that were not his own.

"David tried to destroy family ties. He made some members of The Struggle stop all contact with their relatives. He even said hurtful things about my closeness with Adan and attempted to separate us. By advising me not to tell you I was your aunt, he kept us apart, too. All of us were supposed to be connected to one and only one person—David."

She pinched her lips.

"That's where David's power over me stopped. No one could make me give up my son or my nephew. That's why I kept inviting you over, and why I wanted you here when they released you."

"I wanted you here, too," Wacko said.

"Adan and the Professor knew. Who else?"

"Just Max and Rabbi Shapiro."

His employer!

"It's one reason the Rabbi's been so kind to you, hiring you instead of asking volunteers from the congregation to do the yard work. Simon left money to the synagogue to establish a fund to pay you."

"I'm a pity hire?"

Flora raised her eyebrow.

"No, no. The Rabbi wanted to keep you from drifting away from the congregation, since so many of your relations are members. Not just the children. Their mothers, too."

His brow wrinkled.

"What do you mean?"

She stared at him as if to say, "Don't you get it?"

"You and Adam are first cousins."

Adam was his first cousin, too. That hadn't occurred to him. His heart thumped with pleasure. He loved the toddler. Now, whatever happened, they would always be joined.

"Since Adam and the Professor's other children in the congregation are half-siblings, they are all half-cousins to you too. Rachel's son Abe, Jenny's son, Izzy, and the others."

"Izzy?"

"Yes, Izzy is some sort of cousin to you."

"There are no words for people we're related to by the generation below us. So we can't say what kind of cousins you are," Wacko said.

"I'm related to Izzy."

The wonder of it ballooned in Uri's chest. Fresh tears sprung from his eyes. His fears about Izzy preferring the Professor to him vanished in an instant. He wasn't nothing to the boy. He was a blood relative.

"It's not just children from The Struggle. David once mentioned he has other offspring. He's in his late fifties. The Struggle might not have been his first cult. There could have been several others if he started forming them in his twenties. There may be children from each and from women he met in casual ways."

Vel snapped into Uri's mind. The Youth Group had been a kind of cult. The girls wanted to be sexual with Vel. If he allowed it, there might have been deliberate pregnancies. Everyone had been so desperate for Vel's approval, they could have competed to have his children. If Vel was as unethical as the Professor, he'd make a career out of what started in high school. Flora made sense, suggesting The Struggle wasn't the Professor's first time leading a close-knit group.

"Adam is a half-sibling of all of David's children. Through Adam, you are cousins with every one of them."

That night, Uri stayed up for hours, mulling over what he learned. He had an aunt and many cousins, a family. For more than a decade, he thought he had no one. In a vague way, he recalled his mother telling him about his east coast relatives. That's why she wanted him *bar mitzvah'd,* to be reunited with her parents so that he would have grandparents, uncles, aunts, cousins. She joined the synagogue to give him a people—the Jewish people. She didn't want him to wind up alone, as he would if Flora hadn't come into his life and if he hadn't stayed in the Youth Group through his teen years. His mother provided for him after all, not with money, which she didn't have, but with a community. Her death also provided him with family, although he didn't know it until now.

If Simon lived and married Flora, he would have been told years ago. They might have adopted him. Simon would have seen through the Professor and protected Flora and him from The Struggle. And if his mother hadn't died, she would have married Simon. They might have moved east, reconciled with her parents, and enjoyed extended family life.

Adan, asleep in the other bed, was the awl puncturing his inflated wonder. No one would want the brat for a cousin. Uri still imagined Adan might be responsible for half the things the FBI accused the Professor of and for the death of Simon. Uri's grandparents were racist bigots. The children spawned by the Professor carried his genes and might turn out to be molesting scumbags like their father. Was this the family Uri searched for since his mother's death?

Each thought had an underside. He never had to be alone again. But it was better to be alone. He could celebrate the milestones of life and holidays with a family. But those who didn't behave ruined those events. Relatives could love him, despite his scarring. But the story of Jacob and Esau was an example of how families often devolved into hatred, betrayal, and exile.

As the first light glimmered through the curtains, Uri gave up trying to turn off the conflicting views that deprived him of sleep and went down to the kitchen. Wacko was there, making coffee.

"You're up early. Want a cup? I made enough fer two," he said.

"Couldn't sleep."

"That's my problem."

He put both cups on the table, and they sat.

"When did you find out that Flora is my aunt?"

"Soon after we started dating. I began training Adan, and she hoped I'd help you when they released you. But first you'd have to be told."

He took a thoughtful sip of his coffee.

"Look, kid. I want to marry your aunt. But I need to get out of the fight club business and do something legit. She's a lady, very classy, and I don't want to bring her down by getting arrested."

"Like me and the Professor."

"Well, yer right."

"Adan might wind up inside. He thinks he won't get caught. That's where he's plain stupid."

"Flora wouldn't get over it."

"What do you want to do?"

"Stay in the entertainment business, which is what I know. I'm thinking of promoting wrestlers. That's legit, especially if it's through the WWE. I've got connections there."

Uri guessed what was coming next.

"With your size and looks, you'd be a natural as a wrestler. All you need is a costume. You already got a rep and a name—Demon Jake. I'd train you. For the next ten years, you'd have a career in the ring. After that, you'd coach."

"I don't want to hurt anyone, anymore."

"Wrestlers don't hurt anyone. It's all fake. They're more like stunt men than fighters. I'd show you all the moves. It's just show business, Demon. Not the Olympics."

"Let me think it over."

"What else are yer going to do with yerself?"

"Before yesterday, I didn't care. Now that I realize I have a family, what I do matters more. I want Flora to be proud of me."

"We both want to do right by her."

"She might not approve of wrestling."

"If she knows it's just show business...."

"You convince her first. If she goes for it, I'll talk to her about me joining you. Maybe."

"Fair enough, Demon."

Between dinner the night before and coffee that morning, Uri gained an aunt, cousins, and the possibility of a career. A future shined down on him. He kept waiting to wake up in the bed next to Adan and discover it was all a dream, that instead of nourishing light, it was the same dull, overcast sky, that his only future was mowing lawns, and that he was alone, mattering to no one.

As the day wore on, he stayed awake. He wasn't dreaming. Everything that happened in the preceding hours was real. And the best part of it was finding out blood attached him to Izzy.

CHAPTER 37

Crossing the threshold of the prison through the visitor's entrance with other civilians differed from being handcuffed and transported through the admissions gate. Although he had done his time without difficulty, Uri shuddered, despite knowing he would be within the stone walls for not more than an hour.

He had spent half the day traveling by bus, along with families, women with children, and unaccompanied others. Crying babies, kids running up and down the aisles, and the hiss of the bus doors interrupted his attempts to sleep. When he left Flora's house early that morning, he had showered and put on a clean shirt. As time passed, his appearance became more disheveled, as he perspired, dropped crumbs from his sandwich, and splattered himself with the coffee, purchased at the bus depot, whenever the driver braked.

The thought that the Professor would look worse comforted him. After his last begging text, Uri expected him to have aged and weakened. He might be hunched, unshaven, with downcast eyes and signs of the humiliation and degradation he experienced inside.

While waiting in the visitor's booth, he took several deep breaths to calm himself. This encounter would test his resolve to avoid entanglement with the Professor. He would state the reason for his visit with no chit-chatting. This was to be a business meeting, not friendship, not the renewal of a one-sided commitment.

About fifteen minutes later, the inmates entered single file and peeled off to the booths when they recognized the occupants. Cheerful sounds of greetings echoed in the large room. The Professor came in last. He spotted Uri and headed for him. Despite Uri's expectation, he looked no different, standing straight, clear-eyed, with no visible remorse. He seemed healthier than he had when he sat shut-eyed at the trial. Both picked up the receivers on either side of the smudged glass separating them.

"Well, well. My amanuensis has shown up."

Uri resisted the impulse to make an excuse, explaining why he hadn't visited before, justifying himself in a servile tone. The old Uri would have done that. He wouldn't be that man anymore.

"I found out that Flora is my aunt and that Adan and Adam are my cousins."

"So, you were told."

"You prevented Flora from telling me."

"Did I?"

This was not off to the best start. He was not here to accuse the Professor or get him to admit the truth.

"That doesn't matter. The important thing is that through Adam, I am a half-cousin to all your children."

"I suppose you would be."

The Professor gazed at him with indifference. Who was related to whom didn't interest him. He bided his time until the moment came to pounce. It wasn't time yet.

"It has to be. Adam is your son. He's a half-sibling of your other children. I'm Adam's first cousin. That makes me a half-cousin to all of them."

"Hmm."

They paused. Uri waited for a reaction. Instead, the Professor changed the subject.

"I've started a Bible study group here. It's quite popular. There's a waiting list to get in. I'm considering opening a second group on another evening. Everyone inside has access to a Bible, so that's no problem. However, the prison system doesn't provide all the things I need."

Uri was supposed to ask, "What things?" That would be a trap. He took a breath.

"I'm not here to talk about your activities inside."

"Oh?"

"I'm here to talk about my cousins, your children."

The Professor waited, saying nothing.

"How many are there?"

"That's hard to say. I lost track of some of the women. I'd guess around twenty-five, but that's rough."

"You sound proud of that."

"God commanded the patriarchs to be 'fruitful and multiply.' God intended the best of His people to reproduce, to populate the Promised Land with the best stock."

"But you aren't the best stock. You aren't even Jewish."

He outraged Uri.

"Who says I'm not?"

"Well, are you?"

"I am what I'm intended to be."

He wouldn't let anything pin him down. Uri realized he would only get vague answers if he kept asking.

"I want to contact your children, the ones not from The Struggle. I'm aware of those."

"Why?"

"Because they're my cousins."

"And?"

The Professor would not understand a driving need for family connections. It would be another trap to explain any deep reasons. He would keep it simple.

"I want to get to know them."

"Because?"

"I just do."

"Hmm."

There was another pause. The snake was ready to spring.

"What would be in it for me?"

"Wouldn't you like your children to meet each other? I could organize that."

The Professor shrugged.

"If that's what I wanted, I could organize it myself."

Now it was Uri's turn to wait until the Professor revealed what incentive he needed to give the names to Uri. It wasn't a long wait.

"As I was saying before, they don't provide everything inside, as you know. Money has to be put in your commissary account to get 'luxuries' like toothpaste and writing paper."

"That's why most inmates work."

"Hmm."

It's not worth it, Uri reminded himself. It was not his place to suggest ways to make prison easier. They had entered the negotiating phase.

"I suppose if you were to donate an amount for each name, I might consider it."

"Like what amount?"

The Professor named a figure.

"I have a part-time job mowing lawns for the synagogue. I can't afford that."

"You'll think of something. You always have when you wanted something from me."

Uri's scars blazed. He was being reminded of all he had done in the past in his shameful quest for the Professor's approval. He rose.

"I'll have to get the names another way."

"You don't have another way."

He took a breath.

"Then I'll have to do without them."

He turned to leave. The room filled with sounds of other visits not going well—arguing, crying.

"Wait! Look. I'm not a hard man. It's just difficult in here. For you, Uri, I'm willing to lower my price, within reason."

He named another figure. It was also unaffordable. But less so than the first figure. Uri nodded and left before the Professor could talk him into anything else.

Back home, he had another conversation in the kitchen with Wacko. He told him about his deal with the Professor.

"*Geez*, twenty-five kids." Wacko shook his head.

"At least."

"It's a lot of money. And who asks for money to name his children?"

"More and more, I'm realizing what a monster he is."

"That's the good news."

"But Wacko. I need to make money and fast, before he changes his mind or ups his price."

"My offer still stands."

Uri watched wrestling on tv for years. He memorized the holds. He was in good shape from exercising in prison. It wouldn't take much to be trained.

"We'll have to tell Flora."

"She knows it's just show business. I already explained it to her."

There was a pause while Uri switched gears.

"When I saw the Professor walk into the visitor's room, there was a moment, just a moment, when I might have melted and promised to put money in his commissary account, asking nothing in return."

"What made you change your mind."

"When he couldn't tell me how many children he has. He doesn't give a damn about them, Wacko. They are no more to him than... than... the phone receivers we talked into. When I saw that, I realized that if his children meant nothing, I meant less than nothing."

"Yer right, there."

"He tried to convince me that God chose certain men, the patriarchs, to 'be fruitful and multiply' in Biblical days, and that he was one of those chosen men in modern times.'

"You might ask Rabbi Shapiro about that."

"The Patriarchs loved their children and knew how many they had. Their problem was having favorites, not forgetting who their children were."

"And they had them in legit ways—the women were their wives or concubines. Today, no one denies women choices about mates, but laws were not the same back then."

Uri stared at the light outside the kitchen window, remembering.

"The Professor was too clever to ask the girls in The Struggle to get pregnant. He has a way of making people want to please him without him asking. The girls thought having the Professor's babies was their idea. I only met one other person who could manipulate people that way, my high school friend Vel. He never asked for anything either. Things were just given to him."

"The name for that is charisma. People who have it draw others to them. If they are *schmucks*, they use their power to do bad things. Some politicians and entertainers have charisma. Prophets do. And leaders of cults for sure."

"The Professor has it."

Wacko wrinkled his brow.

"You know who else has it?"

"Who?"

"Adan."

"For real?"

"I've had my eye on his way of operating. He has Flora wrapped around his finger, and other women, too."

"He's been trouble since he was a little kid."

Wacko nodded.

"Adan's taking over my role promoting fighters in the underground clubs."

"That's no surprise."

"I tried to interest him in wrestling, but he wants the bigger money. And he's very popular with certain types among the spectators."

"The mobsters."

"I feel guilty for mentoring him. Flora still thinks he's legit."

"I'm the one who took him to Punches first. He was crazy mad about it right away, and he was still in high school."

"It's Flora I'm worried about, not Adan. He thinks he's clever enough to avoid arrest. If he's wrong, Flora will take it bad."

"We'll be there for her."

"Yer right, but it won't be enough."

Uri looked out the window again. Cars drove by, seeming purposeful, rushing to their destinations. Now that he knew Flora was his aunt, he took it as his job to look out for her. It would be a way to make up to his mother for his failure to protect her. Protecting Adam would be a way of making up for his failure to protect his first only best friend, the original Adam, Simon's son. Adan might not be changeable, but he owed it to him to try to convince him to do something constructive with his life before he had a record. He was young. He still had a chance.

"I'll talk to Adan."

"Don't hope for much."

He returned his gaze to Wacko. He was rough, but a good man. Soon he might marry Flora and be a kind of father to him, a much better choice than the Professor who took and gave nothing in return. Wacko might not have this charisma thing, but he had Uri's back.

"The Professor said one more thing to me as I was leaving."

"What?"

"If my children are your cousins, I'm your uncle."

CHAPTER 38

That night, Adan stayed home. It was the chance Uri wanted.

"Hey, can we talk?" He asked.

"No. Fuck off."

It was not a promising start.

"C'mon, man. I have things to tell you. Don't be a smart-ass."

Adan was standing facing the window, peering out at something with his back to Uri.

"Like what?"

Uri sat on his bed.

"I've asked the Professor to give me the names of his children. They're all our half-cousins through Adam."

"Those two guys down there. Do you think they're spying on me?"

Uri moved to the window. Two men in brown leather jackets lounged against the street lamp across the street, talking.

"It wouldn't surprise me, considering who you hang out with in the fight clubs."

"You don't know fuck about that."

Adan moved to the side so the curtain would hide him from the street-view. Uri returned to his seat on the bed.

"Do you owe someone money or something?"

"I make enough to pay my debts on time. Those guys are trying to unnerve me. That's all."

"Why?"

"Who knows? Maybe they want a piece of my business. It's fucking territorial out there. Each business covers its own area."

Uri frowned.

"That sounds like drugs. Are you dealing?"

"My finger's in lots of pies. Let's leave it at that."

Adan moved to his own bed.

"The Professor wants me to put money into his commissary for the names of his children. When I get all of them I can, I'm organizing a meeting."

"What the fuck for?"

"To meet them. They're our family, Adan."

Adan snorted.

"Family!"

"Look, man. You always protected your mother. That tells me you're interested in family."

"Only because I'd have to live with whatever asshole she marries or lets move in."

"You're still living here when you can afford your own place, and you're sharing a room with me. What does that say when you have other choices?"

Adan changed the subject.

"Wacko's going to promote you for wrestling matches, right?"

"Yeah."

"It's fake. Everyone knows wrestling's just entertainment. That's why there's no money in it unless you're one of the top wrestlers on tv, with sponsors. You'll be starting out for pennies."

"It's honest. And no one gets hurt."

"That's the fucking problem. No one gets hurt. In fight clubs, spectators pay to see fighters get hurt. Whatever happens is real."

"Those fighters can wind up in the hospital or die. Spectators can get injured, even arrested. Events can get out of control."

Adan turned his head. When he looked back at Uri, the disgusted expression he most often had morphed. He gazed into Uri's eyes with an enticing smile.

"Bro. You know I like you, right?"

Adan likes him? That was a stunner. Uri's body tingled. His impulse was to be flattered. Flora had always insisted that Adan likes, even loves, him, but that was her imagination. Yet, they were cousins. Uri wanted Adan to like him. Or did he? This had to be the charisma Wacko talked about. All it took was a smile and a few words for Uri to feel himself being reeled in.

Adan leaned over the space that separated their two beds and held Uri's upper arm. His face was inches away.

"I liked you, man. Always."

His voice was soft, a near whisper. He stared deep into Uri's eyes until they moistened. Uri couldn't let himself bawl, although he was close to it. If he let himself, he would wind up with his head in Adan's lap or on his shoulder, weeping. He wanted to apologize, although he had done nothing wrong. Until that moment, he hadn't realized how much he wanted Adan's friendship.

Taking a deep breath, he resisted the impulse and waited to find out what the little weasel was up to.

"Forget Wacko and wrestling. Let me be your promoter. I have connections at several clubs. One fight and if you win, you'll make enough money for a dozen commissary accounts and an up-to-date prosthetic hand."

There it was, on the table. It would take minutes to earn the same amount of cash with Adan that would take months with Wacko. Minutes of illegal activity, then he could go legit forever after. One hard slug to take his opponent down, then he would hurt no one again. One punch to release all the anger that had built up over the years of his servitude to Vel, the Professor, even Lois. One time hitting back for all the teasing, humiliation, ridicule, and rejection for his ugly appearance. Once to make someone else hurt the way he had been hurting most of his life.

And Adan would be his fifth only friend after the first Adam, Zhong, Vel, and Don, sharing their bedroom, talking into the night, laughing, planning fight club matches, showing each other what they bought with the prize money.

Except he understood it hadn't been just once before and wouldn't be just once again. If he accepted Adan's offer, Wacko would throw up his hands. Adan would use his cunning charm to convince Uri to fight a second time, then a third. The money would be too much and too easy. Greed would kick in. If he hurt an opponent, he would say all the fighters realized what they were getting into. And no single slug would make up for all he had been through. It would take a hundred slugs, a thousand, all the slugs in the world and still more. He would keep fighting until the police arrested him again, or he was injured. A year or less after he started, he'd be finished.

He began the conversation to convince Adan to choose a different path. Instead, it had curled into a choice he would make about himself and his own future. How had that happened? With effort, he pulled away from Adan's grasp. As if they were in a dance, Adan leaned forward at that exact moment, still drilling his stare into Uri. The only escape was for Uri to stand up, breaking the hold before Adan had him in a lock.

"That's not a good idea. I'm going to wrestle, even if the purse is less. That's what I'm going to do."

"Don't be a loser, man."

"And you should get into the wrestling business with Wacko and me. Or anything besides fight clubs. Rodeos. Dog breeding. Postal worker."

"The fuck. All I know is fighting. And women. You into women?"

"Are you pimping women, too?"

"My finger's in many pies."

He said this before.

"Shit, man. Gambling, fighting, drugs, women. And you're only, what? Nineteen?"

"Call me a fast-learner."

"Is it any use talking to you?"

"Is it any talking to you?"

Adan's smile changed to a worried expression.

"Just do me one favor. Take care of those guys down there spying on me."

It was another trap.

"I won't be your security, Adan."

Just then, Adam toddled into the room, his freckled face illuminated.

"Ada. Play wit me."

Adan stood up and muttered something Uri couldn't hear. Adam jumped around him, reaching up.

"Ada. Ada."

"For fuck's sake."

When Adan didn't respond to him, he became louder.

"Play wit me, Ada. Play."

His older brother enchanted the boy, all the more when Adan ignored him.

Finally, Adan seemed to relent.

"Okay, okay. Sit there, on Uri's bed."

The boy took an excited leap onto the bed.

Adan reached into a draw on his nightstand, taking out a book of matches. He lit them one at a time, throwing each lit match at Adam, who laughed with delight.

For the first few seconds, Uri stood frozen by the door. Then his ability to move returned.

"What the hell?"

He grabbed Adam, holding him high. Adan continued to throw lighted matches in the boy's direction. Uri smacked and stamped each one out.

"Cut it out!"

Adan stopped, stuffing the book in his pocket, looking past Uri. When Uri turned, he saw Flora behind him.

"I heard laughter, so I came up to see what my three lovely boys were doing."

It was clear to Uri that she hadn't seen the "match game." It was time for her to be told the truth about Adan before he harmed her younger son.

"Aunt Flora," he said, passing Adam to her, "We have to talk."

"Believe nothing he tells you, Mom. Uri lies."

"No, he has an imagination and sometimes... Well, sometimes he sees and hears things that don't exist. At least he used to. It doesn't happen so often now."

Adan assumed his most wide-eyed, innocent expression when speaking to his mother.

"Remember. The FBI interviewed me because this looney said I did the things they accused the Professor of. I could have gone to prison because of your nephew's lies, Mom."

"The ones who lie are you and the Professor," Uri said.

"And I thought you were both getting along so well. I refuse to listen to any ugliness from either of you."

With that, she left the room, carrying Adam.

Later, Uri told Wacko what happened.

"I'm scared the fucker will hurt Adam. Even kill him, like he might have done Simon."

Wacko frowned.

"Yeah, I'm thinking he's trying to break up me and yer aunt, too. Telling her I don't have class, and she can do better. I can't argue with that. The boy can be convincing."

"He said the FBI interviewed him after I told them he might have had sex with the teen girls. I didn't know they followed up. Nothing came of it."

"You had no proof. Only a suspicion."

"It's not that I think the Professor is Mr. Wrongly Convicted anymore. He did his share. I just don't know which of them did what."

"The FBI got the Professor for tax fraud and the funny business with money. They must've had underage sex stuff on him for the jury to find him guilty."

Uri stared at the kitchen wallpaper. Black-and-white cows stared back at him, some upside down.

"I wish I had proof about Adan's illegal activities to bring to the prosecutor. He almost admitted pimping and drug dealing. And two guys from some mob were waiting for him earlier today."

Now Wacko's frown changed to a smile.

"I told you I've been keeping an eye on the kid. Sex with teen girls and whatever went down with Simon happened before I met Flora. I have proof of some things, like mob connections, drugs, and pimping, since I took him under my wing."

"You do?"

"Yeah. He has this account book. I found it one time and took photos of every page. He started in high school. The fool kept a paper record."

"The fuck, Wacko! That's so, like, perfect."

"I protected myself. I never trusted the boy not to give me up to the mob or the police."

Uri returned his gaze to the cows. Their enormous eyes seemed troubled.

"The problem is my Aunt Flora. I can't figure out how to protect Adam from Adan and protect her from discovering who her older son is."

"That the tough one."

"But, bottom-line, I can't let him hurt Adam."

"Yer right."

"Let's both sleep on it. We have to decide what to do—and fast."

They parted ways, Wacko heading for the master bedroom, and Uri returning to his room, where Adan waited.

CHAPTER 39

Well into the night, Uri tried to extract a promise from Adan that he would not hurt Adam.

"Hell, I'm just trying to toughen up the kid. Mom coddles him, treats him like a baby. He'll go down if anyone slugs him when he's older."

"It's likely to be you who slugs him."

"He's fucking annoying."

"That's what little kids are like. They want attention. Especially from their big brothers."

The next morning, over breakfast, Uri told Wacko that Adan was still saying Adam deserved whatever happened to him, just for acting like a typical toddler. Adan also dropped jealous hints about his mother's closeness with Adam, of the boy being in the way of his relationship with her. He meant he didn't like any competition for his mother's love.

"That would include me. And you," Wacko said. "He'll take us out one-by-one."

They agreed to talk to the authorities. They made an appointment with someone in the prosecutor's office that morning. Wacko brought copies of Adan's file, and Uri told of witnessing the "match game." Things move fast after that. Child Protective Services did an immediate investigation. A skilled child interviewer got Adam to reveal other instances of his brother's abuse, some of which a medical examination confirmed—bruises, a broken rib.

Flora was told that her older son would have to move out of the house. The only way he would be able to see Adam, if he wanted to see him at all, was during supervised visits. This devastated her. A few days later, when the prosecutor charged Adan with multiple felonies, she spiraled into disbelief and rage.

Wacko suffered the brunt of her anger when she demanded to see the warrant before Adan turned himself in. It divulged Wacko's involvement in the fight clubs.

"You're the one who took him to an illegal place where older men would influence him. An innocent young person in an environment with mobsters and many illegal activities, including violence. And you didn't tell me. You're as bad as the Professor," she said.

In her fury, she broke up with Wacko. He and Adan moved out the same week. She was under threat of losing Adam to foster care for not protecting him from his brother. How did she fail to notice his injuries? She had no answer. Uri understood. The Professor's manipulations blinded him in a similar way, even when Lois insisted on telling him. He found excuses, justifications, or thought his wife was lying, mistaken, misinterpreting. Flora did the same with Adan's long list of crimes.

Uri and Adam were the only two left in her house. If she were rational, she would have blamed Uri for participating in Wacko's betrayal. Uri never told his aunt about his cousin, either. But she wasn't rational. Instead, she turned to her nephew.

"You're the only one I have left. Can I count on you?"

"Of course, Aunt Flora. I'll be right by your side no matter what."

There was a lot to get through. Visits from Social Services to make sure Adam was safe. Adan in jail awaiting court dates. A deal with the prosecutor for pleading guilty, arranged by a lawyer paid for by Flora, who took out a second mortgage on the house.

"Adan isn't guilty. He's just doing what he has to do to get a reduced sentence," she insisted. "It's clear to me that someone framed him."

For the first time since early childhood, Uri basked in a room of his own, now that Adan wouldn't be there to share it. He enjoyed his aunt's dependence on him without trusting it in full. Deep down, she had to know her son was a monster. Deep down, she had to know Uri kept it a secret from her. Deep down, she knew Uri killed her sister. One day, her resentment might surface. Then what?

Both Wacko and Uri understood that by protecting Adam, as well as themselves, they risked their relationships with Flora. That already happened to Wacko.

"But we did the right thing," Uri said.

"Sometimes, when you do the right thing, you suffer for it. Can't be helped," Wacko said, blowing his nose into his handkerchief.

"It's like what happens in the *Torah* when Jacob struggles with the man. He comes out of it a better person, but with an injury to his hip. I bet it hurt him. My hip hurts if I walk too much."

Uri lost friends when he had been violent, and he had lost friends and a wife when he stayed loyal to the Professor. Apologizing hadn't brought them back. But his apologies had been half-hearted, just a step on the road to righteousness. No wonder they hadn't forgiven him. They still feared him.

He vowed to be more honest. It would involve a tough conversation with Flora. He approached her that evening, after she had put Adam to sleep.

"Aunt Flora, can we talk?"

"Of course. Shall we sit in the living room?"

They often held serious discussions there, sitting on the sofa. Flora started with a description of her own misery.

"I failed as a parent, Uri. How did that happen? Adan didn't learn what he should have from me—to resist the crimes those mobsters in the fight clubs pushed him to commit, if he committed any. I didn't teach him to resist Wacko, either. I thought they promoted concerts, things like that. What will happen to him in prison? I'm scared all the time."

"Don't worry. I've been in prison. He'll be fine."

Uri knew this was true. Adan had charisma. It would be more helpful than violence inside. He would wind up with a gang to protect him.

"I'm so disappointed. I thought it would be paradise, the five of us together, a new marriage for me and a step-parent for you three."

Uri wondered whether he should increase her disappointment with his honesty. He had to take the chance.

"Aunt Flora, I have so much to tell you. Some of it may hurt."

"Okay."

She dabbed at her eyes with the end of her cardigan.

"The night before my *bar mitzvah*, I taught Simon's son the 'match game.' When it was his turn, he threw the match at the curtains, and they lit. The fire killed him and my mother, Lora."

He broke into sobs. Flora was crying, too. They leaned on each other. Then Uri straightened.

"There's more. I took Adan to a party when I was a senior in high school. I didn't watch him like I should've. He bought drugs there and put them in the juice at the wedding breakfast. It may have caused Simon's heart attack."

This brought a fresh bout of tears.

"I tried to commit suicide twice and wound up in the hospital. I burned down Simon's house and went to prison. When I did security for the Professor, I beat his enemies. In Punches, I took jobs for mobsters and beat people for money to pay for things the Professor wanted."

"Oh, you poor boy. What your guilt made you do."

"I'm so ashamed."

"We both have much to regret. We can atone together by helping each other."

She gave him a pass, just like she still gave Adan a pass, never mentioning her failure to protect Adam from her older son.

There was only so far she would go. Uri would go all the way, with or without her. He could no longer bear the guilt. Confessing to his aunt was a step.

During his years in Youth Group, before he met the Professor, as *Yom Kippur*, the Day of Atonement, approached, he was reminded of the way to repent: regret the offense, apologize, make recompense, and resolve to never commit the offense again.

He never did this as a package with the friends he battered. He also owed something to those who died—his mother, the first Adam, and Simon—although what still mystified him, beyond the first step of confessing to his aunt.

Meanwhile, he had a routine. Mornings doing yard work at the synagogue, afternoons at the gym training with Wacko. During the evenings, he worked on *Teshuva*—making amends. He sent snail mail letters to the half-dozen men he harmed while doing jobs in nearby towns, when he located them. He found three.

I went to prison for two of a three-year sentence for battering you. It was a sentence I deserved. I'm very sorry for hurting you. I wish I could go back in time and undo what I did. From now on, I will live in peace and try to be a better man.

None of them replied. He never found out if they received his letters or read them. It was as much as he could do. He hoped knowing that they had incarcerated him gave them satisfaction.

Next, he would contact the two ex-friends he had hurt—Vel and Ernie. After doing an inquiry, he found out that Vel was still at State, doing graduate work in the Psychology Department. Ernie graduated and worked for a pharmaceutical company.

He sent a text to Ernie first, saying he wanted to meet him to apologize in a more sincere way.

No need. It's in the past. You already apologized. I've moved on.
Ernie

This was a message he had to respect. He would not force himself on someone who didn't want it.

A few days later, Vel replied.

Yes, I would like to meet. You have something to tell me, and I have things to both tell and ask you.

Vel

They met in the synagogue library on the next *Shabbat* afternoon. It was a safe place for both of them, although safety was Vel's need, not Uri's. Rabbi Shapiro was told in advance in case they required his intervention.

Uri arrived soon after Vel with his hands thrust in his pockets in the classic pose of a man with no plans to attack. He spoke first.

"I've changed since I beat you. I've been in prison for the past two years for battery. That's given me time to think. I'm ashamed of what I did to you, and of how I acted."

Uri's eyes moistened. He hung his head, unable to look at his victim. It was Vel's turn to speak.

"And I want to tell you how your attack changed me. My body healed long ago. My mind is still healing. Have you heard of PTSD? That's what I have. When you beat me, I thought you were going to kill me. You terrified me. The terror stayed with me. Every time a car backfires or I hear a sudden noise, I jump out of my skin. I'm always looking over my shoulder to see who else is going to attack me, even though no one but you ever has."

Uri's scars blazed.

"I wish I had the PTSD and not you."

"That's what I'm studying in grad school. PTSD. Post Traumatic Stress Disorder. Maybe I'll wind up helping others who've been traumatized. I'm not saying that will make your attack worth it. But I'm trying to turn lemons into lemonade."

Vel still had a nondescript look, a man whose appearance was nothing special, yet he had specialness, charisma, a quality that drew Uri to him even while being blamed for Vel's ongoing problem.

"Part of my study involves the perpetrators of PTSD. That would be you, Uri. It would be helpful if you would answer some questions. I hope your time to think in prison produced more than regret. If you don't want to be violent, deal with whatever drove you to be violent. Figure out why you turned to violence."

Uri's stomach heaved. He had never been one to delve into the reasons for his behavior. But he owed it to Vel to try. That would be recompense.

"Okay."

"When did your violence begin?"

After taking a deep breath, Uri answered the best he could.

"I've always been a violent person. Even as a kid, although I wasn't a bully. I didn't know my father, but I imagined he was a brute. I enjoyed thinking he would prove his love by punishing me, hard. Why, I'm not sure. Not long ago, I found out my mother had a boyfriend who hurt me, but I don't remember it. Maybe there's a connection."

"Could be. Go on."

Uri swallowed. He was on the verge of weeping. In a house of worship with someone who was once his only friend, he felt both protected and vulnerable, like he might shatter, and if he did, Vel deserved to be a witness. The words spilled out.

"I was often violent to myself, giving myself cigarette burns and cuts. I tried to commit suicide twice and got boners from fantasies of bigger men wrestling with me, getting me into painful holds. And this kid Adan who was my foster father's son—I let him mistreat me, take my possessions, tell lies that got me in trouble, call me awful names. I just let him, like I wanted it."

Vel blew out his cheeks and nodded his head.

"Go on."

"Everything changed when I met the Professor. It was the only time I mattered to someone I respected. Although it turned out that I didn't matter to him at all. I kept trying to please him, and he kept leading me to darker ways. He made me his security, asking me to take care of his enemies, but never said what that meant. He left it to my interpretation. In the beginning, I just slashed tires, things like that. It progressed to slapping, then beatings. That's where you came in. I beat you. I'm so sorry. So sorry."

He couldn't stop his tears. Vel was being patient with him. How could he have hurt such a gentle person? After a few minutes, when Uri controlled himself again, Vel encouraged him to continue.

"The Professor matched me with Lois from the Youth Group. She had a son by the Professor. Izzy. I raised him until she left me. He was the first person I loved. It differed from the blind worship I had for the Professor. Until Izzy was born, I only knew fantasies of punishment and loyalty to the Professor. I thought that was love. What a *schmuck* I was."

"All your violence came from pain. That's what makes you different from the Professor."

"What do you mean?" He wiped his eyes on his sleeve.

"You have a soul and the chance to become a *mensch*. The Professor has no soul."

Uri had one more thing to tell Vel.

"You were good to me in high school. No one else wanted a friend who was scarred with a glass eye and a stump for a hand. I always wanted more from you. Not just you. Everyone. Anyway, thank you for being my friend back then."

"You're welcome, Uri."

Vel listened to everything Uri said, with no criticism or ridicule. Being heard was an unfamiliar experience. The words were painful, as they should be during *Teshuva*. But also gratifying. He pried himself open himself, dug out the muck, and showed it to another person. It did not shatter him. Instead, he molded together, like a broken ceramic with all the shards glued back in place, cracked, but in one piece.

CHAPTER 40

Uri's third only best friend, Vel, was his friend again. It was not what he expected. He thought Vel hated him, with good reason, and would not accept his apology. That was not how it turned out. Vel still had nightmares and anxiety from what Uri did to him. Yet, he forgave his batterer, even embracing him before they parted.

They did not hang out often after their meeting, having nothing in common. Uri was uneducated, training to be a wrestler, and Vel was in graduate school, on his way to earning a PhD.

At times, they did get together. Vel had a professional interest in the transformation of a felon into a *mensch*, a good person, but he also felt affection for his old high school buddy whose hard life was written on his body, visible for all to see in burn scars, a limp, and other injuries. Each time they met, he asked about Uri's progress in cobbling together a family and abstaining from violence.

"I'm not a pro-wrestler. I'm a kind of acrobat, pretending to hurt my opponent by jumping on him or throwing him against the ropes. If you look, you'll see I'm always hurling myself inches to his side, never straight at him. And he flings himself at the ropes when I give him a slight push. No one is injured."

"You have a stage name, right?"

"Yeah. It used to be Demon Jake. Now it's The Stump. I don't wear my prosthetic or my glass eye when I wrestle. I do all the holds with one arm. Audiences like that."

"What about your half-cousins?"

Uri told Vel about his attempts to locate the Professor's children, how he was related to them, what he did to get their identities. It was a slow process. He still gave Flora the money he earned from groundskeeping at the synagogue. Anything won at beginner's wrestling matches went to the Professor's commissary account in order to eke out the names of his offspring, or their mother's names, one-by-one.

Then there was the laborious task of finding them when the Professor only revealed a first name, or a birthdate, or a town where his baby had been born, or its mother's name, or, if it had one, the synagogue where its *bris,* its circumcision, was performed. Uri had only partial information to work with. It was unclear if the Professor held out to get more into his account or if he never cared enough about his children to remember them. At least Uri did not have to make the lengthy bus trip to the prison anymore. They communicated by phone.

"How many have you found so far?"

"Not any I didn't already know from The Struggle."

"Hmm. You'll need help," Vel said. "Maybe Leah, a grad student in Sociology, would be interested in doing an investigation for her thesis."

She had a special interest in multiple offspring produced by a single father and listened to Uri's description of The Struggle with rapt attention. Her eyes darted across Uri's face as they spoke.

"Fathers like the Professor are often narcissists in positions of power, such as doctors, coaches, fringe religious ministers, and cult leaders. Sometimes obstetricians who use their own semen for in-vitro fertilization without telling the women. But more often, the women are willing participants," she said.

Leah was around Uri's age, with blond hair swept into a ragged ponytail, frameless round glasses, and little sense of style. Most often, she wore oversized sweaters and cargo pants. When they spoke, she looked at Uri, not repulsed by his ugliness.

"Can you help me find the ones related to me?"

She smiled.

"I'll give it my best shot. I'll ask a detective I know for help. What I want is to interview the mothers for my thesis."

They met every time Uri received another scrap of information from the Professor, or when Leah's detective friend revealed another lead. After a while, they also met between those times. They liked each other. Without making it official, they became exclusive by just letting it happen. Neither said a thing about their relationship, or even that it was a relationship.

By the end of a year, they located and contacted half a dozen new names, two the same age as Uri, and the other four between five and nineteen. All were male. Either the Professor only conceived sons, or he was too disinterested in daughters to mention them. Leah speculated the Professor had been in prison during the gaps between children. The detective confirmed this.

Of the six, the mothers of three responded to Uri's initial email. One of their sons was one of the two adults. The other two were under ten. When Uri organized a group meeting, he invited Adam, Abe, Jenny's son, and the three new boys. To his great joy, Rabbi Shapiro gave him Lois' address. She brought Izzy. It was the first time they saw each other since before Uri's incarceration. When she realized how much he changed, she agreed to a visitation arrangement with Izzy. Nothing else reignited between them.

The seven sons of the Professor who attended the group meeting all resembled their father, with brown hair, except red-headed Izzy, dark eyes, round faces, and stocky bodies. It was an awkward get-together. The mothers did what they thought best for their sons, but didn't like being reminded of the circumstances of their conception. Someone who didn't care about them had mesmerized them. Not one was still in contact with the Professor. If any wanted to be, they didn't admit it.

Afterwards, Uri, Leah, and Vel discussed the event.

"Do you think any of the boys will have their father's character?" Uri asked.

Vel thought it possible that charisma was genetic.

"What you're saying is that some might become junior Professors," Uri said.

"It's hard to tell for the younger ones. And we don't know enough about the older ones," Vel said.

"As an almost-sociologist, I believe other factors come into it," Leah said. "The mother's stress, poverty, education, health. You can be a big factor, Uri. If you form a solid relationship with the younger ones, it could tip the balance between genetics and an eventual decision not to be a bad guy like their biological father."

Uri recalled Rabbi Shapiro's words.

If it doesn't end in your generation, you do what you can to make it end in the next one.

"I'm worried about Adam. Adan won't be in prison forever. One day they'll release him. The Professor, too, but that's decades away. Adam might be curious to meet them when he is old enough. They could manipulate him or influence him."

Uri twisted his worried hands.

"Even more important that your influence be stronger," Vel said.

This would become Uri's goal. As the Professor released more information and the detective confirmed their identities, Uri's bond with his half-cousins grew in number. It eased some mothers to understand he was trying to protect their sons from the man who never protected them.

Because he was a wrestler, the boys admired him, even for his ugliness, which was a part of Uri's show business persona. They viewed him as a tough man, like the father Uri dreamed of as a child. But with no harshness. Uri taught them by his example that strength and compassion can co-exist. He showed them his wrestling tricks to assure them he hurt no one.

"It may not be fair, but I have my favorites. They're Izzy and Adam, of course," he said to Flora.

"That's understandable. You've helped raise them from birth."

All the boys inherited their father's instinct about people, so it did not surprise them when Uri showed favoritism. They clamored for his attention when they visited him as a group. He understood Jacob's mistake of choosing Joseph as his favorite among his twelve sons. How could Jacob not have had preferences among so many?

Izzy and Adam realized Uri favored them. That made them the most at risk of becoming like their father, believing in their specialness, that they were better than others. Unless they were the least likely to become like their father because of the genuine love Uri showered on them. It could go either way.

Uri had everything he wanted—a career as a wrestler, a relationship with Leah, and a family—his Aunt Laura and many cousins. He didn't have a father, but he exchanged one father-figure, the Professor, for a much better one, Wacko.

When he was in public, people still shunned him. That would always be the case. To Uri, each injury—the burn scars, the stump left when they amputated his hand, his cauliflower ear, his limp—were reminders of the soulless, suicidal boy he had been before becoming an independent, contented adult.

Or almost contented. In the darkest part of his psyche, something still called to him, sometimes. A book of matches. The siren song of a charismatic encounter with someone superior. The desire for some form of uniqueness other than his ugliness.

As Leah told him, everyone has some sort of darkness they try to keep buried. It is what the struggle of being human is always about.

ABOUT THE AUTHOR

Carolyn Geduld is the author of *Take Me Out The Back* (8/2020) and *Who Shall Live* (10/2021), both published by Black Rose Writing in the United States. Over thirty of her short stories have appeared in literary journals such as *Consequence, Writing Disorder, Steam Ticket,* and *Persimmon Tree.* She is a mental health professional residing in Bloomington, Indiana, where all her fiction is set.

NOTE FROM THE AUTHOR

Word-of-mouth is crucial for any author to succeed. If you enjoyed *The Struggle*, please leave a review online—anywhere you are able. Even if it's just a sentence or two. It would make all the difference and would be very much appreciated.

Thanks!
Carolyn Geduld

We hope you enjoyed reading this title from:

BLACK ROSE
writing™

www.blackrosewriting.com

Subscribe to our mailing list – *The Rosevine* – and receive **FREE** books,
daily deals, and stay current with news about upcoming
releases and our hottest authors.
Scan the QR code below to sign up.

Already a subscriber? Please accept a sincere thank you for being a fan of
Black Rose Writing authors.

View other Black Rose Writing titles at
www.blackrosewriting.com/books and use promo code
PRINT to receive a **20% discount** when purchasing.